THE STORM TOWER THIEF

THE STORM TOWER THIEF

ANNE CAMERON

GREENWILLOW BOOKS
An Imprint of HarperCollins*Publishers*

The Lightning Catcher: The Storm Tower Thief
Copyright © 2014 by Anne Cameron

Black-and-white illustrations by Victoria Jamieson

The text of this book is set in 12-point Times New Roman.
Book design by Paul Zakris

Library of Congress Cataloging-in-Publication Data

Cameron, Anne.
The storm tower thief / by Anne Cameron.
pages cm.—(Lightning catcher ; [2])
Summary: When Scabious Dankhart engineers an outbreak of deadly ice diamond spores, causing chaos and illness, eleven-year-old Angus, who can predict and control catastrophic weather, and his school chums must find the legendary lightning heart—a stone of great power—in order to put everything right.
ISBN 978-0-06-211279-8 (hardback)
[1. Weather—Fiction. 2. Schools—Fiction.
3. Adventure and adventurers—Fiction.] I. Title.
PZ7.C1428St 2014 [Fic]—dc23 2013045268

14 15 16 17 CG/RRDH 10 9 8 7 6 5 4 3 2 1
First Edition

 GREENWILLOW BOOKS

To Paul, Dad, Mum, Jude, Chris, and Teazle

PROLOGUE

EDWIN LARKSPUR'S DISCOVERY

If you have ever been on a midnight tour of London, you will know by now that it has more spooky mysteries per square inch than any other city on the planet, from the Invisible Grave of Gustav the Gruesome to the Rattling Tower of Bones. You will have heard nothing on your tour, however, of the dangerous secret that lurks just beyond the ruins of a peeling paint factory in a grimy part of old London Town . . . a secret so deadly it has been squashed flat under a hundred years of concrete and stone, under three long centuries of discarded, yellowing newspapers, false teeth, and mouse droppings. And there it would have stayed but for an inquisitive archaeologist by the name of Edwin Larkspur.

Edwin Larkspur walked hurriedly through the silent streets of London on a frozen Sunday morning, scratching his left buttock, thinking of the old paint factory where he and his team had first made their incredible discovery. It was being knocked down to make way for a brand-new row of shops, and there, beneath the crumbling foundations, they had unearthed the burned remains of an enormous tower. Hundreds of years old, this mysterious, puzzling structure had clearly been destroyed by a ferocious fire. A few charred bones had been discovered within the ruins, along with two baffling words etched into a twisted scrap of metal: LIGHTNING TOWER.

Edwin shivered as he skidded across a frostbitten parking lot and let himself in through a side gate at the Museum of Ancient Archaeology, where he worked. The whole of London had been gripped by news of his thrilling find. There had been TV interviews and guest appearances on *Archaeology Hour*; he'd even been nominated for a prestigious Ruin of the Year award. There had also been some ludicrous headlines in the newspapers.

MYSTERY REMAINS MAY BE CRASHED ALIEN SPACESHIP!

That had been the most outrageous so far. Along with:

RARE ROMAN TELEVISION ANTENNA DISCOVERED!

But the truth was that weeks after they'd first uncovered the ruins, neither Edwin nor his team (who were far more used to finding Victorian toilet seats and medieval lice combs) was any closer to working out what they had once been.

No official records, maps, or paintings could identify what had stood on this plot of land in the days before the factory. It was almost as if the very existence of the strange tower had been snuffed from the pages of history. The team had also discovered something extremely odd. The mangled remnants were warm, smoldering with an impossibly ancient heat that was hot enough to toast bread and scorch eyebrows. Just the thought of it made Edwin feel queasy. It was as if the whole thing were somehow alive. And he'd secretly started to wish that they'd unearthed a stash of Roman coins instead.

And then, just yesterday afternoon, a week after they had finally dug up the remains and removed them to the Museum of Ancient Archaeology, something even more peculiar had happened. Edwin had returned to his office from the museum library to find a complete stranger rummaging through his private notes. The man had been dressed in a long green coat, with the hood pulled down so low over his face that all Edwin could see of it was a flash of darkly dangerous eyes and the tip of a goatee.

"E-excuse me, sir, but this is a private office," he'd eventually managed to splutter. "Members of the general public are forbidden from entering this part of the museum, and unless you leave this instant—"

Before Edwin could threaten to call the museum security guards, however, the man had pushed past him roughly, knocking Edwin sideways, and disappeared down a long hallway without a backward glance.

Edwin shuddered as he remembered the unsettling incident. From now on, he'd definitely keep his door locked at all times, just to be on the safe side. The museum was closed to the public at this early hour of the morning, of course; in fact, it had been shut for several days now, over the Christmas holidays. But if lunatics in great flapping coats were wandering around . . .

As he finally reached his office, he turned on the lights,

checked behind the door for intruders, then set about making a hot cup of tea—unaware that a man wearing a long green coat had just slipped into the deserted museum and was now treading softly up the stairs behind him.

A CHRISTMAS PODDING

Hundreds of miles away, in a windmill on the outskirts of Budleigh Otterstone in Devon, more trouble was quietly brewing. It was the kind of trouble that lurked behind closed doors, skulked under rotten floorboards, and hid in dark, dingy corners, just waiting to pounce. And at that moment, it was getting ready to pounce on an eleven-year-old boy named Angus McFangus.

Angus had just crept downstairs in his pajamas for an early-morning bowl of his uncle's chocolate turkey pudding. He was standing with his head deep inside the fridge when he heard it.

Click, click, click.

Angus froze, a shiver of fear running all the way down to the soles of his feet. He glanced over his shoulder as a solitary silver pod, the size of a tennis ball, suddenly appeared in the doorway behind him.

It looked exactly like a mechanical crab with a hard metal shell, eight legs, and two vicious pincers. Angus gulped. He was in big trouble. There was no time to make a run for it. He'd have to stand and fight.

He darted across the kitchen and grabbed a baseball bat he'd hidden in the pantry for just such an emergency. The pod edged its way into the room toward him. Angus clutched the bat high above his head, taking careful aim, waiting until he could see the whites of its mechanical eyes, then—*THWACK!*

He swung the bat wildly, smashing a leg clean off one of the kitchen chairs by accident.

CRASH!

He took another swing at it, this time breaking a whole stack of dirty plates on the drainboard, sending shards of shattered crockery flying across the kitchen. The pod ducked, clicking its pincers angrily, then scuttled back into the hallway. Angus flung himself after it, deciding the time had definitely come to call for reinforcements.

"UNCLE MAX!" he yelled. "COME QUICKLY!"

A door swung open at the far end of the hallway, and a head covered in bushy white hair appeared. Maximilian Fidget, a brilliant inventor, was responsible for making some of the world's most volatile and alarming machines, including the hailstone hurler, the Arctic ice smasher, and the cloud-busting rocket launcher. He was also the owner of some equally startling facial hair, which sprouted in great tufts from both his nostrils and eyebrows and the inside of his ears. Thankfully, Angus's own eyebrows were completely tuft free and sat in a perfectly normal manner just above his pale gray eyes.

"Ah, Angus," Uncle Max said, beaming happily at his nephew. "Good gracious, is it lunchtime already?"

"No! It isn't even breakfast yet. The pods are on the loose again," Angus explained swiftly, pointing toward the spiral stairs in the middle of the hall. "I think they went that way!"

"In that case, we must trap them at once, my dear Angus, before they can sever the telephone lines and leave us without the aid of the emergency services." Uncle Max grinned, looking as if Christmas had come again.

Christmas had never been exactly normal at the Devonshire Windmill, but this year's festivities had been positively dangerous. This was due to Uncle Max's latest invention. The pocket-size silver-plated silic-o-pods had been designed to bury themselves deep among the sand dunes of any hot, sunny desert, to collect valuable information about sandstorms and boiling midday temperatures.

Unfortunately, due to a slight technical problem, the pods had escaped from Uncle Max's workshop on Christmas Day and had been roaming around the Windmill in large, thuggish gangs ever since. Electrical wires, bedroom curtains, and Angus's earlobes had all been viciously attacked by the pods, which had also decapitated several innocent garden gnomes sitting on the front doorstep.

"I think it might be best if we take the pods by surprise," Uncle Max suggested, arming himself quickly with a fishing net and a sturdy pair of gardening gloves. "I shall proceed upstairs, if you would be good enough to search the living room, young Angus. If either of us gets into trouble, might I suggest a hearty yell to attract attention?"

"Er, right," Angus said. "So if I get into trouble, you want me to yell my head off?"

"Precisely! If I can tempt the pods into some nice deep buckets of sand, we'll have them safely locked away in my workshop by lunchtime."

Angus couldn't help feeling skeptical. Up until now the pods had stubbornly resisted every temptation put before them, ignoring drawers full of fluffy socks and boxes of used wrapping paper. But as his uncle crept up the spiral staircase, Angus set off back down the hall, wondering where to start his search.

The pods had managed to squeeze themselves into some very unlikely hiding places over the past few days, including a small gap behind the bath taps and the inside of a teapot.

Luckily, Angus knew the Windmill like the back of his hand, because he'd always lived there while his mum and dad worked away in London. Although, as he'd discovered just a few months ago, his parents didn't actually work for some boring government department, as he had always believed. Instead, they were part of a top secret organization of highly skilled lightning catchers, who were frequently sent out to the farthest reaches of the globe to tackle tornadoes, capture hurricanes, and disperse angry thunderstorms, in an attempt to protect mankind from the cruelest weather.

His parents spent the rest of their time at the Perilous Exploratorium for Violent Weather and Vicious Storms, on the secret Isle of Imbur, which was supposed to have sunk into the sea after a terrible storm, hundreds of years ago.

Late last summer Angus had suddenly found himself enrolled as a lightning cub at the very same Exploratorium, where he'd been battered by high winds and ferocious blizzards inside the weather tunnel; had a nasty encounter with some ball lightning in the Lightnarium; and almost gotten himself killed on a deadly fog field trip. And he'd loved every minute of it! He hadn't been quite so thrilled to learn that some strange dreams he'd been having about a fire dragon meant he was a storm prophet, capable of predicting when dangerous weather was about to strike.

Click . . . click . . . BANG!

Angus stopped dead in his tracks as the unmistakable sounds of a scuffle broke out upstairs, directly above his head.

"Uncle Max?" he called as loudly as he dared. "Is everything all right?"

There was no answer, except for some extremely muffled swearing, followed by a thick silence.

Angus hesitated, hoping that his uncle hadn't walked straight into an ambush. He continued into the living room, which was still strewn with the remnants of Christmas. A large tree sat wilting in the corner, along with half a box of chocolates. There was a fresh smoke stain on the ceiling, above the spot where Uncle Max had accidentally knocked over a candle, setting fire to a number of Christmas cards. Angus had hastily rescued the ones he'd received from his two best friends at Perilous, Dougal Dewsnap and Indigo Midnight. They were so badly singed, however, that instead of wishing him a VERY MERRY CHRISTMAS, they now offered him only a VERY RY CHRIS and a HA NEW EAR.

A far less welcome communication had arrived just before the holidays, from the head of the lightning catchers, Principal Delphinia Dark-Angel, who was still considering if Angus should be allowed to continue his training at Perilous. After he, Dougal, and Indigo had uncovered the fabled lightning vaults, Angus had come face-to-face with the most devious villain on Imbur, Scabious Dankhart (who possessed a sinister black diamond eye and who also had a fondness for flinging vicious weather about). Angus had been forced to use his storm prophet skills to stop Dankhart from stealing a lethal never-ending storm and to save his own life.

For some strange reason, this had sent Principal Dark-Angel into a towering rage, and she'd packed him straight off back to the Windmill until she could decide what to do with him.

Angus sighed, deciding for the hundredth time that he'd rather be thrust back into the lightning vaults with a dozen never-ending storms than be banished from Perilous, and his friends, forever.

Click . . . click . . . click.

A solitary pod shot across the floor straight in front of him, pincers gleaming in the Christmas lights, and wedged itself under the sofa. Angus gripped his baseball bat nervously and tiptoed toward it, trying hard not to step on one of the noisy carol-singing slippers that his uncle had made him for Christmas.

There had been no presents or cards from his parents, but Angus hadn't been expecting anything. This was due to the fact that they'd both been kidnapped by Scabious Dankhart and were now trapped in a dungeon beneath his castle. Uncle Max had tried to put Angus in a festive mood, with Christmas puddings, mince pies, and sprigs of holly. Angus had done his best to join in the celebrations, but Christmas felt all wrong without his dad singing carols at the top of his voice or his mum clattering about the kitchen making special yuletide cookies. And he'd missed them both terribly.

Click . . . click . . . click.

He paused in front of the sofa, holding his breath as one long claw emerged from beneath it. The pod was getting ready to make a run for it. It was now or never. Angus carefully laid his baseball bat to one side, waiting for the right moment to pounce, then—

Flumpf!

"Gotcha!" He flung himself on top of the malicious pod, squashing it flat. "Uncle Max, I've caught one!" he yelled as it squirmed desperately beneath him, trying to break free. "Uncle Max?"

"Oooo! NO! ARGHHHH!"

Sounds of a violent skirmish suddenly reached Angus from the room above. Uncle Max was in big trouble this time.

Angus stood up swiftly, dangling the pod at arm's length, well away from all major body parts. With his other hand he grabbed a large, empty cookie tin, wrestled the pod inside it, and tied it securely with a length of tinsel from the Christmas tree.

"ANGUS!"

"Hang on, Uncle Max! I'm coming!"

Angus snatched up the bat again and ran full pelt toward the door, hoping he wasn't already too late. It was only when he crashed straight into something solid that he realized somebody was blocking his path.

"**O**oof!" Angus fell over backward. He stared up at the tall figure now looming over him and almost choked. A very familiar face was gazing back at him, with the same pale gray eyes, the same soft brown hair skimming the tops of his small bear-shaped ears as both Angus and—

"WOW! D-DAD?" Angus spluttered, clambering hastily to his feet. "Oh . . ."

He realized his mistake almost instantly and his face flushed with disappointment. For one delirious moment, he'd been convinced that his parents had somehow escaped from Castle Dankhart and found their way home for a belated Christmas after all. But the man in the doorway definitely wasn't his dad.

"I'm sorry I startled you, Angus." The stranger smiled, leading him back into the living room. "I'm Jeremius McFangus, your dad's older brother. I've heard a great deal about you from your parents."

"You—you have?" Angus asked, stunned, wishing he could say the same thing in return. He was positive, however, that nobody had ever mentioned anything to him before about having an uncle Jeremius.

And yet there was something unmistakably McFangus about him, Angus decided quickly. It was like looking at a slightly thicker, fuller version of his dad, with some deliberate mistakes thrown in. Jeremius had a longer nose, for a start, and broader shoulders; his face was rugged and weatherworn, with a deep, jagged scar across his chin. He was also wearing some thick furs and a heavy coat that made him look as if he'd arrived straight from an Arctic expedition to capture wayward blizzards.

"It appears I've arrived at a bad time." Jeremius frowned, glancing down at the baseball bat that Angus was still clutching. "I also found this trying to escape through the front door." He pulled a struggling pod from his pocket. "One of Maximilian's creations, I assume?"

"Oh, no!" Angus gasped, remembering that his other uncle was still in terrible danger upstairs. "Uncle Max, I almost forgot!"

Before he could explain anything to Jeremius, however, there was another loud thump from the ceiling directly above their heads. Heavy footsteps thundered across it, then—

CRASH!

"Look out!" Angus yelled.

He flung himself behind the sofa, his hands pressed tightly over his ears, as the ceiling suddenly gave way with a loud crack and collapsed, showering the entire room in choking clouds of dust and plaster.

Angus opened one eye warily and peered through the haze. Uncle Max had come crashing straight through a gaping hole in the ceiling. Luckily, the Christmas tree had broken his fall, and he was now sitting on top of it like an overgrown fairy, a length of purple tinsel draped around his ears. Several large chunks of hair were missing from his bushy head, and both his shoes, which looked as if they'd been savaged by a can opener, were flapping about like leathery castanets.

"Uncle Max!" Angus dashed across the room. "Are you all right?"

"I'm perfectly fine, my dear nephew. I may have a few pine needles wedged in some awkward places, but it's nothing that a pair of tweezers and a strong cup of tea won't fix in a jiffy." He climbed down carefully from his perch, showering Angus in ornaments.

"But . . . the pods! What happened?"

"Ah, indeed! I was trying to coax them into some buckets of sand, and they launched a most devious attack." Uncle Max smiled proudly, as if they could have done nothing that would have pleased him more. "Unfortunately, my foot caught in a hole in the bedroom floor as I made a hasty retreat, and the rest, as they say, is history."

Angus stared up at the shattered ceiling, wondering how much longer the Windmill could stand up to such a battering.

"But surely this is Jeremius!" Uncle Max picked his way carefully through a trail of smashed ornaments and plaster, and the two men shook hands warmly.

Jeremius smiled. "It has been a long time, Maximilian. Forgive me for not giving you some warning of my arrival."

"Nonsense! You're most welcome indeed. In fact, you're just in time for some hot breakfast, and then I think perhaps we owe Angus an explanation."

An hour later, after Angus had devoured several rounds of toast smothered in his uncle's special curried sprout marmalade, he was already getting used to the idea that he now had an extra uncle. Still, he couldn't help wondering if he might come down to breakfast one morning to find several previously unknown aunts, cousins, or even grandparents helping themselves to tea and toast.

He had also decided that Jeremius was possibly the coolest uncle in existence. Angus had always loved staying at the Windmill with Uncle Max. But Jeremius had singlehandedly trekked to the North Pole and back again, four times, to collect deep-snow samples. When he was younger, he'd also completed his own training at Perilous, where he'd accidentally set a storm vacuum loose on Principal Dark-Angel, becoming an instant legend.

Angus made a mental note to fill in Dougal and Indigo on all the hilarious details—if he ever saw them again.

"But why hasn't anyone ever talked about you before?" he asked.

There were no photos of Jeremius anywhere in the Windmill. There had never been any letters or Christmas cards. Angus was certain he hadn't heard anyone mention the name Jeremius McFangus until an hour ago, and he was keen to learn everything he could about his dad's mysterious brother.

"It was easier to pretend I didn't exist." Jeremius shrugged. "Sooner or later you would have asked why I never came to visit, and that would have put Alabone and Evangeline in an impossible position. Bound by their lightning catchers' oath of secrecy, they could not have told you where I worked, where I lived, or why I never came round for Christmas dinner."

"But why didn't anyone tell me after I became a lightning cub?" Angus asked. "I mean, I've known all about Perilous and lightning catchers for months now."

Jeremius exchanged a swift glance with Uncle Max. "I'm afraid I've been busy on a solo expedition for the last few months, miles from anywhere. And I wanted to introduce myself in person. I'm sorry, Angus," he added with a sad smile. "This is no way to meet a new uncle for the first time. Your mum and dad should be here, making proper introductions."

They had already covered the painful subject of his parents at length. Jeremius had spent some time discussing their dreadful kidnapping with Uncle Max, who had assured Angus that they had not been forgotten, that they would be found and rescued. But Castle Dankhart sat on the far side of the Isle of Imbur, across a tall range of mountains, and was protected by a moat full of live crocodiles, and nobody had the faintest idea how to mount a rescue yet. Whatever Jeremius said, Angus knew that for the time being at least, his mum and dad would be forced to remain there as prisoners. He swallowed a lump in his throat, trying hard not to dwell on the details, and he allowed another question to pop into his head.

"But if you're a fully qualified lightning catcher, how come I've never seen you at Perilous?"

"After I finished my training, I decided to leave Imbur and work at the Canadian Exploratorium for Extremely Chilly Weather."

"Er . . . to work at the what, sorry?" Angus asked,

wondering why he'd never heard of that either.

"It's nowhere near as impressive as Perilous, of course," Jeremius explained, easing off his fur-lined boots and wriggling his toes in front of the kitchen fire that Uncle Max had lit to keep them all warm. "But snow has always been one of my major interests, and they've got a lot more of it over there. We've done things with blizzards that would make your uncle's eyes water."

Uncle Max chuckled deeply, pouring hot tea into three large cups.

"We've got the biggest underground snow chambers in existence, as well as our own frozen lake, for training on wintry terrain. But don't just take my word for it." Jeremius rummaged through a tatty leather satchel sitting on the floor beside him and pulled out a plain wooden box, with two round lenses on the front like a double camera. "I've got some projectograms here that will show you exactly what we get up to in the frozen north."

"Ah, splendid, splendid!" Uncle Max looked thoroughly excited. "I haven't seen a good projectogram show in years." And he leaped up and closed the kitchen curtains, plunging the room into darkness.

"Um, what exactly is a projecto . . . thingy?" Angus asked as Jeremius opened the box, took out several flat wooden plates, and slotted them into a narrow, sliding bar at the back. He then placed the box on the kitchen table, twiddled with a dial, and—

"Wow!" Angus gasped as a life-size image of Jeremius standing next to an igloo suddenly appeared before them in the kitchen. It floated, shimmering in the air like a slightly see-through three-dimensional mirage. "Can I have a closer look at it?"

"You may explore every last inch of it, if you wish." Jeremius smiled kindly. "Projectograms are completely harmless."

Angus jumped off his chair and walked slowly all the way around the back of the image, which looked so real he was convinced that if he reached out and touched it, he'd suddenly find himself knee-deep in a freezing blizzard. Every individual snowflake glimmered; every last strand of his uncle's frozen nostril hair sparkled with brilliant illumination. He prodded the projectogram curiously with his index finger. The whole picture quivered, causing the legs of the projected Jeremius to wobble gently.

"Normal photographs have no real depth," Jeremius explained as Angus continued to marvel at a row of very real-looking icicles that were dangling from the igloo's entrance. "You can't see round the back of an ordinary picture or work out how deep, thick, or threatening things are. And that's why lightning catchers have also been using stereophotography since the late 1800s—to capture significant images in all three dimensions. Monumental storms, harebrained inventions, and important lightning catchers have all been cataloged in this way and stored at Perilous for future generations to study and admire," Jeremius added. "Projectograms, like this one here, take things one step further by projecting the image."

For the next thirty minutes, Angus sat transfixed as picture after thrilling picture filled the kitchen. There were several projectograms of an icicle-laden Canadian Exploratorium with sloping roofs and impressive towers; of Jeremius in a blizzard, Jeremius with a polar bear, which looked so terrifyingly real Angus was certain he could see the beast's rib cage heaving.

He gazed at Jeremius with renewed awe. Broad and rugged looking, his new uncle seemed distinctly out of

place indoors, and Angus could imagine him sitting far more happily under a tent on an iceberg, with some seals for company.

"As you can see from this picture, the weather has been causing us quite a few problems just lately. It's much colder than normal for this time of year; the storms are far more severe than we'd expect."

Jeremius was talking again; he'd already moved on to the next image. A large, angry snowstorm now occupied the entire kitchen, with flakes so thick and plentiful that the outline of the Canadian Exploratorium was nothing but a blur in the distance.

Angus suddenly remembered that he'd seen something similar on the news a couple of nights before. Christchurch, in New Zealand, which was supposed to be enjoying the beginnings of balmy summer, had been plunged instead into a deep freeze. The weather forecasters had explained it with complicated graphs showing streams of cold air racing up from the Antarctic and had advised everyone to invest in extra knitted socks. Angus had been working his way through a scrumptious box of chocolate creams at the time and hadn't paid much attention.

"Severe icicle storms are the biggest problem at the moment," Jeremius continued, frowning. "London, Washington, Sydney—they've all been hit in the last few days, and goodness knows where the next ones will strike. We haven't seen anything like it in over a century, and it's steadily getting worse."

"Is that why you're here?" Angus asked, finally putting two and two together. "Because of the weather?"

"That's certainly one of the main reasons, yes," Jeremius said. "Principal Dark-Angel has been calling in assistance from across the globe. The icicle storms are starting to cause real problems. And we're getting ready to intervene if the situation deteriorates any further. It's one thing for the Thames to freeze over, but if this carries on and the Egyptian pyramids end up covered in thick sheets of ice . . ."

Uncle Max nodded in agreement. "Quite so. And you leave for Perilous soon?" he inquired, pouring more hot tea. "I have some interesting experiments planned for the pods, if you'd rather rest at the Windmill for a night or two first."

"Thanks for the offer." Jeremius smiled. "But tempting

as that sounds, I'm afraid Principal Dark-Angel is expecting me. I've already arranged to catch a lift with a friend back to Imbur. She's picking me up here, as a matter of fact, at ten o'clock sharp."

Angus peered around the edge of the projectogram at the clock above the stove. It was already twenty minutes to ten. Jeremius had barely arrived, and he was now talking about leaving. Worse still, he was leaving for urgent and exciting lightning catcher business at Perilous.

"What's the other reason you're here?" he asked gloomily, remembering that Jeremius had more than one.

"A very good question. I wouldn't normally travel to Perilous via Budleigh Otterstone, but on this occasion Principal Dark-Angel has asked me to kill two birds with one stone."

Angus suddenly felt the muscles in his jaw clench. Jeremius was now looking directly at him.

"It seems your antics in the lightning vaults caused quite a stir, Angus. I have rarely heard the principal in such a temper. I believe she spent some time considering whether to send you to the Imbur marshes, to complete your training in a swamp."

Angus gulped, imagining the boggy ordeal.

"After she mulled the situation over for several weeks, however, it seems that all has been forgiven," Jeremius said, his face creased into a craggy smile. "I've been sent to personally escort you back to Perilous."

It took several seconds for the miraculous words to sink in. Then—

"You're kidding!" Angus leaped out of his chair, knocking over several cups in his excitement.

Jeremius chuckled. "I've never been more serious in my life. The principal thinks you've been punished enough, and that it would be best for everyone if you continued your training back at the Exploratorium, where she can keep an eye on you. And for once, I happen to agree with her. Perilous is the only place we can hope to keep you out of mischief. In the meantime," Jeremius continued, smiling at the shocked look on Angus's face, "I suggest you start packing. We leave for Imbur in precisely twenty minutes."

"Twenty minutes? Brilliant!" Angus grinned. "Thanks! I mean . . . brilliant!" And he sprinted past Jeremius before his newly discovered uncle could change his mind.

He shot up the stairs, punching the air with a loud whoop. He felt deliriously light and happy all of a sudden, as if the dark clouds that had been lingering over his head had just been destroyed by the cloud-busting rocket launcher. Finally he was going back to Perilous! He couldn't wait to see Dougal and Indigo, to catch up on all the latest news, and to be closer to his kidnapped parents once again. Even the thought of bumping into Pixie and Percival Vellum (two of the most moronic trainees in the history of Perilous) couldn't wipe the huge grin off his face.

He burst into his room and quickly dragged a bag out from under his bed. It was already crammed with a good supply of socks and underwear, which he'd been keeping packed, just in case, along with a bright yellow poncho-like coat and some rubber boots. Angus grabbed a pile of sweaters, along with some extra gloves and scarves, from a drawer and shoved them into the bag. Then he stared around his room, heart still pounding with excitement, wondering what else to pack.

Perched on his bedside table was an extremely unusual and brilliant book about the Isle of Imbur called

Imburology: An A–Z of Fascinating Facts and Frippery, which Uncle Max had given him for Christmas. It contained a genuine lump of petrified earwax from one of the earliest lightning catchers, Eliza Tippins, as well as a yellowing toenail from Crowned Prince Rufus himself, a member of the Imbur royal family. The book was highly informative, if a bit disgusting at times. Angus was keen to show it to Dougal, a great appreciator of unusual books. He wrapped it carefully in a T-shirt and placed it in his bag.

Angus had also received another rather strange present. It had appeared in his bedroom on Christmas morning, with no hint of who might have sent it or how it had found its way into his room. It definitely wasn't from Uncle Max, who always left a gift tag with every present. And Angus didn't have the faintest idea what it was.

The mysterious object was a small, wooden six-sided cube. It was entirely covered with delicate, evenly spaced squares. Each square contained a single letter of the alphabet, a number, or a minuscule symbol that reminded Angus of ancient hieroglyphics. There were highly decorative snowflakes, half-moons, and double-ended lightning bolts, which looked like tooth-extraction tools when he turned them upside down. None of it made any sense.

Annoyingly, the cube didn't appear to do anything, either; it wouldn't move, open, or come apart, even when Angus tried to force it. Nothing happened when he shook it, rolled it across the floor, or shouted at it. And for reasons he couldn't even explain to himself, Angus hadn't told anyone about the appearance of the anonymous present. He had the strangest feeling he wasn't supposed to.

He took it from under his pillow now, stuffed it into his overflowing bag, and, with one last glance around his room, dragged the whole thing down the spiral stairs. Still feeling giddy with excitement, he was just wondering if he had enough time to retrieve his carol-singing slippers from the living room when a large shadow fell across the entire Windmill.

Angus froze. Beneath his feet, the floor began to vibrate gently. An odd noise, which sounded like a vacuum cleaner sucking up pineapples, was getting closer and closer. He'd been so busy packing he hadn't even noticed it. But now it was clear that something big, with powerful, thrumming engines, was approaching the Windmill.

DIRIGIBLE ARRIVAL

Uncle Max strode into the hallway, where Angus stood frozen.

"Ah, I believe your lift has just arrived, my dear nephew. Bring your bag. Jeremius is anxious to leave as quickly as possible. He's waiting for us out on the balcony."

"The balcony?" Angus said, puzzled. "But, Uncle Max . . . what's making that noise?" He grabbed his bag and dragged it back up the stairs after his rapidly disappearing uncle, feeling exceedingly confused.

A wide wooden balcony ran all the way around the top floor of the Windmill and could be reached only by clambering out through one of the bedroom windows. It was often used by Uncle Max for conducting gravitational experiments with giant raindrops or snowflake chains. They had also made use of it, in the hot summer months, for midnight stargazing. But Angus had never caught a lift from it before. Nor did any of this help explain the peculiar noise, which had now reached such an earsplitting volume that it was making his teeth rattle inside his head.

"You're just in time to see it arrive!" Jeremius shouted above the racket as Angus heaved his bag through a bedroom window a minute later, then scrambled out onto the balcony beside him.

"See what arrive?"

Jeremius pointed upward. Angus squinted toward the horizon, fingers stuffed in his ears for protection. For a moment he couldn't see anything except a few clouds scudding across the dull, wintry sky above. One cloud in particular was much lower than all the rest and appeared to be slowing down as it approached the Windmill from the north. It was also traveling against the wind, Angus suddenly realized, as the rogue cloud came to an abrupt halt above their heads with a grinding of gears.

"We're going back to Perilous inside a storm cloud?" he

yelled at the top of his voice, watching it hover.

"Not exactly." Jeremius grinned. "We're hitching a lift with the dirigible weather station. Principal Dark-Angel wants all lightning catchers to return to Perilous as quickly as possible. And this is by far the easiest way."

Angus was just about to ask what a dirigible weather station was when the dense cloud parted and he caught a fleeting glimpse of a vast ship-shaped vessel cleverly concealed inside it, complete with billowing sails, tall masts, and an anchor. Several lightning catchers, strapped into hurricane suits, were trailing behind on thick lengths of knotted cord, bobbing about in the breeze like great party balloons.

Angus gulped, feeling a sudden swoop of nerves. He'd never actually flown anywhere before, not even on a normal airplane, and now he was about to travel by cloud? Would he too be dragged along behind the weather station in a hurricane suit? There was no time to worry about any of it, however. He shouted a hurried "Good-bye!" to Uncle Max, and three minutes later he, Jeremius, and their luggage had already been hoisted up into the large vessel inside a wicker landing basket. And the weather station was on the move again.

"Welcome aboard the dirigible weather station." A bored-sounding lightning catcher greeted them as they stepped out of the basket and handed over their bags. "Passengers are requested not to disturb any members of the crew while the weather station is in flight, except in an emergency. Passengers are also asked to refrain from shouting or waving at members of the general public, should we be forced to land unexpectedly. Cloud sickness tablets are available from the first aid station. We hope you enjoy your flight."

It was much quieter on the inside, Angus was relieved to discover. It also reminded him of a picture he'd seen of an old Spanish galleon, with dark, narrow passageways and creaky-looking timbers.

"But what does the weather station do?" he asked.

Jeremius led Angus past a string of portholes, through which he caught one last glimpse of the Windmill before it disappeared behind misty wisps of gray.

"The weather station disguises itself as a cloud most of the time, passing over towns, cities, and continents largely unnoticed," Jeremius replied. "Its purpose is to collect samples from around the world, from blizzards, tornadoes, and hurricanes, so they can be analyzed and better understood. There are still some mysterious aspects about the weather that even lightning catchers don't understand."

Angus peered curiously into a row of adjoining cabins to the left. A team of lightning catchers was busy studying the contents of some sturdy-looking canisters, each of which had been labeled with words like SILENT SIBERIAN BLIZZARD—HIGHLY VOLATILE and EXTRA GUSTY GREENLAND GALES.

He followed Jeremius up a narrow wooden staircase, and suddenly they were standing on the bridge, with dozens of extra-large portholes in the ceiling and one long windshield at the front for navigating. It was both thrilling and terrifying to watch great whorls of cloud roll past and catch glimpses of the earth, a very, very long way below.

At the very center of the bridge stood a massive ship's wheel. It was manned by three lightning catchers who were all struggling to keep it steady and steer the weather station safely through the skies.

"Hold her steady there! And mind that jumbo jet!" bellowed a woman with a telescope dangling on a chain around her neck. She was dressed in a smart, heavily embroidered coat with gold trim and gleaming buttons.

"That's Captain Claudine Frobisher," Jeremius told Angus. "She knows these skies like the back of her hand. The weather station is frequently used for ferrying lightning catchers right into the thick of things when we've got a major weather catastrophe on our hands . . . and for rescuing them if they run into trouble. Do you remember the great Romanian snowstorms we had four years ago?"

"Er, not exactly," Angus admitted sheepishly, not entirely sure he even knew where Romania was.

"Well, they were some of the fiercest we've had for half a century, but Captain Frobisher scooped up a whole troop of lightning catchers who'd become surrounded by a dangerous storm cluster without losing a single snow boot."

Angus stared at the captain, feeling instantly awestruck.

"I think it might be wise if we make our way up to the passenger observation deck," Jeremius added, steering Angus toward another flight of stairs in the corner. "Things can get a bit bumpy when she really picks up speed. I promise you're in for the ride of your life!"

They were not the only passengers aboard the weather

station. Several other Perilous residents were also being ferried back to Imbur on the same flight.

"That's Catcher Greasley." Jeremius pointed out a short lightning catcher. He had his head pressed against the cool glass of a porthole as he held a spotted handkerchief over his mouth. "And you might already know Catcher Trollworthy," he added as they crept past a silver-haired woman, whom Angus vaguely recognized from his time in the experimental division. She was snoring quietly in her seat.

Angus smiled at a tall fifth-year lightning cub, Juliana Jessop, who was being accompanied by her anxious-looking mother. Two rows in front of them sat a pale, moon-faced man whom Angus had never seen before. He was dressed in a long tweed coat and matching trousers, and his strange, unblinking eyes were magnified through a thick pair of glasses. He instantly reminded Angus of an overgrown owl. The man watched them carefully as they made their way to the front of the observation deck.

"Who's that?" Angus asked quietly when Jeremius offered no explanation.

Jeremius frowned. "He's not someone I know very well. I believe he works in a very quiet part of Perilous.

It's unlikely that you will ever see him in your time as a trainee."

Angus considered asking more, but no sooner had they found two empty seats than they were off.

It was like being on the longest, most stomach-churning roller coaster in the universe. Captain Frobisher threw the weather station around the skies with wild abandon, skimming so low over the Houses of Parliament, in a very misty London, that Angus was convinced they were about to collide with Big Ben. But it was also the most exhilarating thing he'd ever done, and he gripped his seat with white knuckles, swallowing down a mad urge to laugh out loud.

They shot through great puffs of cloud, scattering flocks of seagulls and giving one startled glider pilot a terrible fright when he briefly entered their cloud space.

"But won't he tell everyone about the weather station?" Angus asked as they sailed past.

"It wouldn't matter even if he did." Jeremius shrugged. "Nobody's going to believe a far-fetched story about a great galleon sailing across the skies."

Angus was flung violently off his seat twice, when they

were forced to do two emergency stops to avoid serious collisions with passenger jets. Turbulence shook the entire weather station with such force that he was convinced he was about to lose the contents of his stomach, and he wished he hadn't eaten quite so much curried sprout marmalade at breakfast. By the time they'd hitched a ride on the back of an exceptionally bumpy warm air thermal, he was starting to feel desperately cloud sick and far too queasy to open his mouth and ask for some tablets. But it was still the most exciting journey he'd ever taken in his life. And he found it impossible to stop smiling.

On and on the weather station flew, over endless choppy seas and through ever-darkening clouds.

"Some of the more senior lightning catchers refuse to travel in the weather station," Jeremius said as they banked hard left to circumvent a large flock of geese. "But as you can see, it truly is the fastest way to reach Imbur in an emergency."

He pointed out the window as a familiar island came into view below. Angus felt his heart leap as he caught sight of Perilous in the distance. Perched on top of a tall tooth of rock, and towering over the town of Little Frog's

Bottom, it looked more magnificent than ever in the dramatic clouds. In less than half an hour he'd be back on solid ground, helping himself to some excellent food from the kitchens, looking forward to a long sleep in his comfortable bed. He couldn't wait to see the look on Dougal's and Indigo's faces when he walked straight back into the Exploratorium, with thrilling tales of a long-lost uncle from Canada and a hair-raising ride in a dirigible weather station.

However, even though dusk was now falling, it was obvious that Imbur was in the grip of a ferocious winter. Angus stared out the window at the fields, woods, towns, and rivers below, all covered in thick layers of ice and snow. Several sinister-looking icebergs were floating just off the coast. Farther to the west the weather had closed in, completely smothering the mountains in a shroud of icy white, making it impossible to see anything beyond them, including Castle Dankhart. Angus felt a twinge of disappointment. He'd been hoping to catch a brief glimpse of the castle where his mum and dad were being held.

"Icicle storms." Jeremius frowned, staring hard at the squall. "We could be in for a bumpy landing, I'm afraid.

Captain Frobisher might have to set us down in Little Frog's Bottom instead."

"But I thought we were going straight back to Perilous," Angus said.

"The weather's closing in too fast. It might be unwise to approach Perilous in these conditions. The weather station would be flying blind, with a ton of ice barnacles stuck to its bottom, and strictly speaking, this isn't an emergency. Captain Frobisher won't risk it. Stay here while I find out what's going on."

Jeremius hurried away without another word. Angus stared out at the vicious storm, which already looked closer. The rest of the passengers on the observation deck were also watching its progress with trepidation. Two bearded men were pointing nervously out the window. But the man with the moon-shaped face and the thick glasses was paying no attention to the storm whatsoever. He was staring directly at Angus instead.

Angus turned away quickly, with a strange prickling sensation on the back of his neck, as if he could still feel the stranger's gaze.

Jeremius reappeared a few moments later.

"I was right. Frobisher says it's too hazardous to land over Perilous tonight. She's heading for shelter on the far side of the island and will keep all the passengers there until morning," he informed Angus hurriedly. "She's agreed to set us down at an old friend's house in Little Frog's Bottom first. It's risky, but if we leave right now before the icicle storm can reach us . . ."

Back down through the lower decks they dashed. Angus swayed to and fro as the dirigible weather station was buffeted by the wind, and he couldn't help wondering why they didn't just stay on board overnight with the other passengers.

They finally entered a room where a spacious eight-person landing basket was being hastily prepared for their departure by the same lightning catcher who had welcomed them aboard. Angus swallowed down a nervous hiccup. Being hauled up from the balcony of the Windmill in a basket was one thing, but riding it hundreds of feet straight down into a volatile storm?

"Passengers are advised to keep their mouths shut at all times during the descent, in order to avoid frozen gums, chipped teeth, and glacier tongue syndrome." The lightning catcher recited the list of safety instructions at top speed, passing their luggage over the wicker railings as Angus and his uncle climbed inside. "Exit the basket as soon as it has landed, and evacuate the area immediately. In the unlikely event of an emergency, a warning claxon will sound and a safety device will be deployed." He pointed above their heads to a rather flimsy-looking parachute, which was torn and frayed around the edges. "We hope you've enjoyed your journey on the dirigible weather station. Good-bye!"

"Just keep your elbows tucked in and don't look down," Jeremius said calmly, as if riding wicker baskets through bitter storms was perfectly normal. "Ready?"

Angus nodded, wondering if he'd ever been less ready for anything in his life.

A second later the loading doors beneath them opened. There was a great blast of freezing air, and suddenly they were being lowered into an angry storm cloud. Down through the skies they plummeted, through thick, gray, swirling mists that made it impossible to see anything. Angus closed his eyes . . . which made things ten times worse, and he quickly opened them again before he was

sick. The basket lurched to the left, causing a fresh wave of turbulence to hit his stomach.

"The wind's changed direction!" Jeremius yelled above the howling gale. "We're flying straight into the icicle storm!"

Angus flinched as something hit the ropes above their heads and shattered, showering them both in frozen splinters. And suddenly they were being pelted with dozens of lethal-looking icicles. Long, sleek daggers of ice flashed past his ears, grazing his knuckles as he gripped the basket.

"Keep your head down!" Jeremius roared.

Angus ducked below the outer rim of wicker, shielding his head with his arms. The wind buffeted them from all sides, flinging the basket about violently, and Angus was almost tossed over the safety rail. He caught a brief glimpse of the ground below and gulped—the town of Little Frog's Bottom was zooming up toward them far too rapidly, a jumble of twisted chimneys.

"We're coming in for a heavy landing!" Jeremius warned. "Brace yourself!"

Angus planted his feet firmly on the floor of the landing

basket, moving his frozen fingers away from his face to clutch the ropes above his head.

"OOOF!"

The basket hit a flat roof with a sickening crunch and shattered like a bundle of twigs. Angus was instantly flung high into the air like a human rocket, his arms and legs pedaling furiously. A split second later he was plummeting back down toward the roof again, heading straight for a deep pile of soft snow. . . .

THUD!

Cold slush filled his ears. Purple stars danced before his eyes as he lay awkwardly on his front, the wind knocked out of his lungs. He wriggled his fingers and toes. Nothing seemed to be broken. The icicle storm had now stopped. And everything had gone strangely quiet.

"Uncle Jeremius?" he called anxiously, rolling onto his back, trying to remove himself from the snowdrift. And he hoped that his uncle had also made it down to earth in one piece. *"Uncle Jeremius!"* he called again, more urgently.

The voice that answered him, however, belonged to a different person entirely.

"**W**hat in the name of Perilous are you doing here?"

A startled face stared down at him from above, eyes wide behind a familiar pair of small, round glasses.

"D-Dougal?" Angus blinked in surprise. "What—where are we?"

"Number thirty-seven Feaver Street. You've just landed on the roof of my house!" Dougal said, looking just as shocked to see Angus. "Why didn't you tell me you were coming back? Has Dark-Angel given you a second chance or what?"

"I hate to interrupt this happy reunion." Jeremius suddenly appeared behind Dougal's shoulder from the shadows of a chimney, brushing snow off his coat. Angus was extremely relieved to see that he'd survived the landing unharmed. "We need to get out of this weather as quickly as possible." Jeremius scowled up at the threatening skies above them. "I'm afraid there is another icicle storm on the way."

It took several minutes to sort through the splintered wreckage of the landing basket for their luggage. Dougal then led them swiftly across the snowy roof, past several chimneys and a skylight, through a sloping trapdoor, and down a staircase into a long, narrow hallway.

"Dougal is a friend of yours?" Jeremius asked as soon as the door was safety shut behind them.

"Yeah, you could say that." Angus grinned, feeling that "friend" was a totally inadequate word to describe what Dougal was. In the space of four short months at Perilous, they had completed a treacherous fog field trip, been attacked by a raging storm globe, and done a dangerous dash through the weather tunnel together.

Short and slightly rounded, with jet-black hair and glasses, Dougal was more than just an ordinary friend. Angus knew he was the best friend he was ever likely to have.

"And your father is at home?" Jeremius turned toward Dougal as the next icicle storm began to pelt the roof noisily above their heads. "I need to ask him if we can stay here for the night."

"You're staying? Brilliant!" Dougal grinned. "Dad's in the kitchen."

Jeremius nodded, then disappeared down the stairs without another word.

"Who on earth is that?" Dougal asked, gawping after him with a stunned expression.

"My uncle Jeremius. He works at the Canadian Exploratorium for Extremely Chilly Weather."

"You're kidding! I've always wanted to visit the Canadian Exploratorium. They do amazing stuff with blizzards."

"So you knew there was an Exploratorium in Canada?" Angus asked.

"Yeah, they've got them all over the place, in Iceland, New Zealand, Africa, Scotland. . . . Most of them are much smaller than Perilous, though. You didn't think we were the only ones, did you?"

Angus shrugged, smiling. "Yeah, I suppose I did."

"Anyway, never mind about that now. Why haven't you ever mentioned Jeremius before?"

"It's a long story," Angus said.

His whole body ached from colliding with Dougal's roof. But now that he was suddenly faced with the happy prospect of staying at Feaver Street for the night, he couldn't wait to tell Dougal everything.

He followed his friend down the stairs, peering around at the high ceilings and florid wallpaper. The house was large and rambling, with corridors and staircases disappearing off into the darkness every few steps. It reminded him of an old-fashioned museum, with flickering gas lamps, faded rugs, and one choked-looking houseplant that obviously hadn't seen the sun in years.

Most of the rooms looked dusty and unused. The curtains were drawn, and a musty smell lingered in the air. Mr. Dewsnap's office was a large room on the ground floor and had a far more homey feel about it. It was overrun with tottering piles of books, on top of which various cups of tea, half-eaten sandwiches, and unopened letters had been abandoned.

Mr. Dewsnap himself leaped up from the scrubbed wooden table as Angus and Dougal entered the kitchen. Dougal's father was short and rather plump, and his jet-black hair was flecked with gray. He was dressed in a long, patterned housecoat that resembled a quilted bedspread, and he wore a pair of small, round glasses perched on the end of his nose.

"Aha! Angus, my fine young fellow! 'Tis a great pleasure to meet you at last." Mr. Dewsnap shook him heartily by the hand. He spoke with a lyrical, singsong sort of voice, as if he were addressing the audience in a theater. Angus took half a step backward in surprise. He'd been expecting to meet somebody much more scholarly and serious, someone a lot more like Dougal, in fact.

"Jeremius has just been telling me about your thrilling journey in the weather station," Dougal's father said. "I've lost track of the number of times your uncle has turned up at Feaver Street with tales of crash landings and daring escapes from turbulent storms."

Dougal was frowning. "Hang on a minute. If Angus's uncle has been here before, how come I've never met him?"

"Because he has always descended upon us at an unearthly hour of the night, long after you have gone up to your bed."

"It's true, I'm afraid. I have made more than a few midnight trips to Feaver Street," Jeremius said, shaking a shocked-looking Dougal by the hand.

Angus stared at his uncle in surprise, wondering if there had also been mysterious midnight visits to the Windmill. And if so, why hadn't anyone told him before now?

"Jeremius also has a remarkable talent for trouble," Mr. Dewsnap continued. "A talent that I am beginning to believe runs through the entire McFangus family." He stared over his glasses at Angus. "Dougal hasn't stopped talking about your daring adventures in the weather tunnel since he came home for Christmas."

"Dad!" Dougal turned pink with embarrassment. "I've only mentioned it once or twice."

"To me, perhaps, but I distinctly recall you telling the mailman and Mrs. Stobbs. Oh, you didn't speak of the actual lightning vaults, of course," Mr. Dewsnap said quickly, before Dougal could interrupt again. "But the poor fellow who came to deliver the Christmas turkey

received a lengthy blow-by-blow account."

"Yeah, well . . ." Dougal threw himself into a kitchen chair, scowling. "It serves him right for asking, then, doesn't it?"

"Ah, but it doesn't stop there." Angus got the feeling that Mr. Dewsnap was now teasing Dougal for the fun of it. "Principal Dark-Angel has already written to me twice since the beginning of the holidays, complaining about your 'talent for troublemaking.'"

"But . . . we didn't go looking for trouble on purpose, Mr. Dewsnap," Angus said, coming to Dougal's defense. "It just sort of found us, and then we couldn't really ignore it."

"Indeed?" Mr. Dewsnap smiled. "Spoken like a true friend, and a true McFangus. But then I would expect nothing less."

"Dewsnaps and McFanguses have been firm friends and allies for centuries now," Jeremius explained from the corner of the kitchen, where he had already kicked off his boots and was toasting his socks in front of a glowing fire. "It appears to be something of a tradition."

"Hang on a minute," Dougal said, sounding amazed.

"So you're saying that me and Angus were always destined to become friends or something?"

"Let's just say that there was a distinct possibility of its happening, yes. Ever since the great Deciduous Dewsnap and Marmaduke McFangus joined forces on a highly dangerous expedition to the celebrated fog tunnels of Finland, we have discovered that we enjoy each other's company immensely."

"One of our ancestors was called Deciduous?" Dougal smirked.

"Indeed. A fine and noble lightning catcher and one of the most illustrious Dewsnaps in the history of this island."

"With a name like that, he'd have to be." Dougal caught Angus's eye, and they both looked away from each other swiftly.

But Angus was glad that his family and Dougal's family had had the tremendously good sense to become friends centuries ago. He was positive that only good things could come from such a happy connection.

"Now, by a stroke of exceedingly good fortune, you have arrived just in time for dinner," Mr. Dewsnap said.

Thanks to the rapid nature of their departure from the Windmill and their hair-raising ride in the weather station, it had been many hours since Angus had even thought about food. But he now realized that his stomach was spectacularly empty. Mr. Dewsnap quickly laid two extra places at the table, and ten minutes later Angus was tucking into hot chicken pie and roast potatoes. And while Jeremius chatted with Dougal's dad at one end of the table about the Canadian Exploratorium, Angus filled Dougal in on everything that had happened.

For the next fifteen minutes he thoroughly enjoyed describing every detail of his uncle's dramatic arrival, the projectograms in the kitchen, and their adventures in the dirigible weather station.

"Wow!" Dougal gasped as Angus tried to put into words what cloud sickness felt like. "And I can't believe your dad's got a brother! Hey, just think of all the birthday presents he owes you!"

Angus glanced down the table, wondering if Jeremius was really the kind of uncle who sent presents. And whether he might wake up on his twelfth birthday with a delivery of caribou from Canada?

"So what's been happening here while I've been away, anyway?" Angus asked. He helped himself to another slice of chicken pie, just as eager to hear Dougal's news.

Dougal shrugged. "You haven't missed much. It's been a quiet Christmas. . . . Mind you, there was a bit of an explosion in the experimental division just after you left," he said matter-of-factly. Explosions were a common occurrence in the hazardous department. "Somebody fired up the cloud-busting rocket launcher by mistake, and it smashed into a pile of emergency weather rockets. And then there was the fog field trip," he added, cringing. "A whole week stuck in a bog with Pixie Vellum—it was the worst seven days of my life."

Angus could picture every last detail of the trip as Dougal described swarms of irritating swamp flies, expeditions through thick no-way-out fogs, and the brilliant moment when Indigo accidentally filled Percival Vellum's rubber boots with worms.

He couldn't wait to see Indigo and Perilous again.

"Er, there's something else you should probably know," Dougal said, suddenly looking uncomfortable. "Just after you left, a rumor started going around that you'd come

down with a nasty bout of crumble fungus and that Dark-Angel had sent you straight home to stop it from spreading."

"What?" Angus exclaimed, trying not to choke on his dinner. "That's just brilliant. Now the whole Exploratorium thinks I'm infected. Why didn't Dark-Angel say something?"

"Because I reckon she was the one who started the rumor in the first place," Dougal said. "She couldn't tell every-one about the lightning vaults and the real reason she'd sent you home, could she? And she didn't want everyone asking awkward questions. She also told Catcher Sparks that your real name is Angus McFangus."

Angus stared at Dougal, feeling doubly stunned. For the entire previous term, Principal Dark-Angel had forced him to use the false name of Angus Doomsbury, to pre-vent Dankhart from discovering his true identity. That also meant that nobody else at Perilous, except for a few lightning catchers, knew he was the son of Alabone and Evangeline McFangus. But now . . .

"Clifford Fugg was standing outside Dark-Angel's office," Dougal said, explaining. "He'd just chucked a cold rice pudding at Theodore Twill's head, and he overheard the whole conversation. Then he told everyone else, naturally."

"So the whole Exploratorium knows who I really am?"

Dougal nodded solemnly.

"And does—does everyone know what's happened to my mum and dad?"

"Definitely not. Dark-Angel's keeping that one close to her chest. She's been telling anyone who asks that they're on a top secret assignment in Nova Scotia, and that's why she made you use a different name. She didn't want everyone bothering you about it, you know, asking for details and stuff."

"The Vellum twins don't know I'm a storm prophet, do they?" Angus asked, the horrible thought suddenly occurring to him.

But Dougal shook his head. "They haven't got a clue. They definitely would have said something by now if they'd caught a whiff of that."

An hour later, after three large helpings of chocolate cake, Angus was finally starting to feel warm and dry once again. A comforting fire glowed in the grate as the snow and ice storm raged outside. It was also very enjoyable indeed just listening to Jeremius and Mr. Dewsnap catch up on all the news from Perilous.

"You may be interested to hear that Amelia Sparks and her team in the experimental division have begun testing a controversial thunder-muffling device, which I'm sure will cause endless trouble," Mr. Dewsnap said, handing around cups of tea. "A new librarian, Miss Organza Vulpine, has now been appointed, personally vouched for by Miss DeWinkle. And you've been following the story of Edwin Larkspur, of course." He chucked a folded newspaper across the table at Jeremius, who took a large gulp of tea before studying an article on the front page.

"Who's Edwin Larkspur?" Angus asked, trying to read it upside down.

"He's an archaeologist who has unwittingly stumbled upon the remains of one of the original lightning towers, in London," Jeremius explained. "It happened a couple of weeks ago now."

"You mean he's found one of the actual towers, from 1666?" Angus said. And he thought of the picture he'd seen in Principal Dark-Angel's office the day he'd first arrived at Perilous. It had shown a London of olden times, with huge, imposing, pyramid-shaped lightning towers scattered across the city. They'd been built by the earliest lightning catchers, who had then inadvertently caused the Great Fire of London when one of the towers had been repeatedly struck by lightning. As far as the rest of the world was concerned, the fire had been started by an unfortunate baker in Pudding Lane, and before the truth could emerge, the remaining lightning catchers had sought refuge on the Isle of Imbur, where they'd built the Exploratorium.

"Why didn't you show me all this stuff about archaeological remains?" Dougal folded his arms, looking annoyed.

"Because you have been far too busy basking in the glory of your own adventures." Mr. Dewsnap took the newspaper from Jeremius and spread it across the kitchen table so Angus and Dougal could see a large photo of Edwin Larkspur. He was holding up a twisted lump of metal that looked like a melted bicycle frame.

"But haven't any of the lightning catchers ever gone looking for the ruins themselves?" Angus asked, fascinated.

"Oh, yes, on many, many occasions," Mr. Dewsnap said,

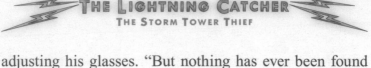
adjusting his glasses. "But nothing has ever been found until now. Although I do recall reading about a particularly eventful dig, in 1873, that accidentally uncovered an ancient collection of chamber pots at the bottom of an old sewer. It caused a terrible stink at the time."

Angus grinned at Dougal.

"For many years now it has been widely believed that the fire destroyed every last scrap of evidence that the towers ever existed," Mr. Dewsnap said, "which is what makes this discovery even more extraordinary, of course. It could give us some valuable information about the very first lightning catchers."

"Principal Dark-Angel is arranging to have the relics brought back to Imbur?" Jeremius sipped his tea thoughtfully.

"Naturally." Mr. Dewsnap nodded. "She cannot take any chances. If Larkspur should realize the true significance of his discovery, if word should ever get out that the twisted lumps of metal were once lightning towers . . ."

Angus understood instantly. It wouldn't take anyone very long to trace the whole story back to Imbur, and then the lightning catchers would be discovered. It would be the story of the century. And it would ruin everything that Perilous had secretly achieved over the last three hundred and fifty years.

It was eleven by the time Mr. Dewsnap finally sent Dougal and Angus up the stairs to bed.

"This is my room." Dougal hovered anxiously as Angus stepped into a small, cozy room at the top of the house. "I was sitting up here reading when I heard you crashland on the roof. I thought there'd been an avalanche or something."

A fire crackled merrily in the grate, and several pictures of Stonehenge were scattered about the walls. Dougal was desperate to visit the ancient site one day. A small Christmas tree sat in the corner, twinkling with baubles.

Angus spent several minutes admiring Dougal's favorite books.

"Hey, speaking of books, I've got something interesting to show you." He rummaged through his bag and pulled out the tome on Imburology that Uncle Max had given him for Christmas.

"Whoa! This is amazing." Dougal traced the fancy

scrollwork on the front cover with his fingers.

"It's got loads of brilliant stuff about famous Imburcillians inside," Angus said, "and some really horrible yeti hair samples."

"Honestly?" Dougal gazed longingly at the book. "Can I borrow it for a bit? I promise I'll look after it."

Angus shrugged. "Yeah, okay. Just don't stick your nose anywhere near the swamp-water sniff strips on page fifteen," he warned. "It'll put you off food for days."

Dougal showed him into the spare room next door a few minutes later. It was warm and friendly, with a stack of extra blankets piled at the foot of the bed. Angus climbed under his covers wearily, still thinking about Edwin Larkspur and his amazing lightning tower discovery, and fell asleep before his head hit the pillow.

He was awakened early the following morning by the sound of Jeremius in the bathroom down the hallway, singing a loud, cheerful song about a lonesome polar bear. Angus jumped out of bed and got dressed, eager to see Little Frog's Bottom in the daylight before their return to Perilous.

Breakfast was a chaotic affair, with Dougal dashing up and down the stairs every five minutes to pack something he'd forgotten. Jeremius then spread the entire contents of his leather satchel across the kitchen table, in order to show Mr. Dewsnap some rare samples of fossilized hailstones that he'd picked up in Siberia. And he accidentally smashed a teapot in the process.

It was only an hour later, after a prolonged hunt for Dougal's spare glasses, which eventually turned up in the pocket of the coat he was wearing, that Dougal and Angus said their good-byes to Mr. Dewsnap. And then they waited for Jeremius outside the snowy front door.

It was obvious in the daylight that Dougal's house sat on the crest of a hill. The road sloped away from it sharply, offering a spectacular view across the crooked rooftops of Little Frog's Bottom. It was the first time Angus had ever seen the town from this vantage point.

"Little Frog's Bottom is shaped like a spiral," Dougal explained, pointing out the deep swirl of frosted streets beneath them, "so it takes ages to get into the center of town. There're loads of shortcuts and alleyways, if you know where to find them. But Dad doesn't bother going into town

much; he says he can get everything he needs right here."
Dougal indicated the row of shops directly across the road.

There was a secondhand bookshop, which, according to a painted sign in the window, had the largest collection of miniature books in the world. A few doors down, a bakery had an enticing display of giant sugared Imbur buns. An inn called the Frog and Fly Catcher was offering special winter broth and toasted bread rolls for three silver starlings. And a sign swinging above the door of the dusty-looking shop next to it simply said FINE BONE MERCHANTS. Wooden shutters had been drawn across the windows from the inside, giving it a mysterious and slightly creepy air.

"Nobody's ever opened a bone merchant's in Budleigh Otterstone." Angus grinned, thinking of the normal street where Uncle Max lived. He quickly decided that he preferred the shops in Little Frog's Bottom.

"The same people own an even creepier bone merchant's in town," Dougal said, shivering. "Dad won't let me in there, though. He says it's not suitable for lightning cubs, whatever that means. Hey, come and stay for a bit when it gets warmer. We'll sneak out of the house before

Dad's awake and I'll give you a proper tour of the town," he promised.

"Brilliant! Thanks, yeah, I will." Angus grinned again, already looking forward to it.

It was several minutes later when he suddenly realized he'd left his gloves on the kitchen table and let himself back in through the front door to collect them.

"And find out what's taking Jeremius so long, will you?" Dougal called after him. "It's freezing out here."

After the bright snowiness of the street outside, the hall-way seemed extra dark. Jeremius and Mr. Dewsnap were still talking in the kitchen. Their voices sounded strangely hushed, Angus thought as he walked toward them. Almost as if they didn't want to be heard.

". . . Dark-Angel's convinced the icicle storms are no accident. They're far too random to follow any normal weather pattern, turning up in Africa one day and Greenland the next."

Angus stopped dead in the middle of the hall. Jeremius hadn't mentioned anything about deliberate storms back at the Windmill. He hovered, wondering if he should creep back outside and pretend he hadn't heard a thing, or give in to his curiosity and eavesdrop guiltily on their conversation.

"Icicles usually take time to form," Jeremius explained. "Meltwater drips and then refreezes slowly, drop by drop, into a solid stalactite of ice. They are not supposed to fall from the sky like rain. We've had reports from the Sahara and Tuvalu, places where ice and snow have rarely, if ever, been seen before. They now have foot-long daggers of ice pelting the ground, causing all sorts of injuries. We're lucky no one has been killed yet, but if this continues, it's only a matter of time. Dark-Angel is calling in every available lightning catcher to deal with any rogue storms. But so far there's been very little we can do to stop them from occurring."

"And Delphinia is certain they're being set off deliberately?" Mr. Dewsnap asked, keeping his voice low.

"What other explanation could there be? We've been monitoring the situation closely at the Canadian Exploratorium, of course, but then, several days ago, I received an urgent message that confirmed our worst fears. It was sent straight from the dungeons of Castle Dankhart."

There was a sharp intake of breath from Mr. Dewsnap.

"But, my dear fellow, you cannot possibly mean . . . it could not have come from . . ."

"The message came from my brother, Alabone," Jeremius said.

Angus felt a sharp stab inside his chest. A message from his dad! It was the first time anything had been heard from either one of his parents since their kidnapping. Desperate for any information, he crept closer to the door, wondering why Jeremius hadn't mentioned this startling news to him or Uncle Max.

"The note was smuggled out in a hurry, it is brief, it says nothing about the state of their health or well-being, but Alabone's handwriting looks firm and strong."

"Then we must take comfort from that, at the very least. But what does the message say?"

"Alabone sometimes overhears careless conversations, whispered plans from those who pass through the dungeons to the experimentation chambers underneath Castle Dankhart," Jeremius answered quietly. "For some weeks now there have been dark rumors and mumblings. Dankhart is up to something. The icicle storms are coming from him. He's using the chaos they cause to keep the

lightning catchers busy, their resources thinly stretched across the globe."

"But what on earth could the scoundrel hope to gain by such a plan?"

"Dankhart's intentions are not clear. Still, it wouldn't be the first time he's used the weather as a distraction. He's already done it once before, with the newts and frogs, when he was looking for the lightning vaults, so why not use it again?"

"And you are positive that Alabone has sent this warning himself?" There was a note of caution in Mr. Dewsnap's voice now. "Have you considered that it could be a clever forgery, a trick designed to cause yet more chaos?"

"I have considered it. But Alabone signed the note with a simple sequence of numbers, a code we used as children. No one else ever knew of it. There can be no doubt that the message is genuine. Here, take a look for yourself."

Angus edged even closer to the door, desperately hoping to catch a glimpse of the words his dad had written. He could hear Jeremius taking something out of his deep coat pocket. There was a pause, then—

"He used a Farew's?" Mr. Dewsnap said, sounding surprised.

"It was the safest way. If the message had been intercepted before it reached me . . ."

Before Angus could even ponder what this strange comment might mean, Jeremius was talking again.

"As you can see, Alabone has also asked me to keep Angus safe. If Dankhart is up to something, Perilous is the only place I can hope to keep him out of harm's way, assuming I can curb this talent for trouble he seems to have developed."

Mr. Dewsnap chuckled.

"Especially as Dankhart now knows that Angus is a storm prophet. There's no telling what he might do with such information."

Angus frowned, puzzled. Why would Dankhart give two hoots about the fact that he could predict a lightning strike or two, or even ten? What possible interest could it be to a person who could already do extraordinary things to the weather?

"I was already on my way to the Windmill when Dark-Angel sent a message asking me to help with the icicle

storms and bring Angus back to continue his training. But I would have brought him back here in any case, whatever her decision about his future at Perilous."

"Rightly so," Mr. Dewsnap said. "Until we are sure what Dankhart is planning, there can be no better place."

"And speaking of Perilous . . ." There was a scraping of chairs as both men stood up. "We really must leave before the weather closes in again and we are forced to stay here another night."

"You are more than welcome, old friend. McFanguses will always find a cheery welcome and a bed for the night here at Feaver Street."

Angus turned silently on his heel, his head now crammed with a confusion of troubling thoughts, and he crept back down the hall before Jeremius caught him listening.

5

THE S-SNOWBALL TEST

The journey back to Perilous was an exceptionally chilly one. They took an ancient open-topped, steam-powered coach, which they caught from the end of Feaver Street. Dougal sat immersed in the Imburology book. Angus watched Little Frog's Bottom disappearing behind them, and in his mind he went over and over the revealing conversation he'd accidentally overheard. At least he understood now why Jeremius had made such a sudden appearance at the Windmill, after eleven years of silence. From the very depths of the Castle Dankhart dungeons, he'd been sent a stark warning. Dankhart was up to his old tricks once again, this time sending icicle storms out to the

far reaches of the world. But why? What was he hoping to achieve? And why had Jeremius kept the shocking news about Angus's dad's message to himself? Surely he should have told Angus something so important.

Angus shivered and pulled his coat tighter. Maybe he should just explain about the accidental eavesdropping and simply ask to see the note for himself? He quickly decided against it. Jeremius was cool and exciting. Angus already liked him immensely. But there was something about him that didn't quite add up.

Twenty minutes later they finally reached the foot of the towering rock upon which Perilous sat. The only way to reach the top was via a stomach-churning contraption called a gravity railway. Angus had ridden on this terrifying mode of transportation only a couple of times before, once when he'd been unconscious, but it was definitely his least favorite part of life at the Exploratorium. He kept his eyes firmly shut as the carriage shot upward at a disturbing rate, and he was extremely pleased when they finally reached the top.

He staggered out of the carriage and stared at the familiar stone building before him. It was enormously grand and impressive. A weather station sat on the flat roof. Ornate steel-and-glass weather bubbles, where he, Dougal, and Indigo had learned about the seventeen different types of fog, burst through the outer walls like enormous soap-suds. Beyond a door in the courtyard wall, there was a set of steep stone steps that led down to the spectacular cloud gardens. Angus grinned. Staying at the Windmill with Uncle Max was brilliant, apart from when he was being attacked by vicious pods, but at Perilous he truly felt like he belonged.

It was obvious, however, that the whole Exploratorium was in the grip of a deep freeze. Lethal-looking icicles dangled off every roof and window frame, and huge piles of fresh snow were clogging the doorways.

"Why's the weather so much worse up here?" Angus wondered aloud as they skidded with their luggage across the icy courtyard and into the entrance hall, to escape the freezing chill.

"Obvious, isn't it?" Dougal said, taking off his gloves. "Perilous is higher up than everything else around it, so it gets the worst of the weather first. You'd be freezing, too, if you had your head stuck permanently in the clouds."

On the inside, the thick stone walls of the Exploratorium were as warm and welcoming as ever, with huge fires blazing in every grate.

"Right, you two. I'd better go and report to Principal Dark-Angel." Jeremius appeared beside them and stamped snow off the bottoms of his boots. "I trust you can make it down to your own rooms without getting into too much trouble?"

"Yeah, we'll try." Angus grinned.

"In that case, I'll see you both later."

Angus watched as Jeremius headed up the stairs, and then turned quickly to Dougal. All private conversation inside the carriage had been impossible, but now that they were alone, he could finally tell Dougal about the shocking news he'd overheard earlier that morning.

"Listen, there's something I've got to tell you. I—" His words were cut short, however, by a loud groan coming from Dougal. "What? What is it?"

Angus stared around the entrance hall, half expecting to see Catcher Sparks marching toward them with a pile of moldy old armpit warmers to scrape before lunchtime. But the only person he could see was a short, plump woman with soft brown curls that bounced on top of her head as she walked. She was wrapped up warmly in thick woolen tights and a sturdy tweed dress. She waved her bag at Dougal, trying to attract his attention. Dougal, however, was now staring determinedly in the opposite direction, pretending to read an angry notice banning all indoor snowball fights.

"There you are, my lovely." The woman smiled kindly down at Dougal. "I've brought you an extra scarf to help keep out this dreadful chill. I don't know how I'd ever face your father again if you caught a cold in this drafty old Exploratorium and it went straight to your chest." She opened her bag, pulled out a long knitted scarf in nauseating shades of peach and mauve, and handed it to a glum-looking Dougal.

"Thanks, Mrs. Stobbs." He sighed.

"And there's a spare one here for your friend too," she added, offering a green-and-red-striped scarf to Angus.

"Er, thanks a lot." Angus draped it round his neck, grateful for the extra knitwear.

"If you need any gloves or hats, you know where to find me, my lovely. Now I'd best be off," she said, snapping her

bag shut. "Principal Dark-Angel's expecting me to polish her furniture this morning, and this weather's playing havoc with my beeswax."

And with one final wave, she disappeared down a stone passageway to the right.

"Who was that?" Angus asked as soon as she was out of earshot.

"Mrs. Stobbs, our housekeeper," Dougal explained, looking uncomfortable. "She works for Dark-Angel most of the time, but she comes round our house twice a week to help out with the housework," he added quietly. "Dad didn't cope very well with the ironing and stuff after Mum died."

Angus stared at Dougal, who was suddenly avoiding his gaze. Why had he never asked Dougal about his mum before? It was obvious now, though, that something must have happened to her—Dougal only ever spoke about his dad. It was also obvious why most of the rooms in the rambling house at Feaver Street felt unloved and abandoned. Dougal and his dad simply couldn't fill them on their own.

"Listen, I'm really sorry. I—I should have asked you

about your mum ages ago," he mumbled awkwardly. And he suddenly felt ashamed of the fact that he hadn't, especially as Dougal had risked serious injury, even death, to help him uncover the truth about his own parents.

"Forget it." Dougal's cheeks glowed pink with embarrassment. "Mum died when I was really young. Dad doesn't like talking about it much."

"Mrs. Stobbs seems . . . nice," Angus added, scrambling around for something else to say.

Dougal shrugged. "She bakes good cakes and stuff, I suppose, but she fusses over things a bit. And she likes to knit," he said miserably, trying to stuff the scarf into his pocket and out of sight. "Come on, let's get out of here before she forces me into a pair of knitted earmuffs as well."

Before they could even escape the entrance hall, however, their progress was halted yet again by a stern voice.

"McFangus! Dewsnap!"

And they spun around to find Catcher Sparks, their master lightning catcher, striding toward them. Her hair was pulled back into a tight bun. She was dressed in a long brown leather jerkin that buckled all the way up the front and looked tough enough to stop a stampeding rhinoceros in its tracks. Angus gulped. Catcher Sparks had been responsible for making them do some of the most disgusting work of their training so far, including scraping snot-repelling handkerchiefs by hand. And she was advancing upon them now with an extremely purposeful look on her face.

"And where, may I ask, have you two been?" she snapped, towering over them with a steely-eyed stare.

Angus exchanged mystified looks with Dougal. "We— we haven't been anywhere, miss. We've only just arrived back at Perilous."

"In that case, you'd better come with me, the pair of you," she ordered, starting in the direction of the staircase that rose up through the middle of the hall.

"But, miss, we haven't done anything wrong," Angus said automatically.

"I am aware of that, McFangus. All lightning cubs are being taken straight to the Antarctic testing center in the supplies department upon their arrival back at Perilous."

"Er . . . to the what?"

"I haven't got time to stand around here explaining.

Come along." She marched them across the hall briskly. "And do something with that thing dangling out of your pocket, Dewsnap; it's making the place look untidy."

"What do you reckon an Antarctic testing center is?" Angus mumbled as they followed her.

"I don't know, but anything with the word 'Antarctic' in it can't be good, can it?" Dougal replied, looking worried.

Catcher Sparks took them up to an impressive marbled hall at the top of the staircase. Angus hadn't expected to find himself back in the Octagon again until the next morning at the earliest. He stared at the eight familiar doors set deep into the thick walls with a sudden feeling of apprehension. He'd already spent quite some time in the experimental division, where his eyeballs had almost been sucked out of their sockets by a powerful storm vacuum. In the Lightnarium, he'd narrowly avoided being burned to a crisp by some ball lightning, and he'd also discovered he was a storm prophet. He stared at the faded golden fire dragon that had been etched into the door of the deadly department many years ago. It flickered at him, shimmering. He looked away from it quickly.

The only two doors he'd never set foot inside led to

the Inner Sanctum of Perplexing Mysteries and Secrets, which nobody ever entered, and the supplies department. Up until now, he'd always considered supplies to be the least dangerous of all the departments at Perilous.

"All lightning catchers are exceedingly busy at the moment," Catcher Sparks explained as she bustled them straight inside. They walked past several closed doors, marked FORECASTING DEPARTMENT SUPPLIES, EXPERIMENTAL DIVISION SUPPLIES, and RUBBER BOOT OVERFLOW. "As I'm sure even you two have noticed, the weather has been behaving in a ferocious manner just lately. Imbur itself is in the grip of a treacherous winter," she said with an involuntary shiver. "And as a result, extra cold-weather supplies are being issued to each and every person at this Exploratorium."

She stopped abruptly outside a door marked LIGHTNAR-IUM SUPPLIES. She knocked once and let herself in, leaving the door open behind her.

"Valentine Vellum has asked me to drop off an order form for a dozen pairs of tinted safety goggles," she said, addressing a startled-looking man inside. "As I was already passing, I agreed on this occasion. But please do not expect me to behave like a carrier pigeon in the future."

Angus caught a fleeting glimpse of neatly stacked shelves and boxes through the open door before Catcher Sparks snapped it shut again. She continued down the corridor as if nothing had happened.

"Not everyone reacts to the cold in the same manner, however, and it is therefore necessary to test your individual thermal capacity. That is why I am taking you to the Antarctic testing center."

She shuffled them through a door marked with a single silver snowflake and into a small waiting room. "Wait here," she ordered, and disappeared through another door at the far side.

The room was bare and cramped and gave no hint of what might be awaiting them in the testing center. Unfortunately, it was also occupied by two of Angus's least favorite trainees in the entire Exploratorium, Percival and Pixie Vellum.

Angus had loathed the hairy, gorillalike twins ever since their very first meeting outside the weather tunnel the previous term. They were watching him and Dougal now, with identical sneers on their ugly faces.

"What is that hideous thing, Dewsnap?" Percival pointed at the scarf, which Dougal was hurriedly trying to stuff deeper into his coat pocket. "Don't tell me you and Dungbeetle are knitting your own underwear now? Or is it a Christmas present from Midnight, your girlfriend?"

"Shut it, Vellum." Dougal scowled. He shoved his way past the twins and sat on a chair in the far corner with his arms folded.

"There's no need to be so touchy," Percival continued as Pixie snickered beside him. "I was only wondering what you and Dungbeetle got each other for Christmas."

"It's none of your business," Angus snapped, wishing Catcher Sparks had left them in a different waiting room. He made a move toward the only empty chair left.

"You're not sitting anywhere near me, *McFangus*. I might catch something." Percival inched away from him, looking revolted. "Everyone knows you've got crumble fungus."

"Yeah, we don't want your disgusting germs in this Exploratorium. Dark-Angel should have expelled you,"

Pixie added, shuffling to make extra room for her brother.

"She should expel you two first for being moronic." Dougal scowled again at the twins.

But for once Percival didn't rise to the bait. Instead, he stared at Angus with an annoying smirk until Catcher Sparks returned a few minutes later.

"You two." She jabbed a finger at the twins. "Come with me." She watched them suspiciously as they stood up and slouched through the open door. "McFangus, Dewsnap, wait here until we're ready for you."

"Of all the idiots to get stuck in this room with . . ." Dougal moaned as soon as the door was closed. "I'm starting to wish we hadn't bothered coming back. What kind of a welcome is this?"

But Angus had more pressing concerns. "Are you sure those two don't know anything about my mum and dad?"

"Course not! They're two of the biggest blabbermouths in the whole Exploratorium. If they knew something that interesting, they'd be telling everyone in sight."

"Then why is Percival looking so smug all of a sudden?"

Dougal shrugged. "That's just his normal expression. Anyway, I'm more worried about what's going on behind that door than what's going on inside Percival Vellum's brain."

Five, ten, fifteen long minutes passed with no sign of Catcher Sparks or the twins. There were, however, some very odd noises coming from behind the closed door. They heard a series of sharp squeals and then a strange whooshing sound that sent shivers up and down Angus's spine.

Dougal looked steadily more nauseated as the minutes passed. By the time Catcher Sparks finally came back, his face had turned the same sickly color as the pom-poms on his scarf.

"McFangus." Catcher Sparks was now wearing a long coat with woolen gloves and snow boots. "Come with me."

Angus followed her through the door, with one backward glance at Dougal. He was hit instantly by a blast of icy air, and he was surprised to find that the entire room was covered in a thick layer of hard, glittering frost. It reminded him of the igloo he'd seen in the projectogram show at the Windmill.

Thankfully, there was no sign of the Vellum twins anywhere. But he did recognize Doctor Fleagal, a short, stout, chatty man who usually worked in the sanatorium. He was sitting behind a desk with a fat pile of notes in front of him.

"McFangus, isn't it?" He smiled in a genial manner, as if there was nothing at all odd about sitting inside a frozen room. He was wrapped up warmly in a thick cloak and fur hat, with extra flaps to cover his ears. "If you could just slip behind the curtain and put on the shorts provided, we'll get started straightaway."

"S-shorts?" Angus gulped, hoping he might have misheard the instructions.

Catcher Sparks sighed impatiently. "Just do as you're told, McFangus. We haven't got all day."

Angus changed quickly into the shorts and then stepped back into the room. The air was bitingly cold on his exposed skin, and he folded his arms across his chest, trying to hold some heat in around his vital organs. His feet were already like blocks of ice.

"It's important to know how your body reacts to the cold, to measure your personal cold threshold, in order to give you the right equipment," Doctor Fleagal explained, coming out from behind his desk. He took a small color chart from his pocket and held it up against the skin on Angus's arm. "Hmm. You, for instance, appear to be a healthy shade of blue with undertones of raspberry and pink, suggesting a high tolerance to cold weather." He jotted down the results in his notes, then shoved something thick and spongy between Angus's teeth. "Bite down hard on this teeth-chattering gum, if you please."

Angus was already having trouble making any part of his face work properly; the quivering in his jaw was uncontrollable.

"Under normal circumstances, all you younger lightning cubs would simply stay inside with hot-water bottles and cups of cocoa until these dreadful storms had passed," Doctor Fleagal added, taking the temperature at the tip of Angus's nose. "But as you will be starting a new phase of your training this term, we cannot afford to take any chances."

Angus wondered what new phase he was talking about. Was Catcher Sparks planning a camping trip on a glacier, perhaps?

"Now for the all-important snowball test," Doctor Fleagal said, and he sat back down behind his desk.

"S-s-s-snow-b-ball?" Angus shivered, struggling to get the word out through his numb lips. Violent shivers were now rippling through his entire body, and he was almost positive he could feel an icicle forming on the end of his nose.

"It's nothing to worry about, Angus. An automatic snowball-lobbing machine will simply hurl a few frozen missiles in your direction so we can study the effect of ice particles on your skin." Doctor Fleagal indicated a machine beside him that looked dangerously like something Uncle Max could have invented. It was quivering ominously.

"All lightning catchers are put through these exact same tests before they are sent to some of the coldest places on earth. It is an essential part of their assessment."

Angus did not find the information comforting.

"If you could just stand perfectly still and allow a couple of snowballs to hit you, three or four should do the trick."

The first snowball shot over his head before he was really ready. He dodged the second one clumsily, bare feet slipping on the icy floor, and fought off a strong desire to pick it up and throw it straight back.

"Stand still, McFangus, or you'll do yourself an injury,"

Catcher Sparks ordered in an irritated voice.

Angus stared at her for a split second. But it was just long enough for the next slushy snowball to catch him square in the chest.

Thud!

A second one smashed into his ear before he could get out of the way, causing him to lose all feeling in his lower lobe. A third hit him hard on his arm.

"Ow!"

And then it was over.

"Excellent, McFangus." Doctor Fleagal was already on his feet, inspecting Angus's skin through a magnifying glass. "There's a slight stinging on the limbs, but no raised bumps or cracked ribs. We could place you on one of the Antarctic teams tomorrow, and I doubt you'd even require any automatic earlobe warmers. You can put your clothes back on now. Take this to the supply room through the door at the back," he added, tearing a slip of paper from his notes and handing it to Angus. "They will sort you out with the extra winter clothing that you require. And I must insist that you drink at least one mug of hot choco- late before leaving the supplies department."

Angus got dressed with difficulty. His fingers were far too cold to tie his shoelaces, and he quickly gave up. He slipped into the adjoining room before Doctor Fleagal could turn him into a human snowman.

The supply room was instantly warmer. Shelves and drawers filled with assorted woolens stretched all the way up to the ceiling. A bored-looking man in green coveralls took the slip of paper from him silently and issued him some electric blue thermal underwear while Angus gulped down a creamy hot chocolate. There was also a red sweater, two underarm hot-water bottles, a pair of fur-lined snow boots, and an assortment of knitted socks and hats.

"For goodness' sake, Dewsnap!" Catcher Sparks suddenly yelled from the frozen room next door. "Stop whimpering; it's just a snowball!"

Angus couldn't help wondering if it might have been easier all around to sneak back into Perilous in the dead of night, when everyone else was fast asleep. Because so far it hadn't been quite the cheery return he'd spent the whole of Christmas dreaming about.

Fifteen minutes later Dougal had also been issued with

a huge pile of extra woolens, as well as a miniature ice scraper to deal with any frosty buildup on his glasses. And they headed back down through the Exploratorium to dump their new gear in their bedrooms.

It was obvious that most trainees and lightning catchers had already been through the same ordeal in the Antarctic testing center. Some were sporting black eyes and nasty ice rashes; others were wincing heavily with every step. Everyone appeared to be wearing thick sweaters, pom-pom-covered hats, and fur-lined boots.

"This place gets more mental every day," Dougal grumbled, gingerly touching an angry red circle on his cheek where a snowball had struck him.

Angus was glad when he finally entered the relative safety of his own room. It was warm and cozy, with a fire already burning in the grate. Somebody had placed an extra rug on the floor and a pile of blankets at the foot of his bed. He smiled. Freezing snowballs or not, he felt as if he'd come home at last.

"Where do you reckon Indigo is?" he said, dumping his own bag and his cold-weather gear on the duvet. "Should we look for her up in the kitchens first, or ask someone to knock on her door in the girls' corridor?"

"Er, I don't think that will be necessary," Dougal said, suddenly looking awkward.

"What do you mean?"

"You'd better come and see for yourself." He nodded toward the Pigsty. "It might look a bit different from the last time you saw it," he warned, throwing Angus an apologetic look.

Angus and Dougal had discovered a tiny hidden room, nestled between their two bedrooms, on their very first day at Perilous. They had quickly named it the Pigsty because of the state they'd found it in. Since then, they had spent many comfortable hours there, sitting before the fire, reading books and discussing the thrilling events that had occurred at the Exploratorium. And Angus had grown extremely fond of it.

Now, however— He stopped suddenly and stared, shocked by the changes that had taken place to the tiny room. Colorful pictures of lightning storms and snowflakes had been pinned to the walls. An old rug covered the floor; there were neat little cushions in every chair. Most surprising of all, Indigo was sitting cross-legged on the floor, flicking through a small book, her long horse chestnut–colored hair tied up out of her way. She looked so pleased to see them both, however, that it was hard to be annoyed with her.

"Angus!" she gasped, turning pink with surprise. She quickly slid her book back into her bag, making sure it was closed properly, before jumping to her feet. "Principal Dark-Angel let you come back! But why didn't you tell us?"

"I didn't get much of a chance," Angus said, grinning at the shocked look on her face.

Indigo was normally rather shy and nervous, except when faced with impossible dangers and certain injury. It had taken her ages to make friends with them both. This was mainly due to the fact that Scabious Dankhart was her uncle, a detail that she was keen to conceal from everyone else at Perilous.

"Oh, but it's wonderful to see you both! And it's so good to be back at Perilous! Did they make you go through that horrible snowball thing when you arrived? I've been waiting down here for hours."

"What exactly are you doing here, Indigo?" Angus

asked. "I thought girls weren't allowed inside the boys' rooms."

"It wasn't my fault," Dougal said hurriedly. "I didn't invite her in or anything. She just sort of found me in here."

"Found you?"

"It was more like an ambush, actually," Dougal explained. "I was sitting in here one night, just after Dark-Angel sent you back to Devon, when I heard somebody tapping on the ceiling." He pointed upward. "And then, before I knew what was happening, this trapdoor opened above my head."

"I found it hidden at the back of Felicity Keal's wardrobe," Indigo interrupted.

Angus frowned at them both, confused. "What were you doing in Felicity Keal's wardrobe?"

"Well, technically speaking, it's my wardrobe now. Felicity's a second year, she wanted to swap rooms with me because hers looked out over the gravity railway and it gave her vertigo every time she glanced out the window, and I honestly didn't mind."

Angus stared straight up at the ceiling. He'd never even

realized that there were any lightning cub rooms on the floor above his own.

"And then one day I was clearing some space in my wardrobe and I discovered a trapdoor," Indigo gushed, face alight with excitement. "There was a folding ladder for me to climb down. And I've only made a few changes to the Pigsty," she said, glancing around at the cushions. "I thought it needed a bit of cheering up."

"Yeah, it looks loads better now," Angus lied. He definitely preferred it the way it had been before, dust and all.

"And I really haven't set a single foot inside either one of your bedrooms, so technically, I'm not breaking any rules. Isn't it amazing?"

"Blinking marvelous," Dougal said, rolling his eyes with a faint grin.

After a slightly rocky start to their friendship, Dougal had finally decided that Indigo could be trusted at the end of their last term, when she had played a crucial role in their race to uncover the lightning vaults. It was obvious, however, that he was less than thrilled with the idea that she would be sharing their Pigsty from now on.

"Honestly, it's been an absolute nightmare," Dougal said

in a low murmur as Indigo bent down to rake through the glowing coals in the fireplace. "I never know when she's going to appear. I thought about boarding up the trapdoor, obviously, but now she's in, there's just no keeping her out."

He stopped talking abruptly as Indigo came to stand beside them again.

"So what did happen with Principal Dark-Angel?"

They sat in front of the fire as Angus repeated everything that had occurred from the moment his uncle had turned up at the Windmill to the daring descent from the weather station as it hovered over Feaver Street.

"And then we came back here this morning and got pelted with snowballs by Doctor Fleagal," Dougal finished, rubbing the sore patch on his cheek. "They could have just asked us if we were feeling a bit chilly."

"Something else happened this morning, too," Angus said, suddenly remembering the conversation he'd overheard at Feaver Street. This was the first real chance he'd had to tell either of them that Dankhart was responsible for setting off icicle storms around the globe. And he quickly told them both everything he could remember about the secret message from his dad.

"I can't believe the maniac's at it again!" Dougal gasped as soon as Angus had finished. "I mean, first he bombards us with newts, frogs, and shooting stars, and now this."

"But these icicle storms are far more dangerous," Indigo said, looking worried. "They could seriously injure someone."

"Or worse," Angus agreed, remembering his uncle's concerns about someone's being killed. "According to Jeremius, my dad's been hearing rumors for weeks now. Dankhart's definitely up to something."

"Yes, but what?" Indigo frowned.

Dougal sighed heavily. "Why can't Dankhart just do some nice, harmless experiments on fluffy snowflakes for a change, or go on holiday and give us all a rest? Why does he have to behave like a raving lunatic the whole time?"

"Jeremius is also worried about the fact that Dankhart knows I'm a storm prophet now," Angus said, staring down at his fingers. "It's one of the reasons he brought me back to Perilous."

"But what's that got to do with anything?" Dougal asked, mystified.

Angus shrugged. "He just said he didn't know what Dankhart might do, now that he knows about me."

"Well, have you seen any fire dragons lately?" Dougal lowered his voice. "I mean, did you see any when you and Jeremius got caught in the icicle storm?"

Angus thought back to the terrifying descent from the weather station and shook his head.

"Then it's not worth worrying about, is it?" asked Dougal.

Angus wished he could feel so sure. He hadn't seen any of the strange, mysterious creatures since his encounter with Dankhart in the lightning vaults. He'd generally tried not to think about storm prophets or fire dragons. But he couldn't stop them from creeping into his dreams, where they blazed with such intense heat that he woke up dripping with sweat. And he was certain he hadn't seen the last of them yet.

"There's something else," he said, quickly deciding to share his doubts about his new uncle. "Why didn't my uncle just show me the note from my dad? I mean, why be all secretive about it?"

Dougal shrugged. "Maybe he didn't want you to know about Dankhart's causing trouble again."

"Or worry you about the icicle storms," Indigo added.

"Yeah, maybe, but how do I know I can trust him if he isn't going to show me important stuff like that? And what if he's hiding other things?"

Angus shifted in his seat, hugging his knees to his chest. He still couldn't shake off the feeling that his uncle wasn't being completely honest with him. Had he really been on a solo expedition for the last few months, or was there another reason why he'd only just introduced himself? There had also been mysterious midnight trips to Feaver Street that even Dougal had been unaware of. Could his uncle be trusted?

"What's a Farew's, anyway?" Angus asked, suddenly remembering another part of the conversation at Feaver Street. "Jeremius said my dad sent him that message in a Farew's."

"A Farew's is a safe way of sending urgent messages to people when you don't want them read by anyone else," Dougal explained. "Its real name is a Farew's qube, though, because it's shaped exactly like a small wooden cube. It's covered in all these markings and carvings, and— What's up with you?" Dougal broke off, looking puzzled. "You look like you've just found a snowball down the back of your pants."

Angus was on his feet in seconds, charging back to his room. He emptied the contents of his bag onto his bed, not bothering to pick up the shoes and socks that rolled onto the floor, and grabbed the wooden cube that had appeared in his bedroom on Christmas morning. He hadn't given it a single thought since leaving the Windmill. He stared at it now, hardly daring to hope, his heart hammering loudly.

"Where in the name of Percival Vellum's bad breath did you get that?" Dougal scrambled out of his chair as Angus rushed back through the door, holding the qube in the palm of his hand so they both could see it.

"It turned up in my bedroom at Christmas, and I've been trying to work out what it is ever since."

"Well, it's definitely a Farew's qube, all right." Dougal took it from him eagerly for a closer inspection. "And if your dad just sent a message to your uncle inside one of these . . ."

"Then the chances are there's a message inside this one, too," Angus said, gulping.

"It's a bit of a major coincidence if there isn't. These things are really rare."

"So how do we get it open?" Angus asked impatiently, desperate to hear what his parents had to say to him.

"Ah." Dougal's face suddenly fell. "I haven't got the foggiest idea."

Angus was so used to Dougal's being clever with words, puzzles, and the unraveling of secret clues that he'd hoped his friend might open the qube before their very eyes.

"Couldn't we just force it open?" Indigo asked. "I mean, if the message is important."

But Dougal shook his head. "If you do that, anything inside gets automatically destroyed, I remember my dad saying. It's one of the measures to stop other people from reading a private note."

Angus, however, was tempted to take his chances. And he quickly decided that if none of them had come up with any ways of opening the strange qube by the morning, he was going to hit it with the biggest hammer he could find and hope for the best.

6

THE RESEARCH DEPARTMENT

Angus lay in his bed the following morning, half expecting Dougal to come bursting into his room with the Farew's qube already cracked and the secret message revealed. And it wasn't until he finally poked a toe out from under his covers that he realized something felt different. The air in his room was now distinctly chilly. A thin layer of ice had formed on the inside of his bedroom window. The glass of water on his bedside table had also frozen solid. It was obvious that the temperature inside the Exploratorium had dropped dramatically overnight.

He got dressed quickly, feeling glad for the first time that he now had a pile of extra woolens to keep him warm.

He was just pulling on a thick pair of stripy knitted socks when he noticed that someone had slipped a note under his bedroom door. Angus recognized the prickly handwriting on the envelope instantly; it belonged to Catcher Sparks. He opened it cautiously, wondering if he and Dougal were about to be sent for a second round of testing in the Antarctic center before breakfast. The note began in familiar frosty tones.

McFangus—DO NOT come to the experimental division this morning. You have now reached a new phase in your training as a lightning cub, and for the next few months you will be working in the research department instead. Report to Catcher Grimble in the Octagon at eight o'clock precisely. DO NOT BE LATE. And NEVER forget that I am still your master lightning catcher. If I hear any reports of bad behavior or deliberate stupidity from Catcher Grimble, THERE WILL BE CONSEQUENCES.

Angus gulped and stuffed the letter into his pocket. He swiftly checked his weather watch—a highly valuable piece of equipment that he'd been given on his first day as a lightning cub and that showed exactly what the weather was doing. At that moment a flurry of fat snowflakes and frosted ice crystals were floating across the gray watch face, clearly indicating that Perilous was in for some extremely cold weather. It also showed that he had precisely seven minutes and twenty-eight seconds to dart up to the Octagon before he was in deep trouble.

He grabbed his new fur-lined snow boots, dragged a comb through his hair, then dashed out into the curved hallway. There was no sign of Dougal, however; his bedroom was already empty. So Angus sprinted up the spiral staircase alone, hoping that Catcher Sparks hadn't suddenly decided to split them up and send them to different parts of the Exploratorium.

When he finally stumbled into the Octagon, he found Catcher Grimble waiting for him. Gray haired and shriveled, he reminded Angus of a punctured balloon, with knees as ancient and knobbly as his walking stick.

"Sorry . . . I'm late . . . sir," Angus gasped, trying to catch his breath.

"Late?" the lightning catcher bellowed, taking a pocket watch out from the folds of his leather jerkin and studying

it through a pair of thick glasses. "Why, I'll have you know that in sixty-seven years at this Exploratorium, I've never been late for anything! Not once!"

"No, sir, I didn't mean—"

Before Angus could explain himself, Catcher Grimble was talking again, his loud voice echoing around the Octagon.

"Now, Catcher Sparks has sent you on from the experimental division, I believe," he said, consulting a list of names, his nose pressed hard against the paper. "Ah yes, here we are, you must be . . . Agnes Munchfungus." He squinted at Angus over the top of his list. "Quite extraordinary, the names some of you lightning cubs have these days!"

"Er . . . actually, sir, I'm Angus McFangus." Angus hastily checked over his shoulder, hoping there were no other lightning cubs lurking about in the Octagon. Because if anyone heard him being called Agnes Munchfungus . . .

"Splendid! Well, then, Agnes," Catcher Grimble plowed on, completely ignoring everything Angus had just said. "I think you will find that life inside the research department happens at a rather less frantic pace. It is a delightful oasis of peace and tranquillity, a place for quiet contemplation and study in the midst of other much noisier, smellier distractions at Perilous. I must therefore ask you to keep your voice down at all times," he boomed, making Angus's eardrums vibrate painfully. "If you would follow me, Miss Munchfungus."

Angus had already visited the claustrophobic department once before with Edmund Croxley, less than an hour after discovering that he'd been enrolled as a trainee lightning catcher. He followed Catcher Grimble through the familiar tightly packed bookshelves, wondering how anyone could possibly find it tranquil. There was barely enough room to breathe among the maze of crumbling records and ancient layers of dust, let alone contemplate anything. He was just trying to decide if he should risk asking for a transfer straight back to the experimental division, even if it meant weeks of cleaning out blocked storm bellows, when Catcher Grimble came to a sudden halt.

"Here we are," he announced cheerfully.

Angus frowned. They'd come to a dark dead end. There was nothing in front of them except a solid wall. Or maybe . . . Angus squinted. He could see a faint outline in the gloom. There was a small click, a thin gleam of light appeared in the wall, and Catcher Grimble shuffled him through a concealed door in the shadows. Angus's jaw dropped in astonishment as they emerged into an enormous hall. Edmund Croxley definitely hadn't shown him *this* on his guided tour!

Long and narrow, the research department stretched far into the distance, like a never-ending library. Monumental shelves stuffed with countless books and stacks of documents towered above them on all sides, with flights of stairs diving off in every direction possible. Some wound in tight spirals all the way up to the ceiling, while others meandered between the shelves and across the aisle down the center of the hall, forming a strange spiderweb of stairs and reading platforms.

High above them, a vast cathedral-like ceiling had been painted with livid storms, lightning bolts, blizzards, and what appeared to be showers of pea-green hailstones. Angus gazed around, feeling faintly dizzy.

"This department is the beating heart of Perilous," Catcher Grimble said suddenly, making Angus jump. He led the way down a wide center aisle. "Without the countless research projects that have been carried out across the centuries, we would understand very little about the weather. Any lightning catcher needing to know more about wind-howling scales or the correct way to measure a monsoon can find information here, within the peaceful haven of the research department."

Angus couldn't help thinking that it would be a lot more peaceful without Catcher Grimble's booming voice bouncing off the walls. And he noticed that several elderly lightning catchers, sitting in various comfortable armchairs scattered among the stacks, were glaring at them as they walked past. It took Angus several seconds to realize that they were also being glared at from above. Some of the armchairs had been raised off the floor on pulleys and were dangling directly overhead. All the chairs had been fitted with seat belts, reading lamps, and alarm clocks, along with an assortment of feathery pillows. Angus grinned as they ducked under a low-flying sofa from which definite sounds of snoring could be heard.

He was equally surprised, a few moments later, to see Indigo and Dougal hovering awkwardly up ahead of them.

"Where have you been?" Indigo asked, looking relieved, as Catcher Grimble wandered over to a desk to speak to a fellow lightning catcher.

"I only found out we were coming here fifteen minutes ago," Angus explained, hastily doing up the last few buttons on his shirt. "How come you two got here before me?"

"Catcher Sparks pushed a note under my door last night," Indigo said.

"And she pounced on me this morning in the kitchens, before I'd even finished half a slice of toast," Dougal said. "She gave me this long lecture about not doing anything stupid and then dragged me up here before I could come and get you. It was worth it, though," he added, suddenly looking far happier than he ever had in the experimental division. "I can't believe we're spending the next few months in the research department. No more messing about with hailstone helmets and armpit warmers. No more machines exploding or inventions going haywire. Most of the lightning catchers who work in here look at least a hundred years old. So it's got to be less dangerous than being with Catcher Sparks, hasn't it?"

Angus smiled. "I wouldn't be so sure."

A few moments later Catcher Grimble joined them once again. "Now that Miss Munchfungus is here, we can begin," he said. "I have some very important work for you to tackle today."

"Miss Munchfungus?" Dougal grinned, nudging Angus in the ribs as they followed the wheezing, shrunken lightning catcher farther into the depths of the research department.

Angus sighed. "Yeah. Just call me Agnes."

Dougal smothered a huge guffaw. Several lightning catchers glared in their direction.

"I don't know what you're smirking about," Indigo whispered, trying hard not to smile. "Catcher Grimble's been calling you Miss Mildew ever since you arrived."

"Miss Mildew?" Angus snorted, suddenly feeling much happier.

"Miss India Mildew, to be precise," Indigo added as Dougal's face dropped. "He's also convinced my name's Douglas Drainpipe. But it's not surprising that he's got us all mixed up with each other. I mean, he can hardly see a thing through those dreadful glasses; he's almost completely deaf; plus, he's obviously lost most of his marbles."

At that precise moment Catcher Grimble stopped up ahead and began an animated conversation with a large potted plant, which he addressed affectionately as Gertrude.

"Oh, dear." Indigo sighed. "I'm not sure how good he's going to be as a teacher."

Catcher Grimble led them up a long flight of stairs and onto a narrow reading platform that was only just big enough for all four of them to stand on. Angus glanced quickly over the side of the railings and instantly wished he hadn't; it was a very long way down.

"Many years ago," Catcher Grimble barked loudly, "the Exploratorium fell prey to a mysterious book thief, and measures were put in place to safeguard our most precious tomes from grasping fingers."

"Measures?" Dougal asked, looking mildly concerned.

"Booby traps, Miss Mildew, booby traps!" Catcher Grimble bellowed, addressing the reading lamp behind Dougal's head. "A number of clever antitheft devices were concealed within the pages of these books to discourage the wretched thief. Unfortunately, no record was kept of where they were hidden, and some of them still remain. It will be your special task, therefore, to scour these shelves and remove any contraptions that you find. You will start with the oldest, most valuable books," Catcher Grimble added, producing three sets of safety goggles and gloves from his leather jerkin and handing them to Angus. "Pass these around if you will, Miss Munchfungus. I'll be keeping an eye on your progress from the Howling Gallery." He pointed across to the opposite side of the hall, where a long bank of comfy armchairs was filling up fast with lightning catchers in various states of consciousness.

"When he says booby traps . . . "—Dougal gulped as Catcher Grimble disappeared back down the spiral stairs—"what do you think he means, exactly?"

Angus dragged an innocent-looking book off the shelf closest to him and studied it cautiously. "I don't know, but it can't be that bad, can it? I mean, they're just records and research papers."

Luckily, the first few books he examined contained nothing more dangerous than a couple of dead moths. And it wasn't until he opened a battered tome called *A Cloud Spotters' Spot Guide*, from 1898, that he was hit by his first booby trap.

"Ow!" He flinched as a small device with jagged wooden jaws leaped from the page and attached itself to his finger, biting down hard. *"Ow! Get this thing off me!"*

"Hold still!" Indigo quickly came to the rescue, but before any of them could speak again— *Poof!*

"Ew!" Dougal had been hit straight in the safety goggles by a cloud of acrid yellow powder.

So it continued. There were rusty alarm bells that dropped straight out of the spine as soon as a book was opened, causing several snoozing lightning catchers to shake their fists in Dougal's direction. There were anti-theft ink squirters, explosions of potent sneezing powder, and clouds of minuscule book mites that buzzed angrily around their heads. But by far the most dangerous booby trap was a set of revolving spine spikes, which twisted themselves so tightly around a loose strand of Indigo's hair that she had to be cut free by Catcher Grimble.

"I don't believe it! This is even worse than the experimental division," Dougal grumbled as he wrestled a finger clamp to the floor of the reading platform and stamped on it hard. "I thought we'd be doing some proper research into cloud formations, at the very least."

"Speaking of research . . ." Angus swatted some annoying book mites away from his face with a hefty tome and sat back on his heels for a rest. "Have you had any luck with the qube yet?"

"Oh, yeah, I cracked it hours ago," Dougal answered sarcastically.

"So you haven't discovered anything?" Angus tried hard to keep the disappointment out of his voice. But he'd been dying to ask Dougal about the qube all morning.

"Well, there is something." Dougal glanced over his shoulder to make sure Catcher Grimble wasn't watching. He then cleared a space on the floor, took the qube out of his pocket, and placed it in front of them. "I've been reading a book Dad gave me last year. It explains how all sorts of secret message devices work. It says that each Farew's qube is specially made for the person who buys it and comes with its own unique code, like a password."

"How do we find out what the password is?" Indigo asked, trying to not to touch anything important. A sticky coating of antitheft gum that she'd just peeled out of a book had attached itself to her fingers instead.

"Easy," Dougal said. "See all the signs and symbols carved into the sides?"

Angus picked up the qube and studied the symbols carefully. He'd already spent a considerable amount of time in his bedroom at the Windmill gazing at the carvings. There were sixteen symbols on each side of the qube, arranged in rows of four. There were tiny letters of the alphabet and numbers, bolts of lightning, half-moons, and thunderclouds.

"All you have to do is line up the symbols in the correct order, so they spell out the password, and then the qube will open automatically."

"But the stupid thing won't budge," Angus said, frowning. "I've already tried loads of times."

"You do it like this." Dougal grabbed the qube and pulled a slender, near-invisible wooden pin from one side of the block. "The linchpin keeps everything locked in place. By removing it, you release the twisting mechanism, and then you can move the squares in any direction you want—up, down, left, right, even in diagonals—to spell out any combination of letters or symbols."

To demonstrate, Dougal picked a tiny letter *A* and

pushed it four squares to the left and three down, forcing all the other squares out of its way in a strange, fluid, rippling motion. "See?" Dougal grinned. "It's simple when you know how."

"But how do we know what the password is?" Angus asked, amazed.

"That's the difficult part." Dougal's smile faded. "I've tried all the obvious words already, like 'Perilous,' 'lightning catcher,' even 'Angus,' but nothing works. So it could be a combination of letters, numbers, or symbols, or letters, numbers, *and* symbols."

Angus stared at Dougal, sudden understanding washing over him. With so many combinations possible, so many passwords that his mum and dad could have made up or chosen, it could take them days, weeks, or even months to figure it out.

"Why is it called a Farew's qube, anyway?" Indigo asked.

"Haven't got a clue," Dougal said. "But *Farew* sounds a bit like *pharaoh*, doesn't it? Like in ancient Egyptian times, and—"

Whatever Dougal was about to add was cut short by

one of the books, which suddenly exploded in a shower of foul, musty-smelling gas, and all conversation came to an immediate halt.

In the days that followed, Angus lost count of the number of booby traps they removed from the never-ending supply of books, as well as the number of times each of them had to be rescued by a lightning catcher. And he began to think longingly of Miss DeWinkle and her impressively boring fog lectures, where he'd allowed his thoughts to drift harmlessly, without fear of being attacked.

Angus also discovered that they weren't the only trainees who'd been moved to a new department. Georgina Fox and Jonathon Hake, two of his fellow first years, had been sent up to the roof, where they'd been set to work chipping icicles off hurricane masts. Nigel Ridgely had sprained his wrist in the Antarctic testing center and had been sent to help the new librarian, Miss Vulpine. Violet Quinn and Millicent Nichols had been moved to the experimental division. And the Vellum twins were now sweeping up bits of flaky seaweed (used for predicting rainfall) in the forecasting department.

"Couldn't have happened to a nicer pair of lightning

cubs." Dougal grinned as they passed the scowling twins one day in the stone tunnels.

Some of the older lightning cubs, too, had moved on to different phases in their training.

"We're doing an advanced lightning identification course with Valentine Vellum in the Lightnarium, and it's totally brilliant," Nicholas Grubb, a friendly, sandy-haired, fourth year said one evening when he met Angus outside the boys' bathrooms. "Three lightning cubs have fainted so far. Plus, we've had two nosebleeds, and we're doing sinister lightning next, so someone's bound to have a truly excellent screaming fit!"

Angus had yet to see two of his favorite lightning catchers: Aramanthus Rogwood, who was rarely seen wandering the stone tunnels and passageways of Perilous, and Felix Gudgeon. After a very wobbly start to their friendship, which was due mainly to the fact that Gudgeon had dragged him out of the Windmill in the middle of the night, Angus had grown to like the gruff lightning catcher enormously. So far, however, he had caught only a brief glimpse of Gudgeon at the far end of the kitchens, hurrying in the opposite direction with Principal Dark-Angel.

Mealtimes were as boisterous as ever. Clifford Fugg and Theodore Twill were constantly being shouted at by an irate Catcher Howler for starting food fights. It was after one such incident, when Angus was forced to skirt around a large lake of cold custard, that he found Dougal and Indigo sitting with another boy, whom he'd had never seen before.

The boy had thick, brown tousled hair and looked several years older than the other lightning cubs in the kitchens.

"Hey, Angus!" Dougal, looking remarkably cheerful, grinned as Angus approached the table. "Guess who this is?"

"Um?"

The boy stood up and shook Angus's hand in a friendly manner. "Geronimo Midnight, Indigo's older, more intelligent brother. I've already heard a lot about you."

"Oh. Er . . . it's nice to meet you, Geronimo."

The boy grinned, and it was obvious, close up, that he and Indigo were related. Both had the same shades of warm chestnut in their hair and the same disturbing resemblance to their uncle, Scabious Dankhart. Last term Angus had decided not to tell Indigo about this unfortunate likeness, knowing that it would upset her deeply.

"Just call me Germ," the boy said cheerfully. "Everyone does."

"Germ?" Angus asked, sitting at the opposite side of the table.

"Mum told you not to call yourself that," Indigo mumbled, looking thoroughly out of sorts. "It sounds more like a disease than a name."

"Thanks, little sis. They'll be lining up to make friends with me after that introduction."

Indigo scowled. "Just don't tell everyone we're related, okay?"

"I'm afraid it's too late for that." Germ grinned mischievously. "I've already pinned a huge sign up on the notice board announcing that you are my one and only sister."

"So, are you a trainee lightning catcher, too?" Angus asked quickly.

"Definitely not. I've already heard enough about double-ended lightning bolts and contagious fog to last a lifetime." Germ jerked his head in Indigo's direction. "I've got absolutely no plans to follow in evil Uncle Scabby's footsteps and fiddle about with the weather."

Dougal choked on a spoonful of rice pudding.

Indigo shushed her brother furiously. "Don't say his name out loud!" She glanced over her shoulder in all directions, making sure nobody was listening. "People will hear you!"

"Stop panicking, little sis." Germ grinned lazily. "I'm not planning on telling the whole Exploratorium; it wouldn't do my social life much good, for a start. I mean, who'd want to make friends with the nephew of that twisted loony? The big family secret's safe with me." He tapped the side of his nose with his finger and winked.

Indigo continued to glare at him, looking thoroughly unconvinced.

"So what are you doing at Perilous if you're not interested in the weather?" Angus asked.

"I've just started work in the sanatorium with Doctor Fleagal. I'm training to be a doctor. So you name it, I'll be popping it, prodding it, lancing it, and slathering it in tons of disinfectant over the next few years. Scabs, pus, and sores, that's where it's all happening." Germ clapped his hands together, seeming keen to get started. "I'll be looking for volunteers to practice my bandaging techniques on, naturally. So, if you two are interested,

I'll be providing entertainment and refreshments."

Dougal grinned. "Thanks, but I'd rather clean some sweaty rubber boots."

"Yeah, I think I'll give that one a miss, too," Angus added hastily. It was extremely easy to like Germ, but he had no desire to spend his evenings wrapped up like an Egyptian mummy.

"Well, if you change your minds, you'll find me in the library." Germ stood up, stretching. "I've got whole books full of warts and bunions to flick through before tomorrow morning. See you lot later."

Instead of heading for the library, however, Germ darted straight over to a table full of giggling fifth-year girls and set about introducing himself all over again.

"Germ's brilliant!" Dougal smiled, still watching him.

"Not exactly shy, is he?" Angus added.

"I just hope he doesn't tell everyone about *our big family secret*," Indigo whispered, staring at her brother with an anxious expression. "If Percival Vellum catches even a hint of our connection with Castle Dankhart . . ."

"Why didn't you tell us Germ was coming to Perilous?" Dougal asked, finally turning back to their table.

Indigo fiddled with the straps on her bag, looking highly uncomfortable. "Because I had no idea he was planning to work here until a few days ago."

But Angus thought he understood the real reason. To Indigo, the subject of her family was a touchy one, for obvious reasons. She therefore kept most important personal information to herself. He changed the subject quickly, before Dougal could grill her any further.

Germ became a regular visitor to their dinner table over the next week, leaving Angus, Dougal, and Indigo very little time to discuss icicle storms, Dankhart, and the mysterious Farew's qube in private. They retreated to the Pigsty every evening, therefore, to study the qube's strange symbols, attempting endless combinations of letters and numbers in an effort to open it.

"How about Delphinia Dark-Angel?" Dougal suggested one night as Indigo quickly moved the letters around the qube to spell out the principal's name.

"Nope." She sighed. "Nothing."

"What about Felix Gudgeon, then, or Jeremius McFangus?" Angus said hopefully.

But Dougal shook his head. "We've already tried both

of those, twice, along with Alabone and Evangeline McFangus. I've started a list of all the words that definitely don't work."

He turned to the back of his workbook and showed Angus a page filled with column after column of their unsuccessful attempts.

Angus sighed, feeling his frustration levels rise. "It just doesn't make any sense. Why would my mum and dad send me a message that's impossible to open? I mean, it must be something urgent or important. It could even be something about the icicle storms."

"Maybe." Indigo frowned. "But why didn't they just tell Jeremius if it was?"

Angus looked away from her quickly. The same question had already occurred to him. Was there something that his parents didn't *want* Jeremius to know? It wouldn't be the first time they'd sent Angus some highly dangerous information. The previous term they'd mailed a map of the lightning vaults to him, instead of to Principal Dark-Angel. But Jeremius was his father's brother. Surely he could be trusted with anything?

▲ ▲ ▲

It was at the end of their second week back at Perilous that their troubles truly began. It had been another very long day in the research department. Catcher Grimble had set them to work on a new pile of booby-trapped books, which contained some of the most vicious anti-theft devices yet. And all three of them had ended up in the sanatorium, being treated for minor cuts and scrapes by a very excitable Germ.

"Books just aren't supposed to be violent," Dougal grumbled, rubbing the sores on his hands as they finally made their way down a spiral staircase and along the curved corridor that led to the boys' living quarters. "I mean, can you imagine if we got attacked by a swarm of fog mites every time we opened up our fog guides?"

Angus shivered, trying hard not to picture it. When he reached his bedroom door, he grabbed the handle wearily, looking forward to toasting his feet in front of the fire before climbing into his soft bed. The door, however, refused to open.

"What's up?" Dougal asked.

"Something's wrong with my door." Angus rattled the

handle again, giving it a shove, but it remained stubbornly shut.

"It's probably just the cold weather," Dougal said knowledgeably. "Try pushing it with your shoulder."

Angus leaned his full weight against it, pushing hard, his heels digging into the floor.

"It's no good. It just . . . doesn't . . . want to—"

CRACK!

The door gave way with an odd jolt. Angus forced it open just wide enough to squeeze his body through sideways, then—

WHOOSH!

His feet shot out from underneath him. Slipping in every direction, he skidded across the floor, which for some strange reason appeared to be extremely icy. And before he could stop it from happening—

SPLAT!

He collided with something white and fell flat on his face, squashing his nose sideways.

He rolled over onto his back, groaning, and gazed at the incredible sight before him. Everything from his bed to the fireplace was now covered in a hard layer of glittering ice and frost. The clothes that he'd left lying on the floor had been frozen into odd, lumpy hillocks; his books and bedcovers were hidden under fresh snowfall; and his whole room now resembled a sparkling winter grotto. Even the door was covered in a thick slab of brittle ice, which explained why it had been so impossible to open.

"What's going on?" Dougal squeezed in through the door behind him. "Why won't your door— WOW!" He stared around at the wintry scene with an awed expression.

Angus grabbed hold of his window ledge and struggled back onto his feet. His nose was throbbing painfully; a thin trickle of blood was now rolling down his face. His trousers were ripped at both knees.

"Did you leave your bedroom window open or something?" Dougal asked.

"Of course I didn't. It's been frozen shut for days."

"Then why does it look like a snowman exploded all over your floor?" Dougal snapped an icicle off the end of Angus's bed and held it up for inspection.

Up until now Angus had always considered his room to be a sort of haven, safe from the explosions and dangers that occurred in every other part of the Exploratorium.

When he'd left it that morning, it had been in its usual slightly untidy state. But now it was clear that somebody had deliberately snuck in and set off the one thing that could have caused this much damage.

"Somebody's been in here with a storm globe," he said, suddenly feeling sure of it.

"What? You're kidding! But nobody we know would be stupid enough to— Hang on a minute. Percival Vellum!" Dougal said abruptly. "He's definitely moronic enough to try it. You should go straight to Dark-Angel, or Catcher Sparks, and tell on him," he added eagerly. "With any luck, we could get him and that gargoyle sister of his expelled before the end of the day!"

But Angus had a better plan. He skidded across his room, yanked the door open properly this time, and darted through it.

"Hey! Wait for me!" Dougal scrambled after him. "Where are we going?"

Percival's bedroom was at the other end of the corridor. Angus stormed straight up to the ugly twin's door. Percival was lounging on his bed, engrossed in a comic called *Lightning Louie: The Adventures of a Storm Hero*.

"Well, if it isn't Agnes Munchfungus and India Mildew," he said. "I heard Catcher Grimble talking about the new girls in his department, and I assumed it must be you two."

"You're so hilarious, Vellum," Angus said, folding his arms across his chest. "But at least no one's going around calling us the Vermin twins."

Percival scrambled off his bed, dropping his comic. "I'm warning you, Munchfungus." He threatened Angus with a muscled finger. "You'd better not spread that name around."

"Talking of spreading things around," Angus interrupted, still fuming, "what did you drop a storm globe in my bedroom for?"

Percival stared blankly at them both. "What on earth are you talking about? I haven't been anywhere near your room."

"Oh, yes, you have," Dougal chipped in, angrily brandishing the icicle he was still holding. "There's snow and ice everywhere."

A slow smirk spread across Percival's face. "Let me get this straight, Munchfungus. Are you telling me that your room's been frozen solid?"

"You know it has, Vellum. You're the one who set off a storm globe. And if you ever set another foot inside my room—"

"For the last time, you couldn't pay me enough to go near your room. I might catch something contagious. Or worse still, someone might see me and think we were friends. I wish I *had* done it, though," he added with a malicious grin. "It would have been worth it just to see the look on your stupid face. Now go away and stop bothering me, Munchfungus. I've got some important reading to do." And he slammed his door shut, still snickering.

"He's lying. He definitely did it," Dougal said, trailing after Angus as he stomped back to his bedroom. "He just doesn't want to admit it and find himself in Dark-Angel's office. If only he'd been thick enough to scratch his name into the ice."

7

THE ROTUNDRA

It took several hours to clean up the mess. Angus eventually managed to wiggle his window open, and he and Dougal then scooped up the snow and flung it out into the evening air, where it swirled around like a fresh winter storm. The snow was oddly sticky, however, with a very strange texture. It clung to Angus's clothes, face, and hands, no matter how many times he tried to brush it off. There was also no sign of any broken glass left behind by the storm globe. But his floor was littered with some extremely gritty ice that refused to melt. In the end he was forced to pluck it off the rug with a pair of sugar tongs that Dougal borrowed from the kitchens.

Finally Dougal lit the fire, and a slow thaw set in, along with a steady *drip, drip, drip* as frozen curtains and blankets began to defrost. Angus moved his most precious possessions into the Pigsty and settled down for the night in one of the armchairs, with a spare pillow from Dougal's bed and a blanket pulled up to his chin. He still felt extremely grumpy.

Thankfully, no more storm globes appeared in his bedroom during the next seven days. His carpet still felt a bit squelchy underfoot, and it would take some time before his bed stopped smelling damp. But he was just starting to believe that nobody else had actually noticed the state of his dripping curtains, when—

"McFangus! A word, if you please."

Angus felt his heart sink. He, Dougal, and Indigo had been making their way quietly across the Octagon after another grueling day with the booby-trapped books. He'd been looking forward to a hot dinner and a large bowl of plum cake, the smell of which had been wafting its way right through the research department all afternoon. But Catcher Sparks was now striding toward them with a ferocious look on her face. Angus gulped; it could mean only one thing.

"I have just had a very interesting conversation with the cleaner who attends to your room." She loomed over him with her arms folded, her nostrils flaring dangerously. "It seems that in the course of making your bed over the last week, she has been forced to wade through some sizable puddles of freezing water on your floor. Your curtains are also dripping wet. Has a fish tank exploded in your room, McFangus, or have you and Dewsnap been engaging in some exceedingly childish water fights?"

Angus swallowed hard and stared at the lightning catcher's pointed chin. "It wasn't my fault, miss. I can explain."

"Water fights are expressly forbidden in every part of this Exploratorium, unless you are assisting with the quenching of lightning fires," she interrupted him angrily. "As a punishment, you will report to me in the experimental division, on a weekend of my choosing, where you will help flush out the storm drains."

"But, miss!" Angus protested. Having his bedroom destroyed by a storm globe was one thing, but getting the blame for the damage and then being punished into the bargain was totally unfair.

"I'm very disappointed, McFangus. If you cannot be trusted to keep your bedroom free of floods in the future, you will find yourself sleeping on a camp bed in the supplies department. Do I make myself clear?"

"Yes, miss." It was pointless trying to argue. He stared down at his snow boots until she'd stalked away, mumbling under her breath.

"Well, that could have been a lot worse," Dougal said cheerily. "She would have gone really mental if she'd heard the words 'storm globe.' "

"I still say you've got to tell Catcher Sparks, or Gudgeon, about the real reason your room's in such a mess," Indigo said quietly. "It just isn't normal."

They had been discussing the strange incident for days now, and Indigo was adamant that they should be taking it seriously. Dougal, however, remained convinced that Angus had been the victim of a pathetic practical joke engineered by the Vellums.

"Look, it's just a bit of snow." Dougal sighed. "And in case you haven't noticed, nothing about this place is ever normal."

Indigo smiled. "But it could be important. Maybe if we

just let Jeremius have a quick look and see what he thinks . . ."

"No way. I'm not showing Uncle Jeremius anything," Angus said quickly, before another debate on the subject could start. He was still trying to decide if his uncle could be trusted. "Look, Uncle Jeremius has already come tearing halfway round the world because he thinks Dankhart's messing about with the weather again. Can you imagine what he'd do if he heard about a mysterious snowstorm turning up in my room?"

"He'd be sleeping outside your door every night with a guard of big snarling snow wolves, for a start," Dougal said earnestly.

"That might not be such a bad idea," Indigo murmured. But she finally dropped the subject.

The weather outside the Exploratorium continued to deteriorate. Little Frog's Bottom now looked like a giant snowball. The windows at Perilous were so thickly encrusted with snow and ice that it was in a permanent state of semidarkness, and anyone who left an outside door open for even a fraction of a second was being yelled at by a furious Catcher Howler.

Inside the Exploratorium, extra fires were lit to help keep the water pipes from freezing solid. Large mugs of hot milk were handed out morning, noon, and night, along with some highly volatile foot warmers, which caused several small sock fires to break out, long after the socks had been discarded. Dougal had taken to wearing the revolting peach and mauve scarf that Mrs. Stobbs had knitted, in a desperate bid to stay warm. Angus had started sleeping in his extra woolens to keep his head from going numb. And everywhere he looked, lightning catchers were desperately trying to stop the weather from causing any more problems.

"The weather cannon's frozen solid, so no one on the island is getting a proper forecast anymore," Gudgeon told them one evening when they finally bumped into him outside the library. Angus had forgotten just how noticeable Gudgeon was, even among the other lightning catchers at Perilous, with his bald head and straggly gray beard and his single silver earring shaped like a snowflake. He'd greeted all three of them with a weary smile. Angus couldn't help grinning back. It was good to see him again. He was wrapped up in a heavy fur-lined coat and matching hat that, from a distance, looked like a sleeping raccoon.

"We've got icicles hanging off the machinery up in the Lightnarium," Gudgeon continued as they listened with interest. "And I'd advise you lot to stay well clear of the weather tunnel, unless you want a horde of angry polar bears chasing after you."

Dougal gulped loudly.

"And it's not just happening here; it's right across the globe. Places that should be sweltering in sunshine have rivers freezing over, and there's no sign of it stopping yet. Principal Dark-Angel's got a good idea of what's causing it, of course."

Angus tried hard not to look at Dougal or Indigo. It seemed quite likely that Jeremius had now showed the secret message from his dad to all the senior lightning catchers and that everyone knew that the icicle storms had nothing to do with rogue weather patterns or climate change. They were coming directly from Scabious Dankhart.

"But can't the lightning catchers do anything to stop it?" Indigo asked.

"Principal Dark-Angel's got an emergency invention being delivered from your uncle Max, Angus. It's already on its way from the Windmill," Gudgeon said, looking troubled. "There're lightning catchers coming in to help from exploratoriums in Alaska, Greenland, Norway. They're used to dealing with this type of weather, so they might have some different ideas. There's a party from the Outer Hebrides arriving any minute now, in fact," he added, checking his weather watch. "They won't be happy if I keep them waiting about in this weather, either."

And he sped away from the library without another word.

With extra numbers of lightning catchers now clogging up the stone tunnels and passageways, getting around the Exploratorium soon became a time-consuming exercise. Mealtimes, however, had never been so exciting. Tables were full to bursting with interesting new arrivals from Scotland, Switzerland, and Sweden, all arguing over complicated weather charts. A very hairy-looking team also turned up from the Canadian Exploratorium. Jeremius greeted his fellow lightning catchers loudly, before they set about comparing the lengths of their beards.

Progress with the Farew's qube, on the other hand, was still painfully slow. They were now trying out long, random combinations of snowflakes, thunderclouds, and lightning bolts. But the qube showed no signs of opening yet. Angus had taken to rolling it across the floor whenever he was alone in the Pigsty, hoping that it might miraculously twist itself into the correct password.

"Any luck yet?" Indigo asked one evening as she came down the ladder from her room, her bag slung across her shoulders.

"Nothing." Angus sighed, setting the qube to one side.

He watched as Indigo settled herself into a chair by the fire, then said, "Listen, Indigo, what exactly do you know about your uncle?"

He'd been tempted to ask her loads of times before, but Indigo was always so embarrassed by the mere mention of her uncle's name that he tried not to bring up the subject unless strictly necessary. But now . . . Dougal was nowhere to be seen. The Pigsty was utterly free from eavesdroppers. There would be no better time to ask.

"I mean, Dougal's told me all about the crocodiles in his moat and stuff," he said quietly, "but hasn't your mum ever told you anything personal about your uncle Scabious?"

Indigo hesitated for a moment, then nodded, her face instantly burning a brilliant, shining pink.

Angus felt his chest tighten.

"I don't know much," Indigo said, her voice a virtual whisper. "Mum hardly ever mentions him in front of me or Germ. But I've heard her talking to Dad." Indigo swallowed. "Uncle Scabious is her older brother. He wasn't always bad. She says he was a good brother when they were younger and had no interest in the weather then. He wanted to move away from Imbur when he was old enough and travel the world. He was going to take Mum with him."

Angus thought back to the thuggish villain he'd come face-to-face with in the lightning vaults and found it impossible to imagine a different, kinder Dankhart.

"But then everything changed," Indigo continued. "My grandparents died in some sort of accident, and Uncle Scabious inherited the castle. Mum doesn't know what happened, but he was suddenly doing all sorts of dangerous experiments with the weather, just like all the Dankharts before him. He wanted my mum to help, but she wouldn't—she just couldn't—and that's when she ran away." Indigo swallowed hard. "I think that's why she didn't want me to train as a lightning catcher. She was worried that I might suddenly change, just like Uncle Scabious did, and start throwing storms around."

Angus smiled. The idea was completely ridiculous. He'd never met anyone less likely to tamper with the weather than Indigo.

"I'm sorry, Angus." Indigo started fiddling nervously with the straps of her bag. "I wish I knew something important, something that would help your mum and dad. Please promise you won't tell Dougal," she added hastily.

Angus nodded. "Yeah, okay, I promise." He understood completely. Although Dougal trusted Indigo, he was still highly dubious about her Dankhart connections and had a hard time hiding his feelings on the subject. "And if you ever hear your mum talking about your uncle again . . ."

Indigo looked away from him guiltily, and Angus got the distinct impression that she already knew more than she'd just told him.

"What are you two talking about?" Dougal entered the Pigsty suddenly and put his bag carefully on the floor.

"The Farew's qube," Angus said quickly, before Dougal could notice the deep blush now spreading up both sides of Indigo's neck. "And we're still getting nowhere fast."

"In that case, there's something interesting I wanted to show you."

Dougal extracted what looked like a small, glossy magazine from his bag and spread it across the floor in front of them both. Indigo snatched up her own bag before Dougal could move it out of the way, her face turning even pinker.

"What's that?" Angus asked, glancing at the magazine.

"It's called the *Weekly Weathervane*. I discovered it on our first day in the research department. It's a private weekly news journal for the inhabitants of Perilous. It only reports on stuff that happens inside the Exploratorium."

"Like what?" Angus asked, interested.

"Anything from the latest breakthroughs in the Lightnarium to what the kitchens prepared for dinner, and it's absolutely brilliant! The first edition came out when Starling and Perilous came to the island, and it's been going strong ever since."

The pages were brightly colored and filled with photographs of icicle storms and a dramatic aerial view of

Perilous shimmering with icicles. There were articles on lightning accelerators, the latest storms in Bermuda, and warnings about an acute rubber boot shortage in the supplies department. There was also a day-by-day summary of the week's most memorable events.

"Anyone can pick up a copy of the *Weathervane* from the research department, but loads of people don't bother, because they think it's boring. I've been reading it every week, though," Dougal admitted, looking faintly embarrassed. "And I found this in the latest edition."

He turned to page five and thrust an article under Angus's and Indigo's noses.

Tucked beneath a large picture of a team of lightning catchers arriving from Iceland was an article written by someone called Catcher J. Willoughby with the headline THEFT OF HISTORIC ARCHAEOLOGICAL ARTIFACTS FROM LONDON MUSEUM.

Angus read the story quickly.

News has just reached us, via the London office, that exciting archaeological remains discovered at the site of one of the original lightning towers have been stolen in a serious robbery at the Museum of Ancient Archaeology. Thieves broke into the museum over the Christmas period, making off with a large number of valuable items, including several rare Victorian toilet seats and a pair of ancient Roman nose hair clippers. Mr. Edwin Larkspur, the archaeologist who first discovered the ruins, was badly shaken by the incident and is suffering from traumatic memory loss. He is presently unable to answer questions.

A full inventory of the stolen items has now been compiled by Mr. Larkspur's fellow archaeologists. The list includes the ruins of the lightning tower. It is now feared that these important historical artifacts could be lost forever.

Principal Dark-Angel was unavailable for comment.

"Oh! Wasn't there anything left of the lightning tower?" Indigo asked, disappointed.

Dougal shook his head. "Not according to the *Weathervane*. The thieves took everything."

Angus searched through the rest of the magazine, hoping to find another article reporting that the ruins had since

been recovered and locked away in a safe vault. After his exciting discussion at Feaver Street with Jeremius and Mr. Dewsnap, he'd been looking forward to seeing the artifacts with his own eyes.

"What's the London office anyway?" Angus asked, suddenly imagining a huge Exploratorium hidden under Hyde Park.

"Dad's mentioned something about it once or twice." Dougal shrugged. "But I think it's just a minor observation station. They've probably got two old lightning catchers sitting in a garden shed somewhere, making notes on elephant-shaped clouds."

The following Monday morning Angus made his way up to the kitchens for breakfast, only to find Dougal, Indigo, and the rest of the first-year lightning cubs waiting together in a nervous huddle next to the serving tables. His spirits sank.

He'd just spent the worst weekend of his life in the experimental division, under the watchful eye of Catcher Sparks, helping to flush out the storm drains—which had smelled so badly of rotting leaves and mildew that he'd only just gotten his appetite back. It had also left very little time for him to help Dougal and Indigo with the Farew's qube. He was definitely not in the mood for any more surprises.

"What's going on?" he asked, grabbing a slice of toast and standing between Dougal and Jonathon Hake at the back of the group.

There was an anxious buzz of conversation in the air. Georgina Fox and Violet Quinn were whispering to each other. Nigel Ridgely was hastily doing up the laces on his snow boots. Dougal had turned the color of porridge. But before he could explain anything to Angus, a familiar figure came striding toward them. Dressed in a sturdy leather jerkin that fell to his knees, with a fur hat and snow boots, Gudgeon looked as if he were dressed for a serious bout of mountain lion wrestling.

"Quiet, you lot!" he barked, glaring around at them all. A deadly hush fell across the kitchens, and Angus noticed that even those lightning catchers who were enjoying a late breakfast had stopped to listen.

"Because of the freezing weather we've been having this winter, Principal Dark-Angel has decided that all trainees should be taught the basics of cold-weather survival," Gudgeon announced. "If you find yourself stranded in Siberia or even stuck out in Stargazer Wood on this island, you will need to know how to cook some hot food, build a shelter, and stop your toes from turning into icicles."

"Please tell me we're not camping out in the weather tunnel," Dougal whispered, looking thoroughly alarmed at the prospect.

"Survival lessons take place in the Rotundra," Gudgeon continued, staring directly at a terrified Dougal, "which is a permanent cold-weather room that sits separate from the rest of Perilous and is impossible to find on your own. So I'll be taking you there myself. But we're not going anywhere until you lot have all signed a new declaration."

A nervous murmur swept through the gathered lightning cubs as Gudgeon handed out sheets of paper. Angus took his own declaration with trepidation. He'd already promised never to catch lightning bolts or giant hailstones, in a declaration he signed when he first arrived at Perilous. And now . . . His stomach did several unpleasant somersaults. The new declaration was short, terrifying, and to the point. It said:

I, the undersigned, solemnly swear that I will never venture out into an icicle storm, and I understand that doing so may result in my own unfortunate death. I also promise not to stand on any iced-over ponds, lakes, or rivers, even if they look solid; not to stand directly under any large icicles; or to perform any other brainless act that could result in a severe blow to the head, frozen vital organs, or death. Finally, I swear on my weather watch NEVER to indulge in the reckless sport of iceberg hopping without the strict supervision of a fully qualified lightning catcher.

"Iceberg hopping!" Dougal hissed, holding his own declaration at arm's length, as if it might transport him to a giant chunk of ice without warning. "Have they completely lost their marbles? I'm not signing this."

Indigo had already handed her declaration back to Gudgeon with a keen, excited look on her face. But she was the only one brave enough to do so.

"Anyone who is too afraid to sign the declaration will be

joining Catcher Greasley in the cloud gardens every night for the next week, digging up twilight choking weed," Gudgeon warned, folding his arms and glaring down at them sternly.

There was a sudden flurry of activity as Millicent Nichols, Jonathon Hake, and Pixie Vellum all thrust their declarations at Gudgeon. Angus signed his quickly, before he could change his mind or lose his nerve. Dougal hesitated for a second longer, then wrote his name with a quivering pen.

"Right, come with me, and stick close together! I don't want anyone getting lost on the way." Gudgeon marched them swiftly out of the kitchens and straight into one of the many stone tunnels and passageways that crisscrossed under Perilous like the rippling veins of a large stone heart. He led them around a sharp bend and into an unfamiliar passageway beyond. Dry and warm, with only a few flickering fissures to light the way, the tunnel was completely deserted, and it headed downward at a very steep angle.

"We've never been down here before," Dougal whispered, staring at the rough stone walls nervously. "You don't reckon this Rotundra place is underground, do you?"

"I dunno." But Angus was starting to fear the worst. Gudgeon only ever appeared for their most dangerous lessons, the ones where they ended up in the Lightnarium and or got flattened by a fognado. He felt his pulse begin to race. What exactly were they about to find in the mysterious-sounding Rotundra? Why had no one ever mentioned it before? And why could it be reached only by descending into the mysterious rocky depths beneath Perilous?

He glanced quickly to the left, where a gaping black hole marked the entrance to yet another unfamiliar tunnel. He wondered what lay at the other end of it . . . and then instantly wished he hadn't.

"I don't like this," Dougal whimpered beside him. "I mean, I *really, really* don't like this."

Ten minutes later they finally reached a narrow door, beyond which stood a brightly lit room. Gudgeon ushered them inside, and a burst of noisy chatter quickly broke out.

"Right, everyone needs to get into a set of cold-weather survival gear before we go any farther," Gudgeon barked

over the rumpus. He pointed to a long rack of bulky coats along the wall. "Conditions inside the Rotundra resemble those in the polar regions, which means unless any of you are related to snow foxes, you'll need protection from icy winds and treacherous blizzard conditions."

Within seconds Angus was sweltering inside his new floor-length coat. His feet were roasting in his thick boots. Even his weather watch, which now had a furry cap to protect it, was wilting under the sweltering heat.

"It's like being swallowed by a giant hamster," Dougal complained from beneath the thick layers.

Indigo appeared beside them, only her eyes visible under her hood.

A minute later they followed Gudgeon out of the changing rooms and down a long, low passageway. The temperature grew colder with every step until, at the end, they reached a round, solid-steel safety door glittering with tiny icicles. It was exactly like the one that led into the Lightnarium. Angus swallowed hard.

"Right, stick close to me and don't go wandering off," Gudgeon said over his shoulder. "I don't want any of you accidentally falling off an iceberg."

With a twist and a tug, he pulled the heavy door open. An icy blast of air hit Angus in the face, instantly making his eyes water. After the gloomy tunnels, the Rotundra was also painfully bright, and it took several seconds for his eyes to adjust to the new light levels.

"Wow!" Angus gasped. Indigo stood beside him, and they both stared at the incredible sight.

"Isn't it amazing?" she said, her eyes sparkling with excitement.

The Rotundra reminded Angus of a giant round greenhouse, with thick glass walls and unbelievable views across the island. It clung to a wide, rocky shelf set hundreds of feet below the main Exploratorium, which they could now see towering over them through the peaked glass roof above. And it was utterly spectacular.

Inside, everything was chilled to hypothermia-inducing temperatures. The hilly ground was covered in frozen sheets of hard snow and ice. The wind whistled over a range of rocky outcrops and jagged pinnacles that pushed up through the snow like a range of mini-mountains. In the distance a cluster of bright orange tents had been arranged around a smoldering campfire. It was literally

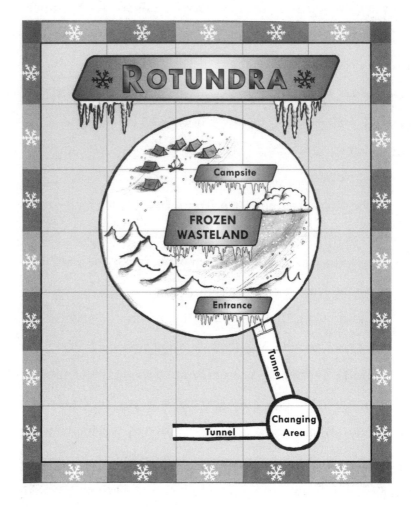

one of the coolest rooms Angus had ever seen at Perilous.

He glanced at his weather watch, which was in an odd state of turmoil, showing great clouds and dense snow-falls one second and icicle storms the next. Before Angus could compare watches with Indigo, however, Gudgeon was on the move again, leading them straight out into the middle of the frozen wasteland, where a tall figure stood waiting for them. It wasn't until they had gathered around him that Angus realized who it was.

"My name is Jeremius McFangus, and I work at the Canadian Exploratorium for Extremely Chilly Weather," Jeremius said, briefly catching Angus's eye and smiling.

Angus smiled back. It was the first time he'd seen his uncle properly since the day they'd returned to Perilous. He'd forgotten just how rugged Jeremius was; he looked completely at home in the harsh, freezing surroundings. It was good to see him again. Angus sighed, suddenly wishing he could confide in Jeremius about the Farew's qube and the state of his soggy bedroom. But how could he, when Jeremius had failed to confide in him about secret messages from the dungeons of Castle Dankhart?

"For the next few months I will be teaching you the basics of cold-weather survival," Jeremius continued. "That means that you will be learning how to keep your wits about you in a blizzard, how to build a fire in subzero temperatures, how to put up a tent in the quickest time possible, and what to do if you suddenly find yourself adrift on an iceberg."

Angus swallowed a lump in his throat, wondering if there were any icebergs in the Rotundra.

"You will use every single one of these skills as fully qualified lightning catchers, when you could be dropped at a moment's notice into the middle of a blinding blizzard, stranded for days in an Icelandic ice cave, or sent to tackle an infestation of Arctic shimmer sharks."

Angus shot a sideways glance at Dougal.

"There are avalanches, ice whirls, and sudden spontaneous snow swamps to deal with, as well as bouts of snow sickness and frost fright. It is thrilling, dangerous, demanding work. And none of it can be undertaken without the proper training. That training begins here, with me, in this Rotundra."

Dougal blanched and wobbled on his feet, looking faint.

Indigo's eyes were gleaming with excitement.

"The glass walls of the Rotundra have been infused with tiny particles of a special coolant that keeps the temperature below freezing at all times, even in the height of summer. This creates a sealed weather system, which follows a predictable pattern on a seven-day cycle, making it perfect for the training you are about to begin."

Angus noticed a tight knot of angry-looking clouds lurking at the far end of the Rotundra, just beneath the glass roof. They definitely hadn't been there five minutes before.

"Before we go any further, I need to make sure everyone knows where the emergency exit is." Jeremius pointed to the back wall in the distance, where a green neon sign shone over a door. Every lightning cub turned to look anxiously. "Although the weather inside the Rotundra is controlled, it can still be a dangerous environment to work in. So if an emergency should occur, a passageway on the other side of that exit will take you safely back to the changing rooms. Now, each of you should take one of these storm timetables and keep it with you at all times during your survival

lessons." Jeremius took a handful of slim, folded storm schedules from his pocket and passed them around.

Angus opened his carefully and studied it. His eye was instantly drawn to something called an abominable snowstorm, which took place every Friday at three o'clock in the afternoon. There was also a daily blizzard that occurred at 6 P.M. and lasted for precisely one hour and seventeen minutes. And . . . he checked his watch. It was now 10:35 A.M. According to his new timetable, in ten minutes' time, they would all be engulfed by something called a snow parade.

"You will also need to study this excellent book," Jeremius said, handing out pocket-size volumes of something called *The Subzero Survival Guide*, by Isadora Sleet. It had a sleek waterproof cover that rustled like a shower curtain when Angus opened it. Inside, there were snow identification charts and ice thickness guides, as well as whole sections on essential survival tips that made his stomach flip over with sudden nerves.

"Take extremely good care of this book," Jeremius said, holding his own battered copy high above his head, where they all could see it. "Do not drop it, lose it in a snowdrift, or use it to light campfires. The information inside this survival guide has saved my life on three separate occasions."

Angus glanced at Indigo and Dougal, who were both staring back at him with wide-eyed astonishment.

"I want all of you to read the first three chapters before our next lesson. Now, if you'll follow me, we'll get started straightaway."

He slipped his survival guide safely back into his pocket and marched them off deeper into the Rotundra.

"All right, Agnes?" Pixie Vellum said as she and Percival barged past. "Found any more snowstorms in your bedroom lately?"

Percival sniggered.

"Get lost, Pixie!" Dougal said. "Your ugly face is making my eyeballs ache."

Angus grinned. Indigo's eyes crinkled at the corners. Pixie scowled and stomped off in a huff, with Percival trailing behind her.

Jeremius took them through the snow until they reached a set of stone steps, concealed beneath a large fake snowman, that led down into a small, round, cavelike room underground. On the far side, Angus spotted another emergency exit tunnel. And a clear glass dome was set into the stone ceiling, directly above their heads, poking back up into the Rotundra like a bubble. It reminded Angus of an aquarium he'd once visited with Uncle Max. Several lightning catchers, armed with ice scrapers and shovels, were attempting to clear a thick covering of hard snow from the outside surface.

"Every Monday, at ten forty-five A.M., a snow parade falls inside the Rotundra," Jeremius explained, gathering them all beneath the dome. "It contains some of the most treacherous and deadly types of snow found on this planet. We shall be observing it today from the safety of the snow dome."

"D-deadly?" Dougal gulped, looking faintly sick.

Angus stared at his weather watch, counting down the last few remaining seconds until . . . five, four, three, two, one.

He gazed up at the snow dome, holding his breath. And suddenly, small flecks of jagged ice were being driven so violently against the glass that he was sure it was about to shatter.

"This is a glacial blizzard, or glizzard," Jeremius

explained as the wind began to howl. "Strong winds loosen hardened specks of snow and ice from the surface of a glacier, which in blizzard conditions can then tear exposed skin to shreds in a matter of seconds."

The glizzard stopped just as suddenly as it had started. Then the sky above darkened, and black snow began to fall, covering the dome in a patchwork of ebony-colored flakes. Angus stared in wonder. It was as if little specks of the night sky had suddenly come adrift.

"Dark snow showers are extremely rare and only occur in the most isolated mountain ranges of the world," Jeremius told them as they gazed at the incredible sight. "They can cause instant disorientation and, in exceptional cases, temporary snow blindness."

The sinister snow only stopped falling when the entire glass dome had been completely blacked out. It was followed by a shower of snowflakes the size of handkerchiefs and a spectacular display of snowbows—tiny frosted rainbows that sparkled and dazzled above them.

"Right, who can tell me what is coming next?" Jeremius said, looking around at the class hopefully.

Dougal was already flicking through the survival guide,

searching for clues. Angus quickly checked his weather watch, the surface of which had now gone strangely blurry. The numbers on the clockface were jumping and dancing around in a very odd fashion. He was just about to ask Indigo if hers was behaving in the same way when he felt it.

The ground shuddered powerfully beneath their feet, causing both the Vellum twins to lose their balance and stumble.

"What's going on?" Violet Quinn whimpered, clinging tightly to Millicent Nichols.

The air quivered; the snow dome shook.

CRACK!

"Oh, no!" Dougal gasped, looking petrified. "It's a frost quake!"

"Correct, Mr. Dewsnap." Jeremius smiled as the ground continued to tremble. "Frost quakes are caused by a sudden freezing of the ground, right down to the bedrock. Moisture already contained within the rock freezes and expands, eventually causing it to crack in an explosive way. It is this rocky blowout that causes the ground to shake. And frost quakes frequently happen during the long winter months on Imbur."

The frost quake slowly subsided, and there was a momentary pause in the weather.

"How long does this stupid storm go on for?" Dougal asked, his voice shaking with nervousness.

Angus was just about to check his timetable for details, when—

BOOM!

Something large and white came hurtling out of the sky and smashed into the glass above their heads with the force of a small cannonball.

"Stay exactly where you are! You're perfectly safe inside the dome," Jeremius shouted above a volley of screams and squeals. Everyone except Angus, Indigo, and Dougal, however, ignored Jeremius completely and fled from beneath the dome, rushing over to the emergency exit tunnel, just in case."What you're witnessing is a snow bomb bombardment," he explained as the large balls of snow continued to explode across the dome. "Formed in the wilds of Alaska, they can appear without warning from clear blue skies and bury a party of lightning catchers in under a minute. Your weather watch is the only warning you will ever get that a snow bomb bombardment is

approaching, so keep your eyes peeled, and don't get caught out by one."

But Angus was no longer listening to his uncle. The hairs had suddenly risen on the back of his neck. There was a strong metallic taste in his mouth, as if he'd just been chewing on a packet of rusty nails and—

BANG!

He staggered backward as his own personal weather warning burst before his eyes. The fire dragon shimmered, a brilliant, blazing sign of danger that burned itself into his retinas like a fireball. And he knew suddenly that danger was hurtling toward them, that the next snow bomb would be bigger and harder than all the rest, that it would come crashing straight through the dome, that it would bury him, Indigo, and Dougal—the only lightning cubs standing in its path—in lethal shards of glass and hardened snow. There was no time to think.

With one hand he grabbed Dougal's hood and dragged him clear of the dome, shoving Indigo roughly away from it with his other hand as the bubble above their heads shattered.

CRACK!

A huge snow bomb hurtled through the gaping hole, smashing into the floor of the cave with the force of a frozen meteor. Jagged glass and ice exploded in every direction, muffling every scream, stopping every scramble for safety in its tracks. Thick clumps of heavy snow began to fall on top of Angus, smothering his face, arms, and legs in a terrifying blanket of white, making it impossible to breathe, impossible to move even the smallest joint of his finger. And then a suffocating silence descended.

"Angus!" There were distant sounds of digging, a cold blast of icy air on his face, and Jeremius broke through the snow.

"Are you all right?" he asked anxiously, dragging Angus back onto his feet, brushing the snow off his coat.

Angus took a deep gulp of air and nodded. "I—I think so."

His neck felt stiff and sore; his legs had jellified, making it exceedingly difficult not to sway on the spot. Dougal was standing beside him, whiter than the remains of the snow bomb. Indigo was holding up her chin bravely, apparently determined not to show how frightened she'd been. The rest of the lightning cubs were still huddled together by the emergency exit tunnel, shaking.

"All three of you have had a very lucky escape," Jeremius said, checking Angus over for signs of injury. "I've seen snow bombs half that size break bones and smother ice bears. We need to get everyone out of here as quickly as possible. Gudgeon will take you back up to the Exploratorium." Jeremius nodded at the gruff lightning catcher, who was already organizing the other cubs. "And I need to find out how that snow bomb broke through the glass dome."

"Come on, quickly now!" Gudgeon opened the steel safety door with a twist and a tug. He hurried everyone into the winding escape tunnel beyond and straight back to the changing rooms before Angus could even scrape the snow out of his ears.

8

TESTING TUNNELS

News of the shattered snow dome spread like a swarm of book fleas. All survival lessons were temporarily suspended while the damage was repaired and a small team of cold-weather experts was sent to investigate the remains of the giant snow bomb. Millicent Nichols, Violet Quinn, and Nigel Ridgely gave long, animated accounts of the hair-raising incident to anyone who asked, leaving Angus, Dougal, and Indigo free to discuss it in private.

"Just for once it would be nice to learn something that didn't involve a high risk of death," Dougal said, demolishing a large plate of ham sandwiches in the kitchens two days after the frightening incident. "I thought

that snow bomb was going to bury us alive."

"Oh, don't!" Indigo shivered beside him. "If it hadn't been for Angus and his fire dragon, I mean, if he hadn't pushed us out of the way . . ." She turned to him with a watery smile.

Angus stared down at his own lunch, embarrassed. He'd found the reappearance of the fire dragon extremely unsettling. It was the first time he'd seen it in months. He'd forgotten the powerful effect it had on his body, setting every nerve and fiber tingling with fire. But at the same time, he was highly relieved that they'd all escaped without broken bones, or worse. And he now had very mixed feelings about the whole episode.

His uncle had come to find them two hours after the terrifying event, to check that none of them was suffering from snow shock. But they'd seen very little of him since. Luckily, none of the other lightning catchers had shown the slightest interest in grilling Angus about the details. And it seemed that in the chaos and confusion, nobody had noticed him dragging Indigo and Dougal to safety seconds before the snow bomb actually struck.

Over the next week life at the Exploratorium slowly

returned to normal, and all talk turned to the news that Catcher Trollworthy had been accidentally sucked into a colossal storm funnel, where she'd then been wedged for several hours. Angus finally turned his full attention back to the Farew's qube. They were still no closer to cracking it. For several days he'd even considered asking Jeremius for help. But the doubts he had about his newfound uncle refused to disappear, and after several long discussions with Indigo and Dougal on the subject, he'd decided against it.

"We've been going about this all wrong," Dougal announced one evening as they sat in the Pigsty with the frustrating qube. He scrunched up the large sheet of paper he'd been scribbling ideas on and lobbed it over his head into the fire. "We've been trying out all sorts of random symbols and combinations, but your mum and dad must have picked a password that means something to them, something important. So . . ." He turned to Angus, looking expectant, pencil poised above a fresh sheet of paper. "Tell me everything you know about your mum and dad!"

"But I don't know anything about them," Angus said

automatically. "I thought they worked in a boring office for years, remember?"

"Yes, but they don't spend their whole lives at work, do they?" Indigo pointed out. "You must know other things about them, like your mum's favorite color?"

"Oh, um . . ." Angus stared around the room, racking his brains. But the truth was, it had been so long since he'd seen them that little details had started to leak out of his head. "Yellow!" he said, suddenly remembering the color of his mum's favorite sundress. "She also loves banoffee pie," he added.

"Excellent!" Dougal said, scribbling frantically. "We need loads more stuff like that. With any luck, they might have used something soppy for the password, like the year they got married or the name of your dad's first pet rock. And if they have"—he looked up, grinning at them— "we'll have this qube cracked by the end of the week!"

Meanwhile, in the research department, Catcher Grimble continued to find more booby-trapped books for them to tackle. And a sudden buildup of ice on the inside of the ornate glass-and-steel weather bubbles meant that all lightning cubs were being sent to help scrape the worst of it off the windows almost every other day.

"If this weather carries on for much longer, the whole of Perilous will be frozen solid," Dougal said at the end of a particularly strenuous ice-scraping session. They were now heading down to the lightning cubs' living quarters. There was just enough time to change their wet socks before lunch.

"Yeah, I know," Angus said. "It's almost as if— Oh no, not again!"

"What?"

"It's my door; it won't open." He gave it a hard shove with his shoulder. "It's stuck, exactly like the last time."

For several minutes they pushed, kicked, and rattled the door, until it finally burst open and an eerie coldness swept over them.

Angus peered inside. For the second time in two weeks, his bedroom was covered in glittering frost and snow. This time, thankfully, at least some parts of his room had escaped the force of the storm globe and remained unfrozen. The floor, however, was covered with the same gritty ice particles that they'd discovered the last time.

"I can't believe Vellum's done it again!" Dougal said,

seething. He took a tentative step into the room.

"Watch out!" Angus warned, dragging him back by his sweater as a shower of lethal icicles fell from the ledge above the door. They shattered inches from where Dougal had just been standing, scattering sharp splinters across the floor.

Dougal gulped, checking himself for injuries. "What's Vellum playing at? I could have been killed!"

"There's no way he's getting away with this twice!" Angus fumed. "I'm going straight up to Dark-Angel before the evidence melts!"

But as soon as he'd said the words out loud, he knew that this time, neither of the twins could have done it. His room had been perfectly normal when he'd left it that morning. He'd been one of the last trainees to enter the weather bubble. And both the Vellums had been present the entire morning. He stared at the frozen clothes on his floor, confused. If Percival Vellum hadn't frozen his room, who had?

"Angus is right," Indigo said. "Percival couldn't have had anything to do with it this time, could he?"

It took Angus five minutes to force his window open,

and the three of them were now scooping the worst of the sticky snow and ice out into the open air, before Catcher Sparks got wind of a second catastrophe.

"You don't think it could have anything to do with Dankhart, do you?" Indigo continued. "I mean, we already know he's trying to cause problems with the icicle storms."

Dougal snorted. "Listen, if your dear old uncle Scabby really had been in Angus's room—"

"Shhh!" Indigo hissed.

"Sorry, but don't you think that if he had been in Angus's room," Dougal said, lowering his voice in case anyone in the corridor outside could hear him, "he'd have left something a lot more deadly behind? Like a swift lightning bolt or two, or a ferocious hurricane?"

Angus couldn't help grinning. "Dougal's got a point. I mean, what's Dankhart planning to do with a couple of snowflakes—tickle me to death? It must have been someone else."

Indigo frowned. "But why would anyone else bother setting off two storm globes in your bedroom?"

"Obvious, isn't it?" Dougal said. "Idiots like the Vellums

don't need a good reason to do something that brainless. It just comes naturally to them."

Vicious icicle storms continued to spread across the globe, now reaching as far as the Australian outback. It was not unusual therefore to find packs of husky dogs yowling in the entrance hall, or collections of storm vacuums blocking the kitchen doors, as preparations were made for new teams of lightning catchers to tackle the brutal weather.

Long queues began to form outside the kitchens at mealtimes as yet more lightning catchers arrived at Perilous. All across the Exploratorium, trainees were being asked to temporarily vacate their rooms for exhausted weather experts who desperately needed to catch up on lost sleep. And Angus suddenly found himself sharing his slightly soggy room with Dougal and Germ, who were now both sleeping on camp beds. It quickly became impossible to find anything in the overcrowded space, making all three of them rather prickly at times.

"What?" Angus snapped when somebody knocked on his door a few evenings later. He'd just spent the last ten minutes rifling through a pile of sweaters, attempting to find one that hadn't already been snagged, singed, poked, or unraveled by the booby traps in the research department. If he didn't find a decent sweater soon, he'd be last in line for dinner for the third day in a row.

"That's no way to greet a visitor, Munchfungus." Percival Vellum came slouching into his room, a sarcastic grin on his face.

It was one of the few times Angus had ever seen the moronic twin without Pixie in tow. Percival looked strangely lopsided without her, as if a large, sniggering boil had been removed from the side of his head.

"What do you want?" Angus asked, quickly getting to his feet. "Catcher Sparks has been making up spare beds in the experimental division, if you need somewhere to sleep. You're not staying in my room."

"I'd rather move into a swamp full of fog phantoms than share any room with you and Dewsnap. I've come to deliver a message from Dark-Angel."

"What?" Angus stared at the twin, surprised.

"She wants to see you. You were supposed to be waiting for someone to pick you up in the entrance hall about five minutes ago."

"But . . . what for?"

"How should I know, Munchfungus? I'm not your personal message service. But Dark-Angel's probably considering chucking you out of Perilous again. With any luck, she'll send Dewsnap and Midnight packing this time, too. So this could be the last time I ever have to look at your pathetic face." And with that, he left the room with an exceedingly smug smile, giving Angus the impression, once again, that he knew more than he was saying.

Angus grabbed a sweater and darted out into the curved hallway and up the spiral staircase, wondering suddenly if Catcher Sparks had spread the word about his soggy room. Was he now in for another round of punishment? He was already certain he was one of Principal Dark-Angel's least favorite lightning cubs. And she definitely wouldn't be impressed with reports that his curtains had started to drip for a second time in as many weeks. He was just considering the unhappy possibility that he might soon be spending an extra weekend with the storm drains when—

THUMP!

He walked straight into something solid.

"Watch where you're going, boy," said a familiar voice.

An arm shot out and grabbed him before he fell over backward. "You almost knocked the stuffing out of me."

"Sorry." Angus stared up at a smiling Gudgeon.

"I was just about to come looking for you myself," Gudgeon said. "You were supposed to meet me here ten minutes ago. I sent Vellum with a message."

"Yeah, I only just got it." Angus frowned. "But I thought it was Principal Dark-Angel who wanted to see me?"

"I'm taking you down to meet her right now."

"D-down? You mean we're going into the tunnels again?"

Gudgeon nodded. "Here, take this in case we get separated." He thrust a complicated-looking map at Angus. It showed the bits of the Exploratorium that Angus already knew, including the Lightnarium, the research department, and the Rotundra, but it also revealed a labyrinth of stone veins and arteries running through the tall rock upon which Perilous sat. "In the early days these tunnels were used by the lightning catchers to carry out all sorts of harebrained experiments," Gudgeon explained as he led the way down the nearest passageway. "After the Lightnarium got built and the experimental division was

added, most of them were abandoned. But that doesn't mean they're safe."

"It doesn't?" Angus asked, stuffing the map into his pocket.

"Some of the tunnels were sealed up tight hundreds of years ago, and no one knows what's lurking inside them now, which is why no one's allowed down here on his own unless he knows this place like the hairs on the back of his knees."

Angus touched the map in his pocket and wondered if he should have taken a good look at it before following Gudgeon. They continued downward at a steep angle for what seemed like hours. And it soon felt as if they'd left Perilous behind and entered another world entirely.

Finally the tunnel leveled off and opened out into a larger cavern, with closed doors set deep into every wall.

"These are some of the deepest and oldest tunnels at Perilous," Gudgeon informed him cheerfully. "They're the only ones still in use today, as a matter of fact."

"But what are they used for?" Angus asked.

Gudgeon grunted. "You'll find out soon enough." He shuffled Angus into a small, dark office. It was filled with shelves, books, and piles of notes and had a well-worn feel about it, as if the same person had occupied it for many years.

"Ah, Angus." Principal Dark-Angel stepped forward to greet him, a forced smile fixed upon her stony face. It was the first time Angus had seen her up close since she'd sent him back to the Windmill. She looked even paler than usual, as if she'd spent the last month underground.

"I trust you are enjoying your work in the research department with Catcher Grimble?" she asked.

Angus didn't answer. Dark-Angel wasn't alone. Two other lightning catchers were standing in the shadows. The first was Aramanthus Rogwood, one of Angus's favorite people at Perilous. Rogwood was friends with most of the McFangus family, including Uncle Max; he had taken Angus to see his parents' room at the end of the previous term. He had also been the first person to realize that Angus was a storm prophet. Rogwood smiled kindly through his toffee-colored beard, his tawny eyes twinkling.

Behind Rogwood stood one of Angus's least favorite lightning catchers, Valentine Vellum. With his cold,

pin-sharp eyes and low, thuggish brow, his resemblance to a gorilla, and to Pixie and Percival, was obvious.

Angus felt a swift swoop of nerves. The last time he'd been in a room with this exact combination of lightning catchers, Valentine Vellum had been planning to zap his brain with some low-voltage lightning bolts.

And suddenly he understood. This had nothing to do with flooded bedrooms. Dark-Angel had allowed him to return to Perilous only because of his mysterious storm prophet skills.

"Angus, I have brought you down here this evening because we have some unfinished business to attend to," she said, confirming his suspicions. "It came to our attention last term that you possess the skills of a storm prophet."

Valentine Vellum coughed loudly. Gudgeon glared at him.

"We decided not to test those skills, however, without the expert knowledge of Doctor Obsidian. I am happy to report that he has now returned from his travels."

Another figure emerged from the far end of the room, making Angus jump. The man's eyes were magnified behind his large glasses. Angus recognized him instantly from the passenger lounge on the dirigible weather station.

"Doctor Obsidian has given the situation a great deal of thought since his return to Perilous," Principal Dark-Angel continued, watching Angus carefully. "He has now devised a totally safe method for testing your abilities that does not require the use of lightning."

"But I don't understand." Angus frowned. "Why do I need to be tested at all?"

Principal Dark-Angel glanced briefly at Doctor Obsidian and then attempted another unconvincing smile.

"Angus, it has been centuries since any storm prophets lived among us here at Perilous, and yet they form such an important part of our history. It would be a shame to waste this opportunity to explore your abilities a little further, especially given the recent events in the Rotundra, wouldn't you agree?"

Angus stared at the principal. The incident with the snow bomb hadn't gone unnoticed after all. Dark-Angel had simply been waiting for the right moment to bring it up.

"The decision is still yours, Angus," Rogwood said. "Doctor Obsidian is extremely capable. He has given his word that you will come to no harm. If you decide not to participate in these tests, however, no one will force you," he added, with a meaningful glance at Principal Dark-Angel.

"Knows his onions, does Orcus Obsidian," Gudgeon said, catching Angus's eye. "If he can't get to the bottom of this dragon business, nobody can."

Valentine Vellum said nothing. He continued to glare at Angus.

Angus gulped and glanced at the odd-looking doctor, wondering if he really wanted to know what any tests would say about him. He'd been deliberately avoiding all thoughts of storm prophets and dragons as much as possible. He also had a strong feeling in the pit of his stomach that knowing more wouldn't necessarily make him feel any happier. What if Doctor Obsidian discovered something dreadful, or dangerous, about him, something that couldn't be fixed? Seeing strange fiery creatures when violent weather was about to strike definitely wasn't normal, even at Perilous.

On the other hand, wouldn't it be better to know what being a storm prophet truly meant?

"Okay, I'll do the tests," he decided swiftly, hoping that he hadn't just made the biggest mistake of his life.

"Excellent!" Principal Dark-Angel smiled, looking immensely relieved. "The tests will take place over the next few months, but they will not interfere with your duties as a trainee. I must have your solemn promise, Angus, that you will not divulge a single detail of this to anyone, including Mr. Dewsnap and Miss Midnight. We do not want the whole of Perilous asking difficult questions about storm prophets."

"I . . . Yeah, I promise."

"Good. Doctor Obsidian will escort you back up to the Exploratorium when you are finished. Come along." She swept Rogwood, Gudgeon, and Vellum hurriedly toward the door before Angus could change his mind.

Feeling dazed by the rapid turn of events, Angus stood awkwardly as they left the room.

"If you will follow me," Doctor Obsidian said, collecting a bunch of keys from the back of the door, "we'll get started straightaway."

He spoke with a soft, whispery voice. And Angus suddenly wished that Rogwood or Gudgeon had stayed

behind with him. Being alone with the odd doctor was already making him feel uneasy. He wished that he were being tested by someone less creepy, who didn't spend most of his time at the bottom of a tunnel.

Doctor Obsidian led the way back into the cavern and through a door standing almost opposite his office. On the other side of it, a narrow stone corridor stretched ahead of them. A sign overhead indicated that they were now entering the testing tunnels.

"Er . . . excuse me, sir, what exactly are the testing tunnels?" Angus asked.

"The experimental division frequently uses these specially fortified rooms for new devices that cannot be allowed to run amok up in the main Exploratorium itself. They can, however, be safely contained down here, as you can see." The doctor pointed to a door on their left as they passed it.

Angus swallowed a loud yelp as angry yellow flames burst out from under the door, snapping at his ankles, followed by a ripple of intense heat. He hurried past to the next tunnel, which appeared to be sealed with thick black rubber; a great sloshing noise was coming from behind that door, as if gigantic waves were crashing against the watertight seal.

Was there a special testing tunnel for lightning cubs with unusual and possibly dangerous skills? Would he also be stuck behind thick doors with rubber seals? Or would Doctor Obsidian simply force him through each of the tunnels in turn, to see if he came out the other end alive?

They stopped abruptly outside the last steel safety door at the end of the corridor. Angus held his breath as the doctor unlocked it and led the way inside. The tunnel was tall, wide, and immense, stretching far back into the shadows.

"The talents of the storm prophet have been a source of fascination since they were first discovered among the early lightning catchers," Doctor Obsidian explained, leading Angus farther into the echoing realms. "Daring experiments were conducted in the lightning vaults and the Lightnarium as we attempted to unravel the mystery of those powers. But this particular testing tunnel was also used by those who wished to practice and develop their skills."

"You mean the storm prophets practiced in—in here?" Angus asked, surprised.

Doctor Obsidian nodded.

The tunnel looked surprisingly ordinary, with rough stone walls and a soft, warm glow radiating from the light fissures. Angus stared, wondering if he should somehow be able to sense the presence of the other storm prophets or whether that, too, had vanished long ago.

"Storm globes were used to great effect in this tunnel," the doctor continued, "and all manner of violent weather could be produced and fought against in relative safety." He pointed upward. A large storm vacuum was hanging from the ceiling directly above their heads, waiting to suck up any weather that grew too big or violent.

"A battery of storm bellows can be employed should the storm vacuum fail or become full during a testing session. There are vents on all sides of the room for the immediate release of any overzealous winds, which are then dispersed harmlessly in the air above Perilous. Drainage systems have also been put in place to deal with any flooding."

Angus stared down at his feet and realized with a start

that he was standing on top of a giant rubber bathtub stopper. He had a horrible feeling he knew what was coming next, and he didn't like his chances.

"Storm globes, however, are highly unsuitable for the testing of an eleven-year-old boy," Doctor Obsidian declared. "I shall be investigating your skills instead with a range of projectograms."

"Pro-projectograms?"

"A storm will be projected around you, Angus. It will feel very real. Your brain will be unable to tell the difference between the projected storm and a real storm, between projected danger and real danger. I have brought you here today merely to demonstrate this process."

Angus felt a huge surge of relief. For once, Principal Dark-Angel had been telling him the truth. There were no powerful lightning bolts waiting to electrify his brain cells, no blizzards or icicle storms ready to swoop in and freeze off his earlobes.

He watched with interest now as Doctor Obsidian walked over to a cupboard set into the wall and took out a box with two cameralike lenses on the front. It was exactly like the one his uncle Jeremius had used, only bigger.

"This projectogram offers a number of weather options and will demonstrate well," said the doctor, sliding a plate into the back of the box with a click. And . . .

Nothing happened.

Doctor Obsidian picked up the box and gave it a gentle shake.

"But I thought projectograms were like three-dimensional photographs," Angus said, thinking back to the ones he'd seen in the kitchen at the Windmill, while the doctor twiddled the lenses on the front of the box.

"These projectograms are more advanced; they work on many sensory levels. When it rains, you will be convinced that you can feel each drop as it falls upon your skin, that you are soaked right through to your socks, and yet you will remain bone dry. When it snows, you feel all the normal sensations of coldness, yet your body remains a constant temperature. When lightning strikes . . ."

He bashed the top of box with his fist. There was a momentary fizzing sound, and a blurry image flickered in front of them. It faded before Angus could tell what it was supposed to be.

"Projectograms are the perfect tool to test your storm

prophet skills," the doctor continued. He opened the top of the box, flicked something inside, and closed the lid again. "Every one of your senses will be tricked into believing the danger before you; you will act instinctively to save yourself and those around you, therefore revealing the depth of your skills and your ability to understand the important elemental forces of any storm."

Angus felt an uncomfortable squirming in his stomach. He didn't really understand anything about the forces of a storm. He'd read some stuff in textbooks about unstable air columns and cumulonimbus clouds, and Dougal had once tried to explain to him about internal turbulence, but as for any natural gifts he might have . . .

"Any appearance of the fire dragon will be recorded with a special measuring device," Doctor Obsidian continued, as if reading Angus's thoughts. "It picks up on the unique electrical activity generated in the brain of every storm prophet when his skills are put to the test, allowing us to assess your natural flare and ability."

Angus had a sudden vision of a panel of judges, led by Principal Dark-Angel, giving him marks from one to ten for his performance. What if the tests revealed that he was a substandard storm prophet, not up to scratch, that his skills weren't worth bothering with? Would that be worse than having the skills in the first place? He glanced over his shoulder at the measuring device sitting quietly in the shadows. It looked like a very spiky space satellite with metal probes and rods sticking out at all angles.

"In this testing tunnel, Angus, you will discover the extent of your great gift, while being perfectly protected."

The words had barely left Doctor Obsidian's mouth, however, when the projectogram finally burst into life. A vivid image of palm trees and golden sands appeared before them for a fraction of a second before—

CLUNK!

The palm trees began to shiver and wobble violently, as if struck by a sudden heat haze. Angus felt a deep rumbling sensation through the soles of his feet; the very walls of the testing tunnel seemed to shiver and vibrate. Suddenly there was a loud crack. Angus ducked, shielding his head with his hands. Sparks flew above, as if someone had just set off a box of miniature fireworks.

"Yes, well, that can sometimes happen with projecto-grams, of course, especially when they haven't been used for a while, but it is nothing to worry about." Doctor Obsidian hastily removed the plate from the back of the projectogram. The deep rumbling sensation ceased, and the testing tunnel settled once again.

"What happened?" Angus asked. There was now an unpleasant smell of singed hair in the room. He had a strong suspicion it was coming from the top of his own head.

"The use of projectograms can occasionally create a minor atmospheric instability, which, in rare cases, can lead to spontaneous lightning sprites."

Angus gulped.

"I think that's enough for our first session," the doctor added, moving Angus hurriedly toward the door. "I will take you back up to the Exploratorium."

Angus followed Doctor Obsidian out into the corridor, feeling slightly less enthusiastic about projectograms than he had a few minutes before.

9

ICE DIAMOND STORM

Angus lay awake for large portions of the night, wondering if he should break his promise to Principal Dark-Angel and tell Dougal and Indigo everything about Doctor Obsidian and the testing tunnel. After all, they already knew everything else that had happened to him at Perilous. And he could definitely trust them both to keep it a secret. He was dying to ask Dougal about the advanced projectograms, but could he justify breaking a promise he'd made in front of Gudgeon and Rogwood just to find out how the things worked?

By the time he dragged himself out of bed in the morning, being careful not to kick Dougal's camp bed, the two halves of his brain seemed to be having a furious battle over the issue, giving him an incredible headache.

Thankfully, he was saved from having to make a decision about anything by the news that a new team of lightning catchers was about to depart from Perilous to tackle yet more icicle storms. He, Dougal, and Indigo followed almost the entire Exploratorium out onto the steps of the main entrance to watch their preparations.

They were met by a scene of utter chaos. The weather had taken another turn for the worse overnight, and the whole courtyard was now covered in a treacherous layer of slippery ice.

Gudgeon was helping untangle a team of husky dogs and sleds that had accidentally wrapped themselves around a stone pillar. There were mountains of empty canisters for collecting weather samples and piles of fur-lined boots, as well as what looked like two yaks, which Angus could not imagine traveling up and down in the gravity railway. Principal Dark-Angel was storming about the courtyard, shouting instructions, her face livid with anger.

"That's not a happy principal," Dougal whispered warily

as she rushed past them. "She's got a face like a cloud full of lightning tarantulatis. I'm definitely staying out of her way."

"I wonder where this team's heading," Indigo asked as Jonathon Hake and Violet Quinn joined them on the steps, both wrapped up against the bitter, icy wind.

"According to Catcher Mint, they're going to Athens to help defrost the Acropolis," Violet informed them.

Jonathon nodded seriously. "Yeah, apparently it's buried under six feet of snow and ice."

"You're kidding!" Dougal looked deeply impressed. "If they don't stop these storms soon, we'll be heading for the next ice age."

"I wonder why they *haven't* managed to stop them yet?" Indigo said fifteen minutes later as they climbed the stairs to the Octagon. "I mean, it's been going on for weeks now, and everyone knows what's causing it," she added, lowering her voice. "But if anything, the storms are getting worse, not better."

"Yeah, I know, but how do you stop Dankhart when he's decided to unleash storms full of icicles?" Angus frowned. The thought that the lightning catchers had so far failed in their efforts was even more disturbing than the storms themselves.

"Principal Dark-Angel must have some ideas," Indigo said with a thoughtful look on her face. As they had just entered the research department, however, she was forced to keep any more comments on the subject to herself. They made their way silently past the dusty shelves, being careful not to disturb any of the napping lightning catchers, some of whom were already snoring and twitching in chairs suspended above their heads.

They had finally finished with the booby-trapped books the day before and had now been put to work in the map room. Angus had never seen anything like it before. A collection of giant books occupied one entire wall, each book filled with maps the size of a modest house. It took the three of them, plus Catcher Grimble, just to turn a single page. Eccentric maps from around the world had been hung from every wall; some were knitted and looked wearable, some were carved into thick slabs of stone, others were so microscopic they could only be viewed through a series of powerful magnifying glasses. Angus's favorite, however, was a living map of the lush, green

African savannas, where real swaths of tall grass rustled, and something growled in the undergrowth every time he brushed past it.

In the center of the room, the floor level sank by several feet, leaving a large square pit where some of the sturdier, toughened maps could be unfolded and walked across. There, real miniature mountain ranges could literally be explored on foot, oceans could be waded through in rubber boots, and clumps of pencil-thin trees had to be stepped over with extreme care, to avoid dislodging any of the pinecones.

Catcher Grimble had already supervised the unfolding of one of these exceedingly lifelike maps, a particularly hilly one of the North Yorkshire moors, and had instructed them to inspect every inch of it for rips, tears, or troublesome wrinkles. And it was the doddery old lightning catcher who met them as they entered the map room once again.

"Ah, good morning, ladies!" He smiled at Angus and Dougal. "I trust you are ready for another day of useful work?"

Angus frowned. Things had not gone smoothly on their

first day in the map room. For a start, he'd tripped over a stone bridge and squashed it flat. Dougal had somehow managed to singe a hole right through the village of Giggles-Thicket while ironing out creases. They'd hurriedly covered it up with a number of woolly sheep.

A faint smell of burning still lingered in the air, however, and Dougal rushed over to inspect the damage. But Indigo approached Catcher Grimble with a thoughtful look on her face.

"Good morning, sir," she said, smiling brightly.

"Ah, Douglas, my boy!" His loud voice boomed around the map room. "Having problems with the crinkles in your map?"

"Actually, sir, I wanted to ask you a question about the horrible storms we've been having," Indigo shouted back.

"Storms? Fire away, then, young Drainpipe, fire away."

"Well, sir, we were trying to work out why—why they haven't stopped yet," Indigo said, phrasing her words carefully. "I mean, it's not normal, is it, having snowstorms in hot countries."

"Normal? Of course it's not normal!" Catcher Grimble spluttered. "I should have thought that much was obvious."

"Yes, sir, but isn't there anything the lightning catchers can do to *make* it stop?" Indigo asked, shouting the last few words so he could hear her correctly.

"Ah, a much more sensible question. There are several ways to stop icicle storms or snuff them out before they really take hold. We have cloud-busting rocket launchers, of course, and I believe Catcher Sparks and her team in the experimental division have been developing a device for sucking icicles straight out of the cloud before they can fall. Stopping it isn't the biggest problem. It's far more important to find out what's causing the blasted weather in the first place. If you ask me, this has all the hallmarks of an experiment gone wrong!"

Indigo exchanged skeptical looks with Angus, who had stopped dusting down a church spire and was now listening intently. It was obvious that Uncle Jeremius had not told Catcher Grimble about the secret message from the dungeons of Castle Dankhart.

"Although there is another possibility, of course," the catcher added, lowering himself creakily into a comfortable leather reading chair. "The weather could be the work of the monsoon mongrels."

"Monsoon mongrels?" Angus asked, puzzled. "What are those, sir?"

"Not *what*, Miss Munchfungus, but *who*. The monsoon mongrels are a most despicable bunch of human beings who work for that blackguard Scabious Dankhart."

Indigo gave a small squeak at the mention of her uncle's name.

"You mean . . . Dankhart's got his own lightning catchers?" Angus asked.

"No lightning catcher would ever help such a villain, Miss Munchfungus. It goes against all our oaths. But there are others who share his disregard for the forces of nature, who are interested merely in the deadly powers that it can unleash, and they have become his servants. The monsoon mongrels have engineered some of the most terrible weather this island has ever experienced. Icicle storms wouldn't be the worst of it," he said.

Angus stared at Catcher Grimble, feeling horror-struck. Why had none of this ever occurred to him before? It seemed painfully obvious now. Dankhart couldn't possibly have created this many icicle storms on his own. He must have had help. . . .

Catcher Grimble struggled out of his chair and strolled over to inspect a quilted map of America before starting a heated argument with a reading lamp.

"Hasn't your dad ever mentioned the monsoon mongrels before?" Indigo asked Dougal quietly a moment later.

"Never!" Dougal gasped, looking just as shocked. "I would have remembered something like that. It gives me the creeps just thinking about it."

"Hang on a minute, I think Gudgeon might have mentioned them ages ago," Angus said. He had suddenly remembered the incident at a ferry port, where he'd been knocked unconscious during a rainstorm and where Gudgeon had been forced to release a storm globe to distract the two men in long coats who had tried to follow them. "I'm sure Gudgeon called them mongrels!"

The shocking revelation that Dankhart had his very own monsoon mongrels occupied every conversation that followed for the next four days. The conversation was interrupted only by the presence of Germ, who had taken to entertaining them most dinnertimes with grisly tales of injuries from the sanatorium.

"It's been nonstop since the bad weather started. People keep slipping over on the ice, so we've had loads of broken wrists and cracked ribs," he informed them happily one evening. "And that's not to mention the sudden outbreak of infectious snow boot boils."

"Infectious snow boot boils?" Angus asked warily.

"It all starts with a nasty little bacterium that lies dormant in your snow boots, for years sometimes, and then one bout of really cold weather and *bam*!" Germ pounded the table with his fists, making all three of them jump. "It wakes up, feeds off the sweat in your socks, goes mental, and attacks your feet. Before you know it, they're covered in these horrible green, oozing carbuncles."

Indigo, who had been tucking into a bowlful of plump green gooseberries and ice cream, dropped her spoon abruptly and pushed the bowl to the far side of the table.

"It's been really gruesome," Germ added, grinning. "Half the lightning catchers in the forecasting department have already come down with snow boot boils, and there's a rumor going around that the boils have now spread up to the roof."

"They're not contagious, are they?" Dougal frowned down at his own boots.

Progress with the Farew's qube was still torturously slow. Sadly, Dougal's prediction that they'd have it cracked within a week had failed to materialize, and he'd now resorted to firing personal questions at Angus whenever they had a few spare minutes together.

"And you definitely haven't got a middle name?" Dougal whispered as they brushed their teeth in the bathroom one evening.

Angus shook his head. "No."

"Or a nickname?"

"No."

"Or something private only your parents have ever called you, like Dragon Boy or Noodle Head?"

"Definitely not."

Dougal sighed. "Did you ever have a goldfish, then, or a dog, or an imaginary friend when you were younger?"

"No!" Angus shook his head vigorously, flicking toothpaste everywhere.

"Isn't there anything else?" Dougal pleaded, looking

desperate. "Like a secret code word for if you ever got into trouble?"

Angus thought seriously about this before shaking his head again with a sigh. He was beginning to wonder if he would ever get to read the message from his parents. He still hadn't ruled out the possibility of simply smashing the qube open with a large hammer, despite Dougal's warnings that this reckless act would almost certainly destroy anything inside it.

As the days wore on, his thoughts were increasingly occupied by the frustrating qube, Dankhart, his parents, and the monsoon mongrels. This gave him a strange vacant expression, which Catcher Grimble took as a sign that he was suffering from something called winter fatigue. Indigo also seemed rather more preoccupied than usual.

"Something funny's going on with Indigo," Dougal said, bringing up the subject one evening as they sat in the library, reading their survival guides. "Have you noticed how she's always checking her bag? I accidentally sat on it the other day, and she practically had a fit. I've still got the bruises," he said, rubbing his arm.

Angus instantly thought back to the moment he'd first seen Indigo in the Pigsty, when she'd slipped something into her bag before they could see it. He'd barely registered the fact at the time; he'd been far more distracted by the Pigsty's transformation. But there had been other, similar moments since then, when Indigo had quickly become prickly and defensive.

"I bet she's got something fishy in that bag . . . something she doesn't want us to see," Dougal said.

Angus frowned. "Like what?"

"I dunno. Maybe she's been sneaking booby traps out of the research department."

"What? No way! What would she do that for?"

Dougal grinned. "She could have mice in her bedroom. I mean, those booby traps are vicious enough to catch a whole lightning catcher, so they wouldn't have much trouble with a few measly rodents."

Angus couldn't help smiling. "She's probably just got something personal in her bag, like a letter or a diary that she doesn't want anyone else to read."

"Maybe," Dougal said, sounding skeptical.

▲ ▲ ▲

A few days later, they were back in the Rotundra for their first real lesson in cold-weather survival. Angus stared at the large expanse of snow and ice as they entered the amazing glass structure, wondering what they would be tackling. He glanced at his weather watch. It showed him nothing but cool, clear skies. For the time being, at least, there were no storms brewing beneath the glass ceiling. The weather, in fact, was eerily calm; not a breath of wind stirred the fur linings on their heavy winter hoods. Not a single flake of snow fell as they trudged across to where Jeremius stood waiting for them.

"Uncle Jeremius!" Angus grinned.

"I hope you three are managing to keep yourselves out of mischief." Jeremius thumped Angus on the shoulder in welcome. He smiled at Indigo and nodded toward Dougal, who had sat down on a rock and was clearly inspecting his feet for signs of snow boot boils.

"I thought we might have seen you wandering around Perilous," Angus said.

"I'm sorry, but I've been spending most of my time in here, teaching cold-weather survival lessons. Besides, it's gotten a bit too crowded up in the main Exploratorium for my liking, so I've been sleeping in a very cozy tent instead." He pointed toward the campsite. "And the rest of the time I've been helping my fellow lightning catchers from the Canadian Exploratorium set up an emergency cold-weather training course."

He glanced over his shoulder, and Angus suddenly noticed something in the distance that definitely hadn't been there before. Occupying almost a quarter of the Rotundra and camouflaged under layers of drifting snow and ice, it looked like a huge obstacle course. There were thickets of giant icicles standing twenty feet tall, enormous walls of frozen water, and a large lake littered with magnificent drifting icebergs.

"It's been set up especially for those lightning catchers who need a quick refresher in cold-weather dangers and survival skills, before tackling any icicle storms."

Angus gulped. Even from a distance the course looked formidable. "S-so you're not expecting us to . . . I mean, *we're* not . . ."

"Relax." Jeremius grinned. "I won't be sending any lightning cubs across those icebergs—unless, of course, one of you does something exceptionally brainless, and then I might consider it."

Angus glanced over at the Vellum twins—two of the most dim-witted trainees in the history of Perilous. Seeing them struggle across the treacherous obstacle course would be one of the highlights of his year. . . .

Two minutes later, their first cold-weather survival lesson began in earnest.

"Before we begin," Jeremius said, gathering the lightning cubs before him, "has everyone read chapters one to three of Isadora Sleet's survival guide, as I asked?"

Millicent Nichols and Georgina Fox both nodded solemnly. Angus had read it through three times in a row, and it had scared the living daylights out of him. The first chapter explained how blizzards formed and contained long descriptions of all twelve different types of snow, including the ones they'd already seen in the snow dome. But there were others he'd never heard of before, such as magnetic snow, sneaky snow, and snow swarms. Chapter two set out a complete inventory of essential survival equipment for any lightning catcher venturing out into frozen landscapes, including crinkleproof maps, emergency food supplies, spare weather watches, and weather flares. And as for chapter three . . . Angus swallowed. Isadora Sleet had personally traveled to Newfoundland to interview the famous world champion iceberg hopper Winifred Wulf for some detailed instructions on how to tackle the tricky activity. Indigo had read it aloud one evening in the Pigsty, leaving Dougal in a state of near nervous collapse.

"So let's see how much you've remembered," Jeremius said. "Indigo Midnight."

Indigo jumped anxiously.

"How does Isadora Sleet define a blizzard?"

"She—she says a blizzard is a severe snowstorm, sir, with extremely low temperatures, high wind speeds, and considerable snowfall," Indigo said.

"Correct. Three things must be present for a blizzard to form. The first is cold air, at ground level and in the cloud where the snow develops. If the temperature near the ground is too warm, the snow will melt on its way down, and you'll suddenly find yourself standing in a rainstorm instead," Jeremius told them. "The second thing required is lots of moisture. Clouds and snow both need it to take shape. Snow is formed high up in the atmosphere when water vapor changes directly to ice without becoming a liquid first. The third thing needed is lift, generated when warm air rises over cold air, forming a weather front. As lightning catchers, you will come into regular contact with all types of blizzards. And those of you who have already consulted your storm timetables will know that at precisely ten o'clock this morning, a fierce blizzard will strike."

Jeremius pointed toward the far end of the Rotundra, where the first signs of the storm were already gathering. Angus checked his weather watch. The surface was now covered in a frosted sheen of ice crystals that clearly warned of dangerous weather to come. The temperature was also dropping by the second.

"In the wild, blizzards can occur without warning. They can obliterate the horizon in seconds, causing massive disorientation. You could be standing three feet from your own campsite and there's a strong chance you wouldn't be able to find it. One of the first things you need to learn about surviving in any cold-weather situation therefore is how to find shelter, quickly. Which is why you must always carry one of these with you." He took a small oblong object from his coat pocket. It was no bigger than

a matchbox and had the letters IEWS printed across it in large black letters.

"Well, that's not going to be much use in a raging blizzard, is it?" Dougal mumbled. "It wouldn't keep a fog mite dry in a storm."

"*IEWS* stands for 'instant emergency weather shelter,'" Jeremius continued, holding up the box so they all could see it. "It was developed by our very own experimental division after an expedition of lightning catchers got badly bruised in a sudden blizzard containing giant Hungarian hailstones. Watch closely, and I'll demonstrate how it works."

Angus took several steps backward. Standing between Dougal and Nigel Ridgely, he watched as Jeremius snapped the small box in two to break the outer casing. He placed it carefully on the ground. Then—

"Wow!" Angus gasped.

Something large and orange sprang up before their eyes at an alarming rate, with sharp spines and rods poking out at odd angles like knees and elbows. Angus jumped out of the way. Jeremius ran round the shelter, staking it down with tent pegs.

"The trick is to secure the tent before it has a chance to deflate or get caught by the wind. It just takes a bit of practice and . . . there." Jeremius stood back so they all could admire his work.

The emergency weather shelter was dome shaped and just big enough for two people to sit in. Angus stared at it, amazed, wondering how one small box could contain a whole tent.

"In less than a minute, you can take cover from any blizzard, icicle storm, or monsoon. Reinforced with toughened reindeer fur fibers, the shelter comes fully equipped with sleeping bags, emergency food rations, and a pack of cards in case you're snowed in for the night. Right, now it's your turn." Jeremius pointed to a box behind him containing dozens of IEWS. "You'll be working in pairs. Find yourselves a space; you've got ten minutes to get your shelters up before the blizzard hits."

"Ten minutes?" Dougal said, inspecting the tiny box as he and Angus made their way to an empty spot in the snow. "We'll be wrapped up in blankets drinking cups of cocoa before that thing gets anywhere near us."

Six minutes later, however, all they'd managed to do was

create several small craters. Angus needed all his arms and legs just to stop the stupid contraption from snapping itself shut again. It was like wrestling with a giant bowl of Jell-O.

"How are you supposed to keep this thing still long enough to peg it down?" Dougal said, looking hot faced and angry, his arms and legs splayed. The orange fabric twitched and jerked beneath him like a wild animal trying to break free.

"Just hold it still for one . . . more . . . minute," Angus said through gritted teeth. He'd already smacked himself in the forehead twice with one of the tent pegs, which stubbornly refused to be beaten into the snow. But this time he was determined . . .

"There! Done!" He stood back, marveling at their triumph.

The shelter was leaning to the left at quite a precarious angle. It also had a small hole in the top where Dougal had accidentally ripped it on a sharp rock, but it was still better than a number of the other attempts around it.

Some of the shelters had snapped themselves shut again, like gigantic carnivorous plants, swallowing several struggling trainees. Jonathon Hake and Nigel Ridgely were chasing after theirs as it sailed across the Rotundra on the wind. Other shelters were simply lying on the ground, flat and deflated like punctured balloons. Only Indigo and Georgina Fox had managed to put theirs up in the correct manner. Angus couldn't help thinking that when the blizzard struck in a few minutes' time, everyone else would be in big trouble.

"Not bad for a first attempt," Jeremius said as he wandered around inspecting their efforts. "You might want to fix that hole, though." He took a repair kit from his pocket and chucked it at Angus. "Sleeping in a drafty tent is no fun, trust me."

"S-sleeping? We're not sleeping out here, are we?" Dougal asked, horrified, as Jeremius moved on to help Millicent Nichols and Violet Quinn, who had somehow managed to put their tent up inside out.

"Personally, I wouldn't spend five minutes in that dismal excuse for a shelter, never mind a whole night."

Angus spun around to find Pixie and Percival Vellum looming over them, like a pair of sniggering yetis. Pixie nudged a tent peg with her boot, and the whole

structure lurched even farther to the left.

"Hey, get away from that!" Dougal said. "We've only just finished it."

"I'm surprised you've still got someone to share a tent with, Dewsnap. I thought Dark-Angel might throw Munchfungus out again. Especially as . . ."

"Especially as what?"Angus asked, clenching his fists tightly.

Percival smirked. "Never mind, it'll keep for another time." And he turned and walked back to his own tent, with Pixie following behind.

"Those two know something."

Dougal frowned. "What do you mean?"

"Percival keeps dropping hints, making snide remarks like he knows something he isn't telling us."

"If that idiot knows how to tie his own shoelaces without help, I'll eat my boots. Just ignore him," Dougal said.

Angus glared after the vile twins.

"What's Vellum talking about, anyway?" asked Dougal. "When did Dark-Angel almost chuck you out again?"

Angus hesitated. Dougal would spot a lie in seconds.

He'd have to break his promise now, whether he wanted to or not.

"Let's get this tent pegged down again and fix that hole before the blizzard hits," he said, glancing nervously over his shoulder at the approaching storm. It was now so close he could feel the first flurries of snow in the air. "Then I'll tell you."

Inside, the shelter was surprisingly warm and dry, with cushions, blankets, and sleeping bags all ready to be used. When the blizzard finally hit, it shook the shelter violently from side to side. The wind roared around it, trying to rip the orange canvas apart. Angus stared anxiously at the repair in the ceiling, but it held firm.

"So come on, then. What was Vellum talking about?" Dougal asked, snuggling down inside one of the sleeping bags.

Angus told him everything that had happened from the moment Percival Vellum had delivered the message from Gudgeon. He pointed out exactly which of the testing tunnels he'd been in on the map that Gudgeon had given him, which he still had in the pocket of his pants.

"I wanted to tell you and Indigo," Angus added hastily,

seeing the surprised look on Dougal's face. "Only Dark-Angel made me swear to keep it a secret, in front of Rogwood and Gudgeon. But if Vellum's going around poking his big nose in . . ."

"I can't believe they've got all those testing tunnels hidden away down there." Dougal shook his head, looking stunned. "But why did they want to test you in the first place? I mean, Dark-Angel already knows you can predict when lightning's going to strike. What else is there to know?"

Angus shrugged. "I wish I knew. She kept going on about how I'm the first storm prophet at Perilous for centuries and how it would be a shame not to do some investigations." He felt an unpleasant squirming in his stomach as he thought of the spiky measuring device and the fact that his performance was going to be judged.

The blizzard continued to rage outside. After thirty minutes, Angus and Dougal had finally exhausted the subject of storm prophets and testing tunnels. They found a board game tucked into a handy pocket in the side of the shelter, along with a packet of freeze-dried cookies. They played three rounds of ScumbleChunk! before the conversation came around to the Farew's qube.

"Well, we definitely won't find a list of passwords just lying around in the library," Dougal said as the howling wind shook the tent.

"We could ask Catcher Grimble for some ideas, the next time we're in the research department," Angus suggested. "But I don't know what kind of an answer we'd get."

"Grimble . . . Hey, you've just reminded me of something!" Dougal sat bolt upright, his head skimming the top of the shelter. "There's a whole shelf full of books on cracking passwords in the research department."

"What? Are you serious?"

"Yeah, I found it the other day by accident. Grimble sent me to fetch the latest copy of the *Weathervane*, and I took a short detour through the weather words, puzzles, and games section, and there it was! But some doddery old lightning catcher was half asleep in a chair, right in front of it, so I couldn't grab anything."

"Why didn't you say something?" Angus asked.

"I was going to, but when I got back to the map room, Catcher Grimble started telling spooky stories about fog phantoms and I forgot. Sorry," Dougal added sheepishly.

But Angus didn't care. "We've got to get up there and have a look!"

Half an hour later, the blizzard finally blew itself out. They emerged from their shelter to find a scene of utter devastation before them. Some shelters, which had been poorly put up in the first place, had been ripped to shreds by the gale-force winds and scattered across the Rotundra. Others had been crushed under the weight of snow. Angus couldn't help grinning as Percival Vellum trudged past them with icicles dangling from his earlobes.

Indigo and Georgina Fox were the only other trainees to come through the storm completely unscathed, with their shelter still intact. Jeremius set each team to work immediately, however, helping to retrieve the debris that had been scattered far and wide. It was another full hour before he allowed anyone to return to the Exploratorium, where a dinner of hot stew and dumplings was waiting for them in the kitchens. Angus quickly filled Indigo in on everything he'd already told Dougal about Doctor Obsidian and the storm prophet tests. There was no point hiding anything from her, now that Dougal knew the details. And Dougal told her about his discovery in the research department.

Strangely, though, Indigo hurried off to her room as soon as she'd finished her dessert, claiming she was far too tired to hunt for books. So Angus and Dougal headed up the stairs to the research department, full to bursting with apple pie and custard, to search for password-cracking books without her.

"Maybe Indigo's right, we should do this in the m-m-morning?" Dougal yawned. "We'll be in the map room all day tomorrow."

Angus was also looking forward to crawling into his nice warm bed; he was almost positive he could hear it calling to him from the trainees' living quarters. A long walk through the research department, which was in completely the opposite direction, was the last thing he wanted to do right now. But he was also convinced that he wouldn't be able to sleep until they'd found something that might point them to the right password at last.

They entered the door in the Octagon and made their way through the familiar cramped maze of shelves. Dougal stopped in his tracks when they reached the main hall. Angus stared around at the deserted aisles. Not a single dangling chair was occupied now. Most of the light

fissures had already been dimmed. Only a small group of lightning catchers, huddled under blankets, remained at the far end of the department. At night, it seemed, the research department was not a warm and comforting place to linger.

"Are we even allowed in here after dark?" Dougal whispered, glancing over his shoulder.

"I dunno." Angus shivered. "I'm not planning on hanging around long enough to find out."

Dougal ran up a short set of spiral stairs and disappeared behind a row of shelves, leaving Angus standing guard alone. It wasn't just that the research department was creepy after dark, he decided, staring into the depths of the deserted hall. It was more that there was an odd chill in the air that he'd never noticed before. It raised the hairs on the back of his neck and sent small shivers running up and down his spine.

"This will do for a start!" Dougal reappeared and handed a dusty book to Angus. There was no title on the cover, just a series of mysterious squiggles and symbols. "Now can we please get out of here? This place is creepier than a bat-filled graveyard at midnight."

They had almost reached the inner door that would take them back to the Octagon again when they heard it. A muffled *thump* came from behind them. The noise reverberated like a shock wave, causing cascades of dust to fall from the highest shelves like a sprinkling of gray snow.

"What on earth was that?" Angus turned. An unnatural breeze was blowing from the far end of the department. It carried a new sound with it. He was almost certain he could hear . . . that it sounded exactly like . . . people running.

He saw them a second later, a stampede of frail and elderly lightning catchers heading swiftly in their direction.

"Look out!" Dougal dragged him to one side as the lightning catchers charged past, hobbling on walking sticks, gray hair and hearing aids flapping behind them.

"Dewsnap, McFangus!" A stern voice cut through the commotion, and Catcher Sparks emerged from the group now heading for the door. "Don't just stand there like a pair of lemons! Run!"

"But— What's going on, miss?"

Before Catcher Sparks could answer, however, an icy

breeze brushed his face, and Angus caught a brief glimpse of a sinister cloud rising above the shelves in the distance. It started rolling toward them with menace.

"Come on!" Dougal gripped Angus's arm and pulled him through the familiar maze of dusty books. They tumbled out into the Octagon a few moments later, gasping for breath. Someone slammed the thick wooden door shut.

"And what, might I ask, were you two doing in the research department at this time of night?" Catcher Sparks was already standing over them, a fierce glare on her face.

"I—I wanted to find a book, miss," Angus explained. He scrambled to his feet and backed away from her before flames burst out of her nostrils. He realized almost immediately, however, that he was no longer holding the book. "Oh no! I must have dropped it!"

"Well, the next time, McFangus, you will restrict your book browsing to daylight hours. Do I make myself clear?"

Angus nodded silently.

"It is extremely fortunate that you did not decide to go wandering off among the shelves. When I think what could have happened when that cloud went off . . ." Catcher Sparks gulped, her voice trailing away. She looked uncharacteristically white. "Any lightning catcher or cub who did not escape the research department in time . . ." She stopped short again, trying to compose herself.

Angus and Dougal exchanged puzzled glances.

"I must inform Principal Dark-Angel immediately. And you two will return to your rooms and stay there until you are told otherwise."

With a single sniff, she strode toward the stairs, leaving a heap of panting lightning catchers in her wake.

"But, miss—" Angus chased after her. "What was that cloud?"

Catcher Sparks stopped and stared down at him. "That, McFangus, was an ice diamond storm, one of the most deadly and unnatural weather forms known to man. It was invented by Scabious Dankhart with just one purpose—to kill anyone in its path."

10

GRIT AND STEAM

News of the ice diamond storm spread like wildfire through the stone tunnels and passageways of Perilous. By the time Angus went up to the kitchens the following morning for breakfast, the whole Exploratorium was buzzing with details of the strange and dangerous incident. The fact that Angus and Dougal had been in the research department at the time, however, did not appear to be common knowledge, and Angus ate his sausage and bacon in relative peace, discussing the events quietly with Indigo.

"Catcher Sparks actually said that D-Dankhart invented it to kill people?" she whispered, stumbling over her uncle's name.

"Yeah, she said it was one of his most dangerous creations."

There had been very little opportunity to discuss exactly what had happened the previous evening. Germ, who was still sharing Angus's room, had invited a whole bunch of his own friends in to discuss the outrageous rumors flying around that Principal Dark-Angel had set the ice diamond storm off herself, to stamp out the epidemic of snow boot boils. And Angus had been forced to turn things over quietly in his own brain until it felt as if it were about to explode.

"Listen, does your mum know *anything* about the ice diamond storms?" he asked quietly, leaning closer to Indigo across the table.

"I'm sorry, Angus. I don't know anything about my uncle's inventions."

"So your mum's never told you about his experiments with the weather?"

Indigo shook her head solemnly. "Never. She doesn't even like reading the forecast in the newspaper. I know he's got nothing to do with our family anymore, but I think she still feels guilty. And now he's planting ice diamond

storms as well." Indigo stopped, suddenly looking very watery eyed and upset.

"Oh, er." Angus fiddled uneasily with his breakfast, not quite sure what to do. "Is everything all right?" he eventually asked. "I mean, it's not just the ice diamond storms, is it?"

"I'm fine." Indigo sniffed. "Honestly." She shot a nervous glance at her bag and quickly changed the subject before Angus could quiz her any further. "Didn't Catcher Sparks explain why the storms are so dangerous?"

"She didn't tell us anything useful." Angus sighed, leaning back in his chair again. "It might help if we actually knew what ice diamond storms were, for a start."

Angus and Indigo both turned automatically to look at the chair where Dougal usually sat. Dougal was always the most likely person in any room to know about anything secret or dangerous. Dougal, however, had not been seen since late last night. Angus had woken up early to find his friend's camp bed already empty. There had been no sign of him in the queue for the bathroom or the kitchens.

"You don't think he's in trouble, do you?" Indigo asked anxiously. "He's never missed breakfast before. What if he's gone back to the research department on his own, to find out more about the ice diamond storms?"

The same worrying thought had already occurred to Angus. But surely Dougal wouldn't have risked it? Not after the dire warning issued by Catcher Sparks. Not without at least one of them tagging along for moral support!

"There's only one way to find out." Angus dropped the last forkful of sausage onto his plate and stood up, determined to find his friend. "Come on, let's head up to the research department and see what's going on. Maybe Dougal's already waiting for us in the Octagon."

But when they reached the marbled hall a few minutes later, there was no sign of Dougal. An assortment of lightning cubs had already gathered, hoping to hear any snippet of new information or catch a glimpse of something interesting. The door to the research department, however, was firmly shut. It was also being guarded by a stern-looking Catcher Sparks.

Determined to find out if Dougal had somehow slipped back inside, Angus pushed his way past Georgina Fox, Juliana Jessop, and Edmund Croxley.

"Er . . . excuse me, miss."

Catcher Sparks glared down at him. "No one is allowed

inside the research department until it's been fully decontaminated, McFangus," she said abruptly. "Considering the lucky escape that you and Dewsnap had last night, I would suggest that a day spent in the library catching up on your homework would be a good use of your time."

There were dark circles under her eyes. It was obvious that she'd been up all night and was in an extremely prickly mood. Still, Angus had to be sure.

"But, miss." He tried again. "Nobody's seen Dougal this morning, and me and Indigo were wondering if he might have gone back into the research depart—"

"I can assure you that no lightning cub, including Dewsnap, has been anywhere near this department," the catcher snapped, looking even fiercer. "You will be informed when your normal duties can be resumed. Now, you will kindly move out of the way. We are trying to rescue what is left of some extremely old and precious research papers before they are lost forever, and you are blocking the entrance."

Angus and Indigo hopped swiftly to one side as a whole team of lightning catchers, including Jeremius and Gudgeon, came charging through the Octagon carrying various bits of strange equipment.

"That's the last of the defrosting devices from storage, Amelia." Jeremius pulled Catcher Sparks to the side as the other lightning catchers maneuvered the equipment awkwardly through the door, gouging several chunks of wood out of the frame. Angus and Indigo hovered, trying not to look as if they were eavesdropping.

"And the de-icers are still having little effect?" Catcher Sparks asked, lowering her voice.

"The structure of the ice diamond storms is completely different from anything we've ever seen before," Jeremius said, "even at the Canadian Exploratorium."

"Only Dankhart would bother inventing ice that doesn't melt," Gudgeon said, shaking his head.

"And we still don't understand why he's doing this?" Catcher Sparks hissed. "I mean, first the icicle storms and now this! What can he possibly hope to gain?"

"Chaos and panic right at the very heart of Perilous," Jeremius said simply. "And so far, he's succeeding. We knew he was planning some sort of trouble, but if we can't even keep our own lightning catchers safe, if he decides to attack the Lightnarium or the kitchens next time . . ."

"Next time?" Catcher Sparks repeated, sounding alarmed.

"You can bet your snow boot boils he hasn't finished with us yet," Gudgeon growled. "Principal Dark-Angel's calling in anyone who can help. Aurora Tweed and Geoffrey Whitworth are coming in from Alaska. They're both experts in unusual ice forms."

Angus was listening so intently to their whispered conversation that he almost jumped out of his skin when he suddenly felt a sharp tugging on his sleeve. He turned around to find Indigo pointing at the entrance to the research department, which was now standing completely unguarded.

"It might be our only chance to see what's going on for ourselves," she whispered, grabbing his arm and pulling him toward the door.

Catcher Sparks, Jeremius, and Gudgeon were still deep in conversation. Nobody in the Octagon appeared to be watching them. Angus followed Indigo as she slipped quickly through the door and disappeared into the maze of dusty books beyond.

"If we get caught, Catcher Sparks will have me

vaporized," Angus hissed as they crept closer to the hidden door at the far end of the chamber. But before they could get anywhere near it—

"Get back!" Indigo warned suddenly, dragging Angus deep into the shadows. The inner door to the department was flung open from the inside, and a team of lightning catchers raced past.

"And I want a path cleared through the middle of that Octagon!" a senior-sounding lightning catcher shouted after them as they disappeared into the dust and gloom. "We've got several storm victims heading straight for the sanatorium."

"Victims?" Angus whispered, turning to Indigo. "You don't think—I mean, Dougal?"

But Indigo shook her head and pointed to the strange procession that was now heading through the maze of crumbling records. Three unfortunate casualties of the ice diamond storm were being rushed toward the door. It took Angus several seconds to realize that they were being carried out in their own armchairs. And it was obvious that they had been overcome by the sinister storm before they could even make a run for it.

The first victim had clearly been in the middle of a humongous sneeze when the storm had struck—it was now suspended in midair beside him, a terrible icy blob. Angus couldn't help staring as they ferried him past. The second had been caught in a state of obvious panic, with his hair literally standing on end, his eyebrows frozen into stiff peaks of alarm. And the third . . .

"Oh!" Indigo gasped as they both recognized Catcher Grimble at the same moment. Angus was extremely relieved to see that the ancient lightning catcher was still breathing, that his chest was rising and falling gently. His eyelids, on the other hand, were frozen shut; his fingers were caked in frosted icicles and horrible crystal fronds. Even the blanket he was sitting under looked white, giving the impression that he'd been transformed overnight into a snowman with knobbly knees.

"These three were up in the Howling Gallery, close to where the storm erupted," one of the chair carriers explained to the senior lightning catcher as they staggered past. "It was impossible to reach them until we'd defrosted the spiral stairs. If they hadn't been asleep under blankets at the time, they would have been totally frozen."

"Get them straight up to the sanatorium," the senior lightning catcher told them. "Doctor Fleagal wants to chip off the worst of the icicles before he tries to thaw them out."

Angus and Indigo made their way quickly back into the Octagon as soon as the coast was clear, ducking past Catcher Sparks before she caught them. Neither Angus nor Indigo spoke until a familiar figure came into view up ahead, and Angus was extremely pleased to see Dougal standing at the top of the spiral stairs that led down to their quarters.

"Where have you been?" Indigo raced up to Dougal with a relieved expression on her face.

"I— What's up with you? Why are you both looking all worried?" Dougal frowned. "I've only been in the library. I went to find a—"

"Well, you could have left us a note!" Indigo whispered, cutting him off midsentence. "We were worried sick, we thought you'd . . ."

"Thought I'd what?"

"Oh, never mind!" Indigo shook her head. "I'll see you two in the Pigsty." She disappeared down the spiral stairs and out of sight.

"What's up with her?" Dougal asked, looking mystified.

"When we couldn't find you this morning, we both thought you'd gone back to the research department on your own," Angus said, feeling immensely glad to find his friend in one piece and not covered in icicles. He quickly described exactly what they'd just seen, including Catcher Grimble frozen solid in his own armchair.

Dougal turned paler and paler as they as they made their way along the curved corridor and slipped quietly through Angus's bedroom into the Pigsty. A cheerful fire was glowing in the grate, making everything look extremely warm and cozy.

"That sounds exactly like the stuff I've found in this book," Dougal said, sitting in one of the armchairs by the fire and wriggling an enormous volume out of his bag. "Like I was trying to tell you before Indigo had a meltdown, I went to the library first thing to find a book my dad told me about once. I'd forgotten all about it until I woke up really early this morning and suddenly remembered it. It took a while to find it, though," Dougal added, flicking through the mildew-spotted pages, each of which had clearly been stamped with the words DO NOT REMOVE

"It was buried behind all these books on glaciers, and then I had to sneak it out past Miss Vulpine. I swear she knew what I was up to, but then she got cornered by Catcher Howler, and I made a run for it. I went straight to the kitchens to find you and Indigo, but everyone had gone."

A sudden grating noise came from above. Neither Angus nor Dougal was surprised to see Indigo descending a ladder from her room. She sat down quietly on a cushion next to Angus, her face now composed, waiting to hear what Dougal had to say.

"Anyway, according to this book, Dankhart toyed with the idea of ice diamond storms years ago, although they were actually invented by one of his monsoon mongrels, some guy called Adrik Swarfe."

"Swarfe?" Angus said. "Haven't we heard that somewhere before?"

"All storm globes contain an assortment of Swarfe weather crystals," Dougal said simply. "Swarfe's first experiments with the ice diamond storms ended in disaster inside Castle Dankhart. An experimental batch got free and killed several of the other monsoon

mongrels. But he must have been refining the idea, and now they're being sent over to Perilous to terrorize the lightning catchers!"

"But how do the storms work?" Indigo asked, frowning.

"It says in this book that a cluster of diamond-shaped spores are contained within an outer shell," Dougal said.

"Spores?" Angus asked.

"Yeah, once the spores have been released from the shell, they quickly rise and form into a raging ice diamond storm. The spores then drift through the air, freezing the atmosphere around them to such a low temperature that anything they touch—any surface made of wood, stone, steel, water, skin, or bone—gets instantly frozen.

"'If you accidentally breathe the spores in, they can freeze your lungs from the inside; they can 'congeal the blood in your veins while your heart is still beating. Just touching a single spore can result in frostbite and uncontrollable shivers, not to mention violent teeth chattering and frost shock,'" Dougal said, reading directly from the book.

"Frost shock?" Indigo asked.

"Yeah, it can make the victims so cold that even if it

doesn't kill them, it takes ages for blood vessels and vital organs to recover their full function. It can take weeks for a patient to even regain consciousness."

Angus shuddered, the cold still lingering in his bones. A picture of Catcher Grimble flashed before his eyes. Was this what Dankhart had been planning all along, to fill the Exploratorium with deadly storms of diamond-shaped spores and kill as many lightning catchers as possible? Angus swallowed a mouthful of bile, feeling sick at the thought. Indigo sat silently beside him, hugging her knees to her chest. But Dougal hadn't finished yet.

"There's more," he said, sounding troubled. "I didn't have time to read this bit earlier, but someone's scribbled a footnote at the bottom of the page. It says that to set the ice diamond storms off, to release the spores, you've got to stamp down hard on an outer shell." He gulped. "And the only trace the shell leaves behind is gritty bits of crystal. Just like the ones we found—"

"—all over my bedroom floor," Angus finished.

"That's not all," Dougal added, before Angus could digest this disturbing information. "According to this, ice diamond storms are extremely volatile before they've been set off. Once the spores have been released, nothing can stop them, but until that moment the slightest temperature change or the smallest vibration in the air can cause the storm to fail. And if it fails, the storm produces nothing but a load of sticky snow and frost instead."

Indigo gasped. Angus felt a dull *thunk* inside his brain as everything suddenly fell into place, making perfect sense.

"But that means—"

"The ice diamond storm in the research department wasn't Dankhart's first attempt," Dougal said, looking deeply shocked. "He's already tried to set off two storms before now."

Angus swallowed hard. "And both of them were in my bedroom."

One storm in his room might be a case of bad luck, but two in just a few weeks? That was no coincidence. It seemed that Indigo had been right all along. This had nothing to do with the Vellum twins. Dankhart had made two attempts to finish Angus off with deadly ice diamond storms.

Angus spent the rest of the day with his brain in an odd state of numbness, which quickly spread to his hands and feet, causing him to trip over his own snow boots more than once. A tense atmosphere had descended upon Perilous. Lightning catchers dashed from the entrance hall to the Octagon and back again, carrying various defrosting devices, buckets, and giant ice scrapers. Principal Dark-Angel was spotted in serious-looking discussions all over the Exploratorium, with Gudgeon, Jeremius, Catcher Sparks, and an endless string of cold-weather experts from Alaska and Greenland.

No more news emerged from the research department, however, and after a very subdued dinner, Angus, Indigo, and Dougal finally retreated to the Pigsty, taking full advantage of the fact that Germ was staying late in the sanatorium. It was now more urgent than ever to retrieve the message from Angus's mum and dad.

"I mean, what if they know something about the ice diamond storms?" Angus said, clearing a space on the floor so they could spread out. "What if they were trying to warn us before it happened? We've got to get that message!" he added, staring desperately at Dougal. Dougal had come up with all the best suggestions so far; he was brilliant at cracking impossible codes and solving tricky puzzles. "There's got to be something else we can try!"

"Okay, okay! Just let me think!" Dougal sat on the floor, legs crossed. He took the qube from his bag and pushed his glasses as far up his nose as they would go.

"Indigo, jot down the names of every lightning catcher at this Exploratorium and anyone else you can remember from Greenland, Iceland, and Canada," he ordered, a look of great determination on his face. "Angus, make a list of every invention your uncle Max has ever made. I'll try some key words from the *McFangus Fog Guide*. And if none of that works, we'll take the qube straight up to the experimental division," he added, high spots of color now rising in his cheeks, "and shove it through the hailstone cracker."

Indigo curled up in her favorite armchair and began scribbling furiously. Angus made a hurried list of every invention he'd ever seen, or almost been killed by, at the Windmill, including a massive pair of knitted wind socks that had deliberately tripped him as he headed down the stairs. He was just wondering if his Christmas carol-singing slippers should be added to the list when—

"I don't believe it!"

Dougal was suddenly on his feet, a startled look on his face.

"What?"

"The Farew's!" he gasped. "Something's happened! I was just picking out random words from the *Fog Guide*, so I tried 'deadly,' you know, because invisible fogs can be deadly, then I added a few fognado symbols on the end for good measure, and"—Dougal gulped—"I think it might be opening!"

Angus was halfway across the Pigsty before Dougal had finished speaking, with Indigo hard on his heels. Dougal set the qube down on a small table where they all could see it. It looked exactly the same as always. Only now it was steaming, from the inside.

"Er . . . what happens when one of these things opens, anyway?" Angus asked, backing away as it gave an odd little hiccup. He'd given no thought to the possible perils of actually collecting the message.

"Now you come to mention it . . ." Dougal swallowed. "If you leave one of these things lying around for too long, or you forget the password and can't get it open, the pressure can build up inside. I think the whole thing's supposed to—"

BANG!

The qube exploded, firing random squares across the Pigsty like bullets.

Ping! Ping! Ping!

Dougal sank swiftly behind an armchair. But Angus stood frozen, his brain addled, not sure which way to dive.

"ANGUS! LOOK OUT!" Indigo knocked him sideways and pushed him behind the other chair only just in time.

BANG!

A second explosion rocked the Pigsty. Strings of tiny letters, numbers, and symbols shot across the top of Angus's head, spelling out the immortal words 24LIGHTNINGPOO*&! It was closely followed by TWINGLE and some extremely colorful phrases about FROGSNOT???

POP! POP! POP!

Indigo grabbed a coal shovel from the fireplace and used it to shield them both as a fresh batch of squares burst in the dying embers of the fire, like extremely aggressive popcorn. Then a sudden silence fell.

"Wow, thanks!" Angus smiled gratefully at Indigo. "If you hadn't pushed me out of the way . . ."

Indigo grinned back, looking faintly embarrassed.

"Is it over yet?" Dougal called from behind the other armchair.

Angus poked his head up warily and almost choked. Tiny squares had been blasted to the four corners of the Pigsty. A collection of miniature lightning bolts was now stuck firmly to the ceiling, and as for the walls . . .

"Whoa!" Dougal said, scrambling to his feet and staring around. "It's like a whole alphabet exploded in here!"

The remains of the qube, however, were now lying calmly on the table, exposing a neatly folded, steaming note inside.

Angus darted over. "I don't believe it! Dougal, you did it! You unlocked the qube! And 'deadly' was really the password?"

"Yeah, with a few fognado symbols bunged in on the end!" Dougal smiled, looking immensely pleased with himself. "After all the complicated combinations we've been trying, it was simple!"

"Listen, thanks," Angus said, suddenly wishing he could think of some far more impressive words to thank his friend.

"Go on," Dougal urged, nudging the remains of the

qube toward Angus. "Whatever's inside it, it was meant for you."

Angus grabbed the small sheet of paper and unfolded it with trembling fingers. Finally, after weeks of waiting, he was about to hear from his parents for the first time since they'd been kidnapped by Scabious Dankhart.

He recognized his dad's handwriting instantly and felt his heart leap. The note had been scribbled in a great rush.

"What does it say?" Indigo breathed in a barely audible whisper beside him.

Angus gulped. "It says, 'Angus, Dankhart is planning to attack Perilous with deadly ice diamond storms, to cause as much chaos and kill as many people as possible. You must find the lightning heart and use it to stop him. *Tell no one what you're looking for.*' " The last few words had been underlined several times. "That's all it says." Angus turned the paper over and found nothing but an inky, smudged thumbprint in one corner.

He handed the note to Dougal and Indigo for inspection, a whole host of new thoughts and questions now battering his brain cells. And the most pressing question of all: "What on earth's a lightning heart?"

11

ANGUS OBSERVED

It took ten whole days before the research department finally opened its doors once again. All ice diamond spores had now been melted, but the trail of destruction left behind was devastating. Large swaths of frost-damaged books, their covers blackened and dead looking, hung limply from the shelves, spines disintegrating. Several flights of stairs reaching up to the highest shelves had simply snapped, as brittle as ancient bones, and now lay in splinters on the floor. Storm vacuums, set to blow instead of suck, had been placed throughout the soggy department and were now wafting warm air around the cavernous hall in an attempt to dry it out. But the floor

was still littered with freezing puddles of meltwater, and an extremely sinister chill lingered in the air around them. Angus could feel it trying to force its way down his throat and into his lungs with every breath he took.

When the three lightning cubs were finally allowed to resume their duties, nobody seemed to know quite what to do with them without the guidance of Catcher Grimble. They were eventually placed under the supervision of a plump lightning catcher called Castleman, who put them back to work in the map room. There they set about squeezing meltwater from a collection of large woolen maps, which had now shrunk to the size of tea towels. It was wet, dull, monotonous work, but as Catcher Castleman was also responsible for taking senior lighting catchers on a tour of the worst pockets of damage, they saw very little of her. They discussed the message inside the Farew's qube without being disturbed.

"If only your dad had said more about what this lightning heart actually *is*," Indigo said as she and Angus wrung out a knitted map of the Netherlands between them and then hung it over the back of a reading chair to dry.

Dougal sighed. "Yeah. I mean, it could be anything.

Maybe it's something top secret the experimental division has been working on, and Catcher Sparks has got it hidden in her office. Hey, it could be an actual heart made from lightning!" he said, eyebrows disappearing under his bangs. "Although I don't know what use that would be to anyone. Or . . . what if it's a massive electrical storm?"

"It better not be." Angus shuddered at the thought. He'd already come face-to-face with one terrifying storm in the lightning vaults, and he was in no hurry to encounter another anytime soon, even if it put a stop to the chaos Dankhart was causing.

"D-do you think we should tell Jeremius about the lightning heart?" Indigo said, holding a dripping map over a bucket.

"No!" Angus and Dougal said together.

They'd been over this thorny issue dozens of times in the last few days alone.

"We've already agreed we can't tell anyone," Angus said, lowering his voice just in case. "I still don't know if Jeremius can be trusted. Besides, my dad told me not to."

Indigo's forehead creased. "But if the lightning heart can stop Dankhart and the ice diamonds . . . I mean, why wouldn't your dad want anyone else knowing about it?

Why didn't he mention it to Jeremius as well?"

"I wish I knew," Angus said.

He grabbed another map from the soggy pile and squeezed it with more vigor than was really necessary. He'd somehow thought that once the message from his parents was revealed, things would become clearer, but instead they'd taken a significant turn for the complicated. And he, Dougal, and Indigo were now faced with several serious problems. How were they supposed to find the mysterious lightning heart when none of them had the faintest idea of what it actually was? Worse still, how would they even know if they'd found it, unless it had a large label attached to it, saying LIGHTNING HEART?

All their efforts to find the lightning heart in the past ten days had failed miserably. Perilous was crawling with extra lightning catchers, and it was virtually impossible to sneak into any room or department unseen. Dougal had narrowly avoided a whole week's work of boot-waxing duty after Miss DeWinkle found him creeping into the library late one evening when he should have been in bed. Indigo had almost walked straight into Principal Dark-Angel after tiptoeing out of the forecasting department.

But Angus had not been so lucky. He'd been caught red-handed by Catcher Sparks as he crept through the experimental division, earning himself another lecture, which seemed to go on forever.

"McFangus! This is the second time in a matter of weeks that I have been forced to speak to you about your behavior. If I catch you, Dewsnap, or Midnight creeping about this Exploratorium again, or if any of you gets caught in an ice diamond storm and comes down with frost shock, I will personally see to it that you spend the entire summer holiday cleaning out storm drains with a toothbrush!"

The three of them had retreated to the Pigsty after that, to avoid any further trouble. Their search for the lightning heart, which had barely even begun, had come to a complete standstill. And Angus had no clue where to hunt for it next. Instead, he read the secret message from his dad over and over each night before going to bed.

His dad had given him a mission, a way of thwarting Dankhart's plans. It was the first time he'd felt useful since his dad and mum had been kidnapped and imprisoned in the dungeons at Castle Dankhart. He couldn't let them down now. He had to find the lightning heart somehow. He had to show his parents that they had not been forgotten.

If he closed his eyes, he could still picture them standing in the kitchen at the Windmill, joking with Uncle Max. He could remember every detail of a brilliant weekend they'd spent at the beach, skimming stones across the calm sea. They'd each kept a small white pebble as a souvenir. But now the picture had started to fade, to blur around the edges. His mum's voice sounded strangely flat and life-less; her laughter belonged to somebody else. His dad's features seemed to grow fainter the more tightly Angus tried to hold them in his memory.

He needed to find the lightning heart, to make new memories that somehow involved his mum and dad, even if they only came from words scribbled hastily in a note like the one he carried safely in his pocket.

Meanwhile, in the rest of the Exploratorium, the ice dia-mond storm was still the main topic of conversation in every department and at every crowded dinner table. Rumors were rife that a secret squad of highly trained lightning catchers, armed with shatterproof storm nets,

had been formed to patrol the stone tunnels and passageways in order to catch whoever was responsible.

Dougal updated them with the latest reports from the
Weekly Weathervane. But details were scarce, and the
magazine soon started running a series of features on
common cold-weather ailments instead.

"It's like they don't want us to know what's going on,"
Dougal said one evening, flipping the pages shut in disgust. "I mean, Doctor Fleagal's top tips on chilblains
aren't exactly going to help much, are they?"

"Looking for loser cures, Munchfungus?" Percival and
Pixie Vellum appeared behind their table. "You won't find
any help in the *Weathervane.*"

"Do us all a favor, Vellum, and go bug somebody else."
Angus sighed.

"Yeah," Dougal added. "Your face is curdling my rice
pudding." Indigo snorted. Dougal grinned at his own joke.

Percival was clearly about to say something highly
insulting in return when he suddenly spotted Germ weaving his way toward them with a hot plate of potatoes.

"Never mind, it'll keep. Come on," he muttered, turning to Pixie, and they both stalked away swiftly.

"How on earth did you manage that?" Dougal asked, amazed, as Germ sat down a moment later. "Those two are usually harder to get rid of than stinkweed!"

"It might have something to do with the fact that Percival came up to the sanatorium the other night with a nasty case of nostril boils. And he probably doesn't want me spreading the news around. Oops!" Germ grinned mischievously. "It looks like the boil's already out of the bag."

"Er . . . nostril boils?" Angus asked warily.

"It's a simple case of cross-contamination," Germ said, with a glint in his eye. "If you've already got snow boot boils, and you pick your infected feet, then pick your nose without washing your hands in between . . . Vellum wasn't so full of himself when he had gruesome rivers of pus streaming from both nostrils, I can tell you."

Angus, Indigo, and Dougal roared with laughter as Percival Vellum sank into a chair at the far end of the kitchens, leaving just the tips of his burning ears visible.

"I thought he was going to start blubbering when we discovered more boils growing behind his ears." Germ turned and waved at the embarrassed-looking twin.

"How's it going up in the sanatorium, anyway?" Angus

asked when they'd finished listening to all the gory details of Percival Vellum's treatment.

"We still can't risk prying two of the oldest lightning catchers out of their armchairs. They're way too fragile," Germ said. "Doctor Fleagal chipped the worst of the icicles off them, but it's going to be a long, slow thaw, I'm afraid."

"But they'll be all right, won't they?" Indigo asked. "I mean, Catcher Grimble's so old."

"Don't worry, little sis." Germ gave her a reassuring smile. "If anyone can get old Grimble up and about again, it's Doctor Fleagal. We're just lucky Adrik Swarfe's little invention hasn't killed anyone yet."

"How do you know about Adrik Swarfe?" Dougal asked, surprised. So far, nobody else in the Exploratorium had even mentioned his name.

"I was cleaning out some vomit buckets a couple of days ago," Germ explained, "and I accidentally overheard Doctor Fleagal and Gudgeon talking about Swarfe and all the nasty little things he invented here, you know, when he was a lightning catcher."

"You're—you're not serious?" Angus exchanged shocked looks with Dougal and Indigo. "Adrik Swarfe was a lightning catcher here—at *Perilous*?"

"Yep," Germ said, shrugging. "But then he had some sort of tiff with Dark-Angel and ran off to join Dankhart and the rest of his cronies."

"You're kidding!" Dougal scoured the *Weathervane* again, as if this astonishing news had somehow slipped between the very pages he'd just been reading.

"It all happened eons ago, years before any of us were even born. Plus, Dark-Angel doesn't like talking about it, according to old Fleagal. She flies into a temper whenever anyone mentions his name. Mind you, I can't say I blame her. Swarfe goes skipping off to join our dear old uncle Scabby—"

"Shhh! Stop saying that!" Indigo hissed, looking terrified.

"—taking all our weather secrets with him," Germ continued. "And look what's happening now. Seriously evil bloke, I reckon."

Dougal shuddered. For several minutes, Angus sat picturing a devious-looking lightning catcher stalking through the stone tunnels and passageways of Perilous . . . until he finally remembered his dinner, and had to eat the rest of it cold.

He left Dougal and Indigo fifteen minutes later to return an overdue book to the library. The new librarian, Miss Vulpine, had already sent him several threatening reminders. He was just about to push through the library doors when—

"Hey, Angus!"

Germ was chasing after him down the corridor. On closer inspection, he looked slightly disheveled, with bits of frayed bandage stuck to his hair and yellow antiseptic stains on both hands.

"Can I talk to you?"

He drew Angus away from the library, looking distinctly uneasy.

"What's up?" Angus asked, puzzled.

"Look, I didn't want to say anything in front of the others, in case you choked on a carrot or something. But your uncle came up to the sanatorium the other day with a deep cut on his finger. Old Fleagal started asking him how he got the scar on his chin. And Jeremius said . . ."

"Said what?"

Germ scratched his head, not quite looking Angus in the eye. "He said it happened two years ago, when he was staying with my uncle at Castle Dankhart."

"What! But he can't have . . . I mean, he must have meant . . ." Angus stared at Germ, feeling as if he'd just been hit in the stomach by a giant Hungarian hailstone.

"Listen, I've been thinking it over, and I reckon there're only three reasons why Jeremius would admit something like that," Germ said. "One, he was making a really bad joke. Two, he's betrayed Perilous, the lightning catchers, and all the weather oaths he's ever taken and is now in cahoots with the monsoon mongrels."

"But he can't be!" Angus said desperately. "I mean, if he had betrayed everyone, he definitely wouldn't go around bragging about it, would he?"

"In that case, it must be option three," Germ said. "My uncle kidnapped your uncle."

If Jeremius had been kidnapped, how had he escaped? And wouldn't he now know how to get Angus's mum and dad out, if he'd already managed it himself? But what other explanation could there be? Angus felt his head spin; new doubts about his uncle flooded his brain. Had he been right not to trust Jeremius all along? How many secrets was his uncle keeping?

"Don't tell anyone else what you heard, okay? Not even Indigo and Dougal," Angus said.

"My lips are sealed as tightly as a jar of stormberry jelly," Germ said, pretending to zip his mouth closed. "Luckily, I'm already an expert in keeping big family secrets!"

Angus stumbled back to his room in a state of such confusion that he tripped over Edmund Croxley without stopping to apologize.

To everyone's surprise, cold-weather survival lessons resumed in the Rotundra just twelve days after the ice-diamond storm. Feeling extremely uncomfortable after Germ's revelations, Angus did his best to avoid his uncle's eye for the entire lesson.

Luckily, icicle storms pelted the peaked glass roof above as they entered the Rotundra, and Jeremius seemed to think that was the perfect opportunity to teach them how to use their own body heat to warm up cold hands and feet. Angus therefore spent fifteen minutes with Dougal's bare toes wedged into his armpit.

"Just be grateful it wasn't Percival Vellum's feet," Dougal said.

At the end of the lesson, they were forced to heat up a bag of powdered instant survival stew for dinner, over a roaring campfire. Concocted by the experimental division, the stew was gray and lumpy with bits of floating gristle, and it tasted, in Angus's opinion, like a bowl of burned turnips that had been strained through a pile of festering socks.

On the way back to the changing rooms, Jeremius took them on a small detour to an observation platform placed right on the edge of the emergency cold-weather training course.

"In some parts of the world, iceberg hopping is considered a competitive sport," he explained as they watched several lightning catchers attempt to leap from one towering mass of ice to the next. "But here at Perilous, it is a crucial part of our cold-weather training. Icebergs are formed when a piece of freshwater ice breaks off the end of a glacier or ice shelf. No two icebergs are the same shape, but they can be flat-topped or tabular, domed, pinnacled, wedged, drydocked, or U-shaped . . . or blocky. Ninety percent of their bulk exists below water, which is where the phrase 'tip of the iceberg' comes from. Many are ten thousand years old or more, and they can weigh up to two hundred thousand tons, but some are much larger. Others are the size of a grand piano and are called *growlers*, due to the noises they sometimes make."

Dougal gulped, looking nauseated.

"Icebergs are deadly. They can roll over without warning, throwing anyone standing on them at the time into freezing water. The training icebergs you see here are a fraction of the average size, and strict safety measures have been put in place, of course. If lightning cubs are ever caught attempting to cross this lake without the strict supervision of an experienced iceberg hopper, they will be expelled from Perilous immediately."

Indigo looked disappointed. Angus watched with sweaty palms as three lightning catchers attempted a daring human bridge maneuver between two wobbling icebergs. He was quite relieved when Gudgeon escorted the lightning cubs back up into the Exploratorium a few minutes later. And he felt a huge surge of affection for his cozy room as he and Dougal entered it at last. A warm fire was blazing in the grate, perfect for toasting his wet socks. He could already see the lump in his bed where a hot-water bottle had been thoughtfully placed.

It wasn't until he'd pulled off one sodden snow boot that he saw it. A note had been shoved under his door and was half hidden beneath the edge of his rug. He hopped across the room on one foot to retrieve it . . . and then instantly wished he hadn't bothered. The handwriting on the envelope was horribly familiar. With a sinking feeling, he ripped it open and read the short message inside:

Angus,

Rogwood will collect you from the entrance hall at 8:30 this evening for your first session with Doctor Obsidian and the projectograms. Please do not keep either of them waiting.

Principal Dark-Angel

Angus sighed. Thanks to the ice diamond storms, the lightning heart, and the unsettling news about his uncle, there had been no spare room in his head to worry about fake storms, the strange pale doctor, or tests.

He handed the note to a curious Dougal.

"You'd think Dark-Angel would have more important things to think about than you at the moment," he

declared as Angus found his boot and pulled it back on.
"They can't force you to do it. Just tell Gudgeon you don't
feel like leaping about after any thunderstorms tonight."

"I can't," Angus said wearily, "I've already agreed to do
the tests."

"Tests, yeah, but this is more like experimentation."

Ten minutes later, Angus made his way up the spiral
stairs again and found Rogwood waiting for him in the
entrance hall.

"Ah, Angus, we meet again." Rogwood smiled kindly
from beneath his braided beard. "I must apologize for
dragging you away from the comfort of your room at such
a late hour. No doubt you were thinking of retiring to your
bed with a good book on lightning puzzles or famous
Imburcillian explorers."

Angus smiled. He'd left Dougal snuggled up in
the camp bed, immersed in *Imburology: An A–Z of
Fascinating Facts and Frippery*. He'd been reading the
chapter called "Ghosts, Ghouls, and Famous Phantoms."

"I presume that Miss Midnight and Mr. Dewsnap are
now fully aware of your extra activities?" Rogwood
asked as they headed down the nearest tunnel and

descended swiftly into the darkness.

"Er . . . yes, sir, sorry," Angus said sheepishly. "I know I promised not to tell anyone, but I, um, didn't want to lie to them."

Rogwood nodded. "Perfectly understandable, under the circumstances. But it might be wise not to mention the fact to Principal Dark-Angel."

They walked in silence after that. As they descended deeper into the gloom, however, the uneasy questions that had been lurking at the back of Angus's mind began to surface once again. What would Doctor Obsidian's tests show about his skills? Would he be compared with other storm prophets from the past? And if so, would he be at the bottom of the weather-wrangling class?

A few minutes later, they were striding along the corridor that led past the mysterious testing tunnels. Cold black flames flared from under a door on the left, and there was an odd, rhythmic thumping noise coming from one on the right. It sounded like a whole troupe of fog yetis doing the Highland fling.

Rogwood ushered him through the last door at the end of the corridor. Doctor Obsidian wasn't the only person waiting for them, however. Principal Dark-Angel, Felix Gudgeon, and Valentine Vellum were also talking in a quiet huddle.

"If you would wait here for a few moments, Angus, I will see if Doctor Obsidian is ready to begin," Rogwood said with a friendly smile, and he went over to join the others.

Angus undid his coat and loosened his scarf, suddenly feeling uncomfortably hot inside his warm winter clothes.

"Ah, Aramanthus, at last." Principal Dark-Angel turned to greet him. "We were just discussing the details of tonight's test."

Doctor Obsidian had stacked a number of projectograms against a familiar wooden box. The odd spiky measuring device sat on its own, a little farther away. Angus gulped, thinking he should have faked a twisted ankle after all.

"The projectograms I have prepared offer a wide range of dangerous weather scenarios," the doctor explained in his whispery voice.

"And you are certain one of these will trigger the appearance of the fire dragon?" Principal Dark-Angel asked.

Doctor Obsidian nodded. "I believe so. Advanced

projectograms work on many sensory levels. Angus will believe the danger before him is real."

"I still don't see why *he* has to be here." Gudgeon glowered, staring at Valentine Vellum with obvious loathing. "What Angus can or can't do doesn't concern him."

Vellum bristled. "I am here at the special request of Principal Dark-Angel, who requires my expertise in the area of lightning strikes."

"Only thing you're an expert in, Vellum, is poking your nose in where it doesn't belong," Gudgeon grumbled, giving him a withering stare.

"That will do, Gudgeon!" Principal Dark-Angel snapped. "I will ban both of you from any further involvement unless you can be trusted to behave in a civilized manner. We are simply here to observe tonight's test."

All four of them turned to look at Angus, who tried to pretend that he hadn't heard a single word of this heated conversation and that he was fascinated instead by a section of bare rock on the wall.

"Doctor Obsidian," Principal Dark-Angel continued, "are you ready to begin?"

The doctor nodded once.

"Good. Then I suggest we stop wasting valuable time."
She turned toward Angus with a frosty smile. "I trust you
are keeping warm in these difficult times, Angus?"

"Er . . ."

But without waiting for his answer, she retired to a seat
against the wall.

"Don't let Vellum put you off," Gudgeon said, giving
Angus's shoulder a friendly squeeze. "It's all hot air and
no brains with that one." Angus managed a weak smile as
Gudgeon sat down with the others.

"If you would come this way, Angus," Doctor Obsidian
said, leading him to a chair where a weatherproof coat
and hat had been laid out next to a pair of rubber boots.

"Weatherproof clothing is not strictly necessary, of
course, but perhaps it will assist with the illusion that
the test is being conducted within a real storm?" he said,
sounding hopeful. "You can put your own boots over
there before we begin." He pointed to an old newspaper
on the floor.

Angus was just about to pull off his boots when he
realized that the newspaper article staring up at him, several months old now, concerned the theft of the lightning

tower artifacts from the museum in London. And he wondered nervously if one day in the distant future, an Imbur archaeologist would uncover the testing tunnel and find the remains of an eleven-year-old boy buried deep within.

He buttoned up his weatherproof coat with fumbling fingers. There was now a vague, unhelpful buzzing in his ears.

"I think we will begin with one of the smaller, less powerful storms, just to get things started," Doctor Obsidian announced. "Remember, Angus, you are perfectly safe."

Angus had no more than a second to wonder what he was about to face when—

Click.

He was suddenly standing in a wooded glade. Tall, shady trees towered above his head, forming a soft green canopy from which a gentle rain was dripping. The entire tunnel had been transformed into a woodland. Angus stared in amazement at the lifelike toadstools popping up through the mossy ground, the thick, knotted tree roots running under his feet like fossilized veins. He could hear the soft pitter-patter of drizzle on his coat, he could feel a cold trickle of rain running down the back of his neck, and yet . . . He ran a hand over his skin just to check. He was still as dry as a bone. The projectograms were even more amazing than he'd imagined. The rain was utterly convincing.

"I will now introduce an element of danger," Doctor Obsidian announced.

Angus felt his muscles tense. He could still see and hear everything that was going on outside the boundaries of the projectogram, which somehow made the illusion even more believable. What would the doctor consider dangerous enough to make him see the fire dragon? And suddenly—

Click.

He was standing on top of a hill, the only high spot for what looked like miles around, and above his head, in the gathering gloom, a violent storm was brewing. Rumbles of thunder echoed around the tunnel. There was nowhere to hide, nothing to take shelter under; he would be forced to defend himself from the lightning bolts that were lining up to use him as target practice. . . .

CRASH!

Angus flinched as the first blinding flash of lightning skimmed past his ears and struck the ground three feet to his left. He looked around for an escape. . . . If he could flatten himself against the wall of the tunnel—

CRASH!

The second bolt of lightning seemed to fill the entire tunnel like a huge electrified cobweb. Angus pressed his hands tightly over his ears, but the thunder that followed was still deafening and made his entire rib cage vibrate. The projectogram was amazing! He wanted to make a run for it, to tell Dark-Angel that he'd changed his mind. He definitely didn't want to take part in any tests, ever again!

For the next thirty minutes, he dodged, ducked, and darted about the tunnel, his heart leaping with every new flash of lightning, his brain aching as he struggled to make sense of it all. But after three bitterly cold blizzards, two gusty storms, and a mini tornado on a tropical island, the fire dragon had still refused to appear.

Angus leaned against the wall of the tunnel, desperately trying to catch his breath as the latest projectogram faded. His legs were aching, his weatherproof hat had been ripped off his head ages ago, and his boots were hanging on by a rubbery thread. He was also starting to suspect that he might be in the middle of some very real weather after all, that Doctor Obsidian had secretly smashed several storm globes inside the tunnel to produce genuine blizzards, tornadoes, and lightning.

What would happen if he simply pretended to see the fire dragon, he wondered, clutching a stitch in his side? Would they be able to tell that he was fibbing?

"I think perhaps one more projectogram, and then we might call it a night?" Doctor Obsidian suggested.

Principal Dark-Angel nodded, clearly disappointed that Angus had done nothing remotely impressive so far.

There was another *click*. A vicious icicle storm appeared and began to pelt Angus with foot-long daggers. He had barely had time to register the danger when the projectogram began to flicker and rumble, sending strange vibrations throughout the tunnel.

"Obsidian! What's going on?" Gudgeon demanded, leaping to his feet. "I thought you said these projectograms were safe?"

"There is a minor instability in the program. It is nothing to be alarmed about; there is no immediate danger. It may produce a few spontaneous lightning sprites, nothing more. I will have it fixed in a few seconds."

But the rumbling continued. The shaking became so strong that Angus could hardly stand on his own two feet. Meanwhile, the weather had gone haywire. One second he was standing beneath a blazing sun that made his eyeballs ache with the brightness; the next, puddles were collecting around his feet from a torrential downpour.

Clunk!

There was a sudden crackle of electricity in the air. A bolt of lightning shot across the ceiling, illuminating the entire room like a thousand-watt bulb. Angus flinched, pressing himself against the wall. And then there was a new sound.

BOOM!

The icicle storms, palm trees, and puddles disappeared. In a dark corner of the tunnel, something strange was happening. A tall plume of glittering diamond-shaped spores was rising toward the ceiling, shimmering ominously.

"Ice diamond storm!" Gudgeon roared. "Everyone get out now!"

Angus stared at the glittering plume, his insides suddenly clenched tight. There was no time to ask if the spores were real. He ran, stumbling, toward the door.

Valentine Vellum had already disappeared through it, saving his own skin first. Gudgeon, Rogwood, Principal Dark-Angel, and the doctor were hard on Vellum's heels.

"Angus! This way!" shouted Rogwood, urging him across the tunnel to the door.

But the ice diamonds were spreading too rapidly, forming a barrier, cutting him off.

He tripped and fell to the ground. "Argh!" An icy blast of glacial air hit him before he could get to his feet again. The horrible cold crept through his clothes, stealing warmth from his fingers and toes, biting into his bones. He watched his fingers turn blue as the frost crept over his knuckles like a fungus.

He was dimly aware that Gudgeon was shouting something urgent at him, then—

BANG!

The fire dragon burst into the tunnel at last! It blazed before him, molten fire dripping from every scale and claw. It hovered, uncertain. But Angus already knew it was too late to stop the deadly spores from freezing the air in his lungs, from slowing the blood in his veins to a sluggish

crawl until the reliable *thump, thump, thump* of his heart
simply came . . . to a gradual . . . s-stuttering . . . halt.

He opened his eyes with a jolt of surprise and blinked up
at the ceiling. He was still in the tunnel. He was also still
very much alive.

"Are you hurt?" Rogwood was leaning over him. "Did
you bang your head when you fell?"

Angus shook his head gingerly. It felt as if a large herd
of elephants had been using it as a trampoline. Everything
between his ears—including his skull, his brain, and big
clumps of his hair—now throbbed painfully. He could
also see two Rogwoods kneeling before him, like a pair of
heavily bearded twins.

"Is the boy all right?" Gudgeon demanded, appearing
beside them, his face creased with concern.

"I-I'm fine," Angus said, sitting up groggily. His
eyes finally slipped back into focus.

"Nevertheless, I would like to check that you are not
suffering from a concussion or any other injuries before
you attempt to stand." Rogwood frowned. "How many
fingers am I holding up, Angus?"

"Er . . . four, no, wait, I mean, three!" He corrected himself quickly as his blurred vision sharpened once again. "Definitely three fingers."

"Hmm." Rogwood examined the bumps on his head silently for several moments before speaking again. "I'm afraid you will have some quite spectacular bruises in the morning, but there appears to be no serious harm done."

"But the ice diamond storm . . ."

"It wasn't real. It was just another projectogram." Gudgeon folded his arms across his chest, looking deeply unimpressed.

"Another projectogram?" Angus said, suddenly realizing that he felt perfectly normal now, apart from the throbbing in his head. His heart was still beating; blood was still flowing through his veins. There was no trace of the freezing that he'd felt in his fingers and toes just a few minutes before. The projectogram had fooled his senses completely. Just as the fake rain had convinced him he was wet, the fake ice diamond storm had convinced him he was about to die.

"Obsidian should have told us," Gudgeon growled. "I thought Angus was in big trouble."

"But that was the entire point of this training session," Valentine Vellum said, sneering at him from the shadows. "You were supposed to believe the storm was real."

"I notice you were quick enough to make a run for it."

Vellum glared at Gudgeon. "That is beside the point. In my opinion—"

"When I want your opinion, Vellum, I'll ask for it. And I won't be asking anytime soon."

"Silence!" Principal Dark-Angel snapped. "It was I who asked Doctor Obsidian to include the fake storm in this test session."

Gudgeon stared at her, stunned.

"Doctor Obsidian," Dark-Angel continued when nobody else spoke, "did you manage to obtain any significant readings from this evening's activities?"

The doctor hurried over to the spiky measuring device. He studied it for several moments, then nodded. "It shows a high level of brain activity only after the spores appeared. There are also some extremely promising sensory peaks that should be investigated further."

A faint smile curled Dark-Angel's lips. "It would seem that simple projectograms of thunderstorms are not enough. Angus's fire dragon will appear only in moments of extreme danger. We will have to be more imaginative in the future if we are to see what he is truly capable of."

Angus stared at the principal, flabbergasted.

"Aramanthus, will Angus be able to resume his training in a few days' time?" she asked, apparently showing a distinct lack of concern for his well-being.

"Certainly, if that is what you truly wish, Delphinia." There was a strong warning in Rogwood's tone. "But I would recommend giving Angus at least two weeks' recovery time. This evening has taken a great deal of effort on his part. It will also give Doctor Obsidian a chance to fine-tune his projectograms."

"I've got a better idea what Obsidian can do with his projectograms," Gudgeon muttered, scowling. "You might as well throw the boy into the Lightnarium if that's how safe these storms are going to be."

"The training sessions will continue as planned, and that is my final word on the subject," said the principal.

And with that, she swept out of the room with Valentine Vellum trailing behind her, leaving Angus more confused than ever.

12

STORM IN A TEACUP

Gudgeon escorted Angus back to his bedroom, muttering furiously under his breath about "dangerous, dim-witted doctors" and their "wretched photographs." As soon as he'd gone, Angus found Dougal and Indigo waiting for him in the Pigsty, where he gave them a blow-by-blow account of his brush with the ice diamond storm.

"But that's a horrible thing to do!" Indigo said, hugging her knees tightly to her chest. "I can't believe Principal Dark-Angel let you think it was a real storm!"

"Yeah, but she was the one who asked Valentine Vellum to zap Angus's brains with some low-voltage lightning, remember?" Dougal looked shocked all the same. "Just tell her you've got snow boot boils next time," he added earnestly. "If she thinks you're contagious, she might leave you alone."

Angus finally went to bed , wondering what Dark-Angel was planning to put him through next time. Would he be forced to protect himself from snow bomb bombardments? Or abandoned on his own in the middle of the Imbur marshes, where fognadoes and fog yetis roamed freely?

At three o'clock in the morning, Jeremius woke him quietly and sat on the end of his bed, trying not to disturb Dougal and Germ, who were both now sleeping soundly.

"Rogwood told me what happened in the testing tunnels," he said, looking angrier than Angus had ever seen him. "I've already had words with Principal Dark-Angel. As your closest relative at this Exploratorium I've forbidden her to conduct any more sessions for the foreseeable future."

"Seriously?" Angus whispered. "Wow! Thanks! That's brilliant!"

"She wasn't happy about it," Jeremius added with a faint grin. "She threatened to send me back to the Canadian

Exploratorium for interfering. She kept going on about the fact that you'd given your permission. But those projecto-grams aren't safe. You could have been seriously injured. I'm sorry, Angus." He shook his head in disbelief. "If I'd known what she was planning . . . Your mum and dad would never have allowed it. Nor would they forgive me if I let anything happen to you. And ice diamond storms, fake or otherwise, are about the worst thing that could happen to anybody."

Angus suddenly felt extremely glad he had an uncle who could stand up to Dark-Angel and stop her from having his brain cells fried, even if Jeremius was keeping dark secrets from him.

"But I don't understand," he whispered as Dougal turned over on his camp bed, snoring gently. "Why is Dark-Angel so keen to have me tested in the first place?"

Jeremius thought for a second before answering. "It has been a very long time since we've had a living storm prophet at this, or any, Exploratorium. Accounts we have of their skills come from documents, some hundreds of years old, and although they are fascinating to read, they don't give us a complete picture. I think Delphinia Dark-Angel wants to see for herself just how capable you are of understanding the elemental dangers of a violent storm."

Yet there was something more. There was another reason why Dark-Angel was so interested in him. Angus was sure of it. He could almost sense it, lurking beyond the horizon like a cloud full of poisonous fog.

"But why does it matter to Dark-Angel so much?"

"After tonight, I'm afraid Delphinia Dark-Angel is unlikely to share her private thoughts with me on any subject," Jeremius said quietly as Dougal stirred in his bed again. "I have a feeling Aramanthus Rogwood may be persuaded to tell us more. But now is not the time to ask." He ran a hand over his tired face. "Perhaps when we are no longer being bombarded with icicles and ice diamond storms?"

Angus nodded, suddenly thinking of something else he'd far rather ask his uncle instead. "D-do my mum and dad know about me being a storm prophet?"

"It is possible," Jeremius said, considering the question carefully. "After what happened in the lightning vaults, there may have been whispers and rumors, even at Castle Dankhart."

"But did they know before? I mean, when I was younger, did they ever say anything about me being . . . different?"

Jeremius shook his head. "Absolutely not. Nobody had the faintest idea. But they will be extremely keen to talk to you about it once they return to Perilous."

For one brief moment, Angus considered telling Jeremius everything about the secret message in the Farew's qube, which he kept safe under his pillow at night, and their desperate search for the mysterious lightning heart. And simply asking, while he was at it, whether Jeremius had ever stayed at Castle Dankhart, betraying Perilous, the lightning catchers, and every McFangus on the planet. But his dad's instructions had been clear. He was to tell no one what he was looking for. Not even his uncle.

A few days later, Angus woke to an unexpected shaft of feeble sunlight shining through his bedroom curtains. He scrambled out of bed, being careful not to stand on Germ, who was still fast asleep. He scraped a patch of ice off his window and smiled.

"Hey!" he whispered, chucking a pillow at Dougal's head. "It's stopped snowing! Get up!"

Twenty minutes later, after wolfing down four toasted bacon muffins in the kitchens, they joined a stream of excited trainees, all heading toward the gravity railway. Principal Dark-Angel had decided to allow everyone access to the grounds immediately surrounding Perilous, so that they could enjoy the watery sunshine.

"Brilliant!" Dougal grinned, pulling on a pair of gloves as they squeezed into the packed carriage. "This will be a nice change from all the dark tunnels, dingy rooms, and libraries we've been cooped up in just lately. I was starting to feel a bit nocturnal."

In the days following the fake ice diamond storm, Angus, Dougal, and Indigo had renewed their efforts to find the lightning heart and had taken the slightly less risky approach of searching for any clues in the research department.

"I mean, your mum and dad must have heard about the lightning heart from somewhere," Dougal commented when they found a section that had escaped the ravages of the spores and started looking through mountains of dusty documents. Unfortunately, they also encountered several unexpected booby traps, which Indigo and Angus managed to subdue before they created a commotion. But all they uncovered was a dated book on lightning catcher fashions through the ages, stuffed behind a heater, and a collection of Imbur Isle seaweed recipes, which only Uncle Max would ever have been brave enough to attempt.

Angus was determined to continue searching, however. His mum and dad were counting on him, and he couldn't let them down. He had to find the lightning heart, no matter what.

He held on to his stomach with both hands as the gravity railway carriage plummeted toward the ground. He was extremely glad when they reached the bottom with a gentle bump.

The air outside the carriage was crisp and wintry. The skies to the east still looked dark and threatening, with clouds full of fresh snow and ice. But for the time being, at least, the storms had stopped.

The views of Perilous were breathtaking. Icicles ten feet long hung from every rocky protuberance. And the whole Exploratorium shimmered in the weak sunshine. Little Frog's Bottom looked like a scene from an old-fashioned Christmas card, covered in thick layers of snow, with smoking chimneys and sloping roofs.

"You'd think we'd be totally sick of the white stuff after everything we've done in the Rotundra," Angus said, grinning.

Everywhere he looked, trainees and teachers were already making the most of their sudden freedom. Edmund Croxley and Theodore Twill were locked in a fierce snowball battle. Catcher Trollworthy was helping a group of third-year girls build an impressively large snowman, complete with leather jerkin and snow boots. Rogwood and Miss DeWinkle were leading a party of novice skiers through a tree-lined slalom course nearby.

"What shall we do first?" Angus said.

"Fancy a game of dodge, you two?" Indigo appeared from behind them with Georgina Fox.

"What's dodge?" Angus asked.

"Don't! It's just like the snowball test we did with Doctor Fleagal, and it's totally brutal!" Dougal exclaimed. "I played it with my cousins once . . . and ended up with a broken nose."

"In that case, you're on!" Angus said. "Me and Dougal against you and Georgina!"

To his great surprise, Angus thoroughly enjoyed playing dodge, and for the first time in ages he managed to put all thoughts of Dankhart and ice diamond storms aside. It was a wonderful release just to dart about in the snow, getting hot, letting off steam, and having nothing more important to worry about than where the next snow attack might come from.

Germ turned up an hour later with a collection of sturdy trays decorated with lightning bolts from the kitchens, which were ideal for sledding. And they spent the rest of the morning racing, spinning, and colliding with one another on the slopes of a bumpy hill.

"Listen, I've been meaning to ask. Have you heard anything more about my uncle Jeremius?" Angus asked Germ when he suddenly found himself alone with Indigo's brother at the bottom of the hill.

"'Fraid not." Germ shook his head, showering Angus with fresh snow. "I've tried wheedling it out of old Fleagal a couple of times, of course. I told him all about my evil uncle Scabby and pretended to get upset about it. I've asked him if he knows anyone who's ever been inside Castle Dankhart and that sort of thing."

"Wow. Thanks," Angus said, impressed. "And?"

"And if old Fleagal knows anything juicy about your uncle, he's keeping it hidden under his stethoscope."

By lunchtime, Angus was ravenously hungry. He could hardly feel his toes, and his ears were stinging painfully. He followed Indigo, Dougal, and a stream of lightning cubs now heading back to the gravity railway, wondering if Principal Dark-Angel would let them do it all over again tomorrow.

By the next morning, however, the brief respite in the weather was over, and the icicle storms returned to Imbur with a vengeance. The temperature inside the Exploratorium dropped dramatically once again. Ferocious winds drove long shards of hard ice against the towering rock, rattling windows and hammering on doors. Angus woke several times every night convinced the building was about to collapse. The situation had not improved when they arrived at the research department one morning to find the door blocked by a stern-looking Catcher Sparks.

"What's going on, miss?" Angus asked, standing on his tiptoes, trying to see over her shoulder.

"There's been another ice diamond storm, McFangus. There's no need to be alarmed," she added quickly. "No one was hurt this time. Luckily for us, the storm failed to go off properly, no real damage was done, but we're not taking any chances. The entire area has been sealed off until it's been thoroughly searched and decontaminated. I suggest you head back to the kitchens and wait there for further instructions."

Angus, Dougal, and Indigo loitered in the Octagon for several minutes, however, hoping to sneak into the department and take a look at the damage for themselves. But it was hopeless.

"For goodness' sake, get out of the way!" Catcher Sparks yelled at them eventually. "The decontamination team can't do their work with you three skulking about."

They returned to the kitchens a few minutes later and were greeted by a scene of total confusion. Large groups of grumbling lightning catchers and cubs were milling about, forming a ramshackle line by the door.

"There's some sort of blockage up ahead," Dougal said, trying to see through the gaps in the crowd. "Edmund Croxley's not letting anyone into the kitchens."

"What's going on?" Angus asked Nicholas Grubb, who was standing with a group of his fourth-year friends.

"Croxley's being an idiot, as usual," Nicholas said, sounding annoyed. "It's all right for him. He's already had his breakfast, but we've all been out doing some early-morning temperature checks and we haven't eaten anything yet."

Edmund Croxley, however, had a different explanation.

"There's been another ice diamond storm!" he informed them importantly when Angus, Indigo, and Dougal eventually managed to push their way to the front. "The kitchens are now out of bounds until the decontamination team has finished cleaning up."

A shocked murmur spread around the waiting crowd.

"But . . . the same thing's just happened in the research department," Angus said.

"Go on, Croxley, let us have a quick look for ourselves," urged Nicholas, who was now standing behind Angus. "We won't tell anyone you let us in."

"Certainly not!" Edmund drew himself up to his full height and stared down his nose at the gathered crowd. "Now listen here, everyone! I've been instructed by

Principal Dark-Angel herself to direct all you lightning cubs back to your living quarters. The principal has assured me that there is no significant damage, the storm failed to go off properly, but they're not taking any chances. All meals will be brought to you in your rooms today."

"I don't care what Croxley says, this is getting really serious," Dougal muttered as they followed the other trainees down the spiral stairs. "Two failed storms in one day? What if one goes off properly next time, in the kitchens or the living quarters, when they're crammed full of people?"

"We can't just sit around here waiting for it to happen again," Indigo said, flopping down in her favorite armchair in the Pigsty. "There must be loads of places we haven't looked for the lightning heart yet."

"Yeah, like the Lightnarium . . . Valentine Vellum's bedroom . . . Dark-Angel's sock drawer," Dougal said, counting them off on his fingers. "Basically all the places you never want to get caught snooping."

Angus flung himself into the chair beside Indigo. So far, their search for the lightning heart had been a spectacular failure. They still didn't have a clue what the lightning heart actually was or how they were going to find it before everyone in the Exploratorium was frozen solid.

In the days that followed, a somber atmosphere descended upon Perilous like an invisible fog. Everywhere Angus went, lightning catchers and cubs were discussing the latest ice diamond storms in hushed voices, wondering where and when the next one might strike.

There were also frequent evacuation drills; at the sound of a noisy warning claxon, they were herded down to the frozen cloud garden, where they shivered in the cold until their names had been checked off a long list.

In the meantime, extra lightning catchers had been drafted into the experimental division, where frantic efforts were being made to invent a device that would stop the ice diamond spores from spreading.

"Well, they've got to try something, haven't they?" Dougal said wisely one day, as they were almost flattened by a group of lightning catchers charging through the entrance hall with what looked like a giant net shopping bag. "Storm vacuums won't work because the spores

would freeze the insides, and storm bellows would just scatter them even farther. I wonder how the lightning heart works. I mean, if your dad's right and it can stop the spores . . ."

"I wish I knew," Angus said. "We've got to find it before it's too late."

Their chance came sooner than Angus expected, at the end of a very dull Thursday in the research department, which had now been thoroughly decontaminated once again. Catcher Castleman had put them to work in the map room, cleaning an eccentric collection of wintry, ice-covered charts that showed the location of glaciers in Iceland. The odd maps sparkled and dazzled brilliantly under the light fissures, doing strange things to Angus's vision. By the end of the afternoon, he had large silvery blobs dancing before his eyes. And as they crossed the Octagon, he accidentally tripped over a pile of storm bellows, scattering them noisily in every direction.

"McFangus! Do watch where you're going." Catcher Sparks appeared from the experimental division as Angus stood up and brushed himself off.

"I'm sorry, miss. It was an accident."

"Accident or not, those storm bellows have just been cleaned and oiled. They might be needed any day now if the weather continues to deteriorate. In fact, Clifford Fugg was supposed to have moved them into the supplies department hours ago," she added, glancing around the Octagon for signs of the absent lightning cub. "I assume you three can be trusted to complete the task without causing any further damage?"

"But, miss!" Dougal began to protest.

"Tell Catcher Merriweather that I sent you. And no dawdling, Dewsnap." Catcher Sparks glared at him. "I expect this pile to be cleared away before any of you go down to the kitchens for dinner."

"I'm going to kill Clifford Fugg!" Dougal moaned as they each picked up an armful of storm bellows and staggered through the door to the supplies department. "It's roast beef and mash for dinner, and if all the mashed potatoes are gone by the time we've finished this . . ."

It took seven awkward trips to and from the Octagon to deposit the entire collection of storm bellows with Catcher Merriweather, who insisted on checking each one over for damage before allowing them to leave.

"Come on!" Dougal urged, taking the lead as they made their way back through the department for the last time. "If we hurry up, there might still be some dessert left . . . unless the Vellums have eaten everything!"

Angus could hear his own stomach rumbling loudly. Indigo had shared a small packet of mint humbugs with them earlier, but the effects had worn off ages ago. He was just wondering if he'd be able to fit a double helping of dessert into one bowl when something caught his eye. He stopped dead in his tracks and turned back to gawp at one of the doors. It looked exactly like every other door in the supplies department, with a black handle and rusty hinges. They'd already walked past it fourteen times in the last hour without giving it a second glance. But now . . . it shone out at him like a wondrous beacon of hope.

"What is it?" Indigo asked, dragging Dougal back with her to see why Angus had stopped.

Angus pointed to the sign on the door, excitement rising inside him. "Lightnarium supplies! Do you remember when Catcher Sparks stopped here on the way to the Antarctic center on our first day back?"

"Yeah, so?" Dougal shrugged, looking mystified. "What's so interesting about the Lightnarium supplies room all of a sudden?"

But Indigo understood Angus instantly. "Oh!" she gasped, pushing her hair out of her eyes. "You mean the Lightnarium, lightning—"

"The lightning heart!" Dougal gulped, catching up quickly.

"Do you really think it could be in that room?" Indigo asked.

Angus nodded, his imagination already running away with him. "It could be a valuable piece of equipment used in the Lightnarium or something really old and rare they discovered in the lightning vaults! It could be sitting on the other side of that door right now, just waiting for us to grab it."

It was the first real idea any of them had had in weeks. Angus was desperate to try anything, especially as there was no way they could sneak into the actual Lightnarium itself to poke around.

"Well, don't just stand there staring at it," Dougal urged. "Try the door; see if it's locked."

Indigo checked up and down the corridor, but the rest of the department was deserted.

Angus knocked quietly first. Then he slowly opened the door. Inside, the room was dark and empty.

Angus flicked on a light fissure overhead as Indigo closed the door behind them. The supplies had been arranged in a very orderly fashion on neatly stacked shelves. Labeled drawers told them exactly what each contained. There was a whole rack of lightning deflector suits and some intriguing wooden boxes that reminded Angus of treasure chests. They looked extremely promising.

"Hey, those are silver lightning moths!" Dougal said, hurrying over to an interesting box on the shelf closest to them.

Angus frowned. "What are lightning moths?"

"They get sent up into live thunderstorms," Dougal explained. "They're used to attract lightning strikes on purpose, to help calculate the strength of the storm. They use them all the time in the Lightnarium. They're self-winding, they can see in the dark, and they're attracted to movement. Look."

Dougal bent down and picked up a solitary moth that had fallen out of the box and had obviously been trampled on. Its six razor-sharp wings looked crumpled and bent. Its body had been squashed and was leaking some kind of oily fluid. Angus, however, was more concerned by the large red warning label that he'd just spotted on the side of the box. It read DANGER! BOX SHOULD BE OPENED ONLY UNDER STRICTLY CONTROLLED CIRCUMSTANCES BY A TRAINED MOTH HANDLER.

"Er . . . I'd watch out if I were you. Those things sound dangerous," Angus warned.

"Exactly." Dougal dangled the moth by one of its wings. "And if this is the kind of thing they've got stored in here, then we're bound to find the lightning heart!"

"Let's split up and look around," Indigo said, already rolling up her sleeves. "Search for anything heart shaped or—"

"—seriously dangerous looking?" Dougal finished. He darted to the far end of the room to inspect a large collection of cardboard boxes that had been stacked into a precarious-looking tower.

Angus headed straight for the treasure chests, his heart suddenly thumping loudly against his rib cage. If they

somehow found the lightning heart, and he could figure out how to use it, he could stop the ice diamond storms before Dankhart could do any more damage.

He took a deep breath and lifted the lid on the first chest. It was completely empty, except for a dried-up apple core. The second chest was stuffed full of boring paperwork. The next two were locked tight, with no sign of the keys anywhere. By the time he reached the last one, he was beginning to lose hope. He raised the lid, peering inside . . . and swiftly slammed it shut again.

"Have you found something already?" Indigo asked, staring at him from between two shelves.

Angus shook his head. "Giant earwigs!" he croaked, and moved away from the chests without looking back.

He headed next for a display cabinet that held an impressive collection of antique fulgurites and other curious objects, none of which looked as if they could be the lightning heart. There were mountains of spare parts for the lightning generators and some shockproof clipboards with rubber-coated pens. There were long, flat drawers full of complicated maps. And short, fat boxes stuffed with faded photographs.

Most of the pictures had been taken long ago, inside the Lightnarium, and displayed the results of various lightning experiments. A few, however, captured the lightning catchers, past and present, who had worked in the dangerous department.

One photo in particular caught Angus's eye. It was dark and blurry, but it showed a much younger Valentine Vellum shaking hands with another lightning catcher. His name, according to the writing underneath, which was partially obscured by a smudged thumbprint, was Adrik Swarfe.

"Hey, come and have a look at this," he called quietly. Indigo appeared instantly, brushing cobwebs out of her hair; Dougal followed close behind. "Swarfe and Vellum look pretty chummy, don't you think?" he said, handing the picture to Indigo first.

Indigo stared at it for a few seconds, then thrust it at Dougal, suddenly turning pale.

"What's up with you?" Dougal asked.

"Nothing." Indigo swallowed hard, looking shaken. "It's just . . . What if Swarfe and Vellum never stopped being friends?"

Dougal stared at the fuzzy photo. "You think Vellum's been helping Dankhart and his monsoon mongrels all this time?"

Indigo looked uncertain. But Angus decided she might have a point. He folded the photo carefully and stuffed it into his pocket, deciding to have a closer look at it later. "Have you two found anything yet?"

"Only this . . ." Dougal took an ornate teacup from one of his pockets. It was decorated with lightning bolts and was sealed with a lid. "I've been trying to open it just to see if there's anything interesting— There! Got it!"

Loud rumbles of slightly tinny-sounding thunder suddenly echoed all around them, rattling the glass in the cabinets.

"Shut that thing up!" Angus hissed as the storm grew louder still. "We'll have the whole supplies department in here, wondering what's going on."

"I'm trying, I'm trying!" Dougal struggled, desperate to force the lid back onto the cup.

But Angus was no longer listening. Another even more frightening sound had caught his attention. Footsteps were approaching down the corridor outside.

"Quick, someone's coming!" he whispered, flicking the light fissure off hurriedly. "Get the lid back on that teacup, now!"

"I can't— Oh, drat!" The cup suddenly slipped between Dougal's fingers and smashed on the floor with one final thunderclap.

"Just leave it!" Indigo hissed. "There's no time to clear up the mess!"

Dougal fled, squeezing himself in among the lightning deflector suits, his feet poking out the bottom. Indigo disappeared into the dark. Angus crouched down behind a stack of boxes, listening with dread as the voices grew louder. He felt a sudden wave of panic as he realized whom one of the voices belonged to.

"—really can't be expected to run your supplies department for you, Merriweather. This is extremely inconvenient."

Valentine Vellum's familiar voice drifted through the closed door.

"When I placed an order with you for twelve pairs of tinted safety goggles, I expected it to be ready on the day I specified."

Angus peered around the boxes and watched the tiny gap under the door in horror . . . as two sets of feet stopped right outside it.

"Are you trying to tell me that if I walked into this supply room right now, I wouldn't be able to find a single pair?"

"That's exactly what I've been trying to explain to you, Valentine," the other voice said with a weary sigh. "A party of lightning catchers from Norway totally wiped us out of goggles before they left. Took the whole lot without asking and left me with nothing but a thank-you note and a box of pickled herring. It'll take weeks for a new supply to be delivered. But come in and see for yourself, if you don't believe me."

The light fissure flickered on suddenly, and the two men entered the room. Angus scuttled farther back into the shadows, trying not to breathe too loudly. Dougal's feet, which were clearly visible beneath the clothes rack, twitched with a spasm of fear.

"Oh, goodness!" Catcher Merriweather stopped suddenly as he crunched through the remains of the shattered teacup.

"What is it now, Merriweather?" Valentine Vellum asked impatiently.

"Someone's dropped a storm in a teacup. Rogwood placed the order—a novelty gift to be handed out at this year's graduation and prize giving. But we can't get the wretched things to shut up once they've been opened. Someone must have been rummaging about in here without permission."

Angus shrank behind the boxes. If Vellum realized something was wrong and came to investigate, not even Jeremius could save them.

"I've warned everyone to keep the door to this supplies room locked at all times, but does anyone listen? Moths!" The man darted across the room and scooped up the box of silver lightning moths that Dougal had left on the floor. "It's far too hazardous to leave these lying around; they must be safely stored on the correct shelves. I'll be having words about this!"

"Your storage problems do not concern me, Merriweather." Vellum sounded irritated. "Either you have the safety goggles or—"

"I have already told you once, Valentine," the other

lightning catcher snapped. "I have nothing but a box of pickled herring."

"Then you are wasting my time. I shall be informing Principal Dark-Angel about the shoddy way you run this supplies department."

"Now listen here—"

Vellum turned on his heel and swept back toward the door. Merriweather followed, hurriedly dropping the box of moths. He flicked off the light fissure, closed the door as they left the room together, and locked it from the outside. The sound of their angry voices faded slowly until the corridor outside was silent once again.

Angus sank back onto his heels, letting out a long, slow breath.

"Let's get out of here," he said as Indigo emerged from the gloom. "Before Vellum changes his mind and comes back again."

"But what about the lightning heart?"

Angus stared around the supply room. Everything in it was dead, shriveled up, dried out, or made of cold, hard steel. And the lightning heart . . . He had a strong feeling that whatever it was, it had to be more alive somehow.

"Forget it. It isn't here." And he knew it was true as soon as he said it. "Come on."

"Hey, wait for me!" Dougal whispered loudly. He fought his way out from his hiding place, his foot catching clumsily, and before Angus or Indigo could do anything to stop it . . .

"Argh!"

Dougal tripped and lurched across the room. He collided with a box of repair kits and sent the lightning moths flying.

"Oh, no!" Dougal squeaked as dozens of silvery creatures rose into the air at once.

The moths did not look friendly. They hovered with the buzz of an angry swarm, their mechanical wings flapping furiously.

Angus backed away slowly. The moths followed, in one fluid motion.

"Stand still!" Dougal warned, scrambling onto his feet again. "The moths are drawn toward movement, remember?"

"Then how are we supposed to get out of here?"

"I don't know, but whatever you do, don't make them angry."

Thwack!

Indigo swatted one of the moths with a handy box lid, sending the rest of the swarm into a frenzy.

"I said *don't* make them angry!"

But Indigo stood her ground bravely, taking another big swing and smashing several more moths with one blow. "RUN!" she yelled over her shoulder, already sprinting for the door.

Angus didn't need to be told twice. He grabbed Dougal by the sleeve and dashed across the room. A spare, rusty key was hanging on a hook beside the door. He grabbed it.

"Get down!" Indigo dropped like a stone beside him.

The lightning moths had turned as one sleek, silver wing and were now diving at breakneck speed, their wings flashing ominously. Angus grabbed a bewildered-looking Dougal and pulled him to the ground as the creatures swooped low overhead, missing their ears by millimeters.

He was back on his feet again in seconds, forcing the rusty key into the lock. It scraped and groaned in protest as he tried with all his might to turn it.

"Nothing's happening!"

"Try giving it a wiggle!" Dougal said.

Angus gripped the key with both hands and desperately twisted it backward and forward.

"Quickly, they're coming back!" Indigo shrieked. *"DUCK!"*

The moths flashed past and crashed headlong into a tower of flimsy boxes. They tore at the cardboard with razor-sharp wings, leaving nothing behind but a pile of powdered dust.

"That's what's going to happen to us if we don't get out of here soon!" Angus hissed. He leaped up again, determined to get the door open.

His fingers felt slippery with sweat as he waggled, jiggled, and wrenched the key. The moths were almost upon them again.

"Hurry up!" Dougal urged.

"I'm trying! Just give me five . . . more . . . seconds—"

Click!

The door flew open. Angus bundled Dougal through it first, not caring if they ran straight into Valentine Vellum, Principal Dark-Angel, and every other lightning catcher on the planet. Indigo flew past him into the corridor, hair streaming behind her. Angus stumbled after her,

slamming the door shut, only just in time.

Thud! Thud! Thud! Thud! Thud!

The door rattled violently on its hinges as the moths hit it hard. And then there was silence.

"That . . . was the worst idea . . . you've ever had!" Dougal panted as he slumped against the wall. "I'm never searching . . . another supply room . . . ever again! They're way too dangerous!"

13

CRISPIN PINNY-PENCHER

Angus slept badly that night, plagued by nightmares about giant lightning moths that all looked exactly like Valentine Vellum. One of the moths, a large, ugly, bearded brute, kept hissing his name over and over again.

"Angussss!" it whispered, jabbing him in the arm with one of its wings. "Wake up! I need to talk to you. Angussss!" The lightning moth pinched him hard. Angus woke up suddenly. The skin on his forearm was burning. Indigo was leaning over him, her face creased with worry.

"I-Indigo?" He sat up, trying to rub the sleep out of his eyes. "It's the middle of the night. What are you doing here?"

"I need to tell you something. It's urgent!" She glanced over her shoulder at Germ and Dougal, who were both soundly asleep. "We can talk in the Pigsty. Bring the message from your dad and that photo of Adrik Swarfe."

"What? What for?"

But Indigo had already gone. Angus carefully took the note and the photo from under his pillow, pulled on his slippers, and tiptoed across the room, accidentally colliding with a chair as he stumbled about in the dark.

"Ow!" He grabbed his foot and hopped the rest of the way into the Pigsty. "Can't this wait until the morning?" he asked.

"I'm sorry, Angus, but I just couldn't sleep. I had to talk to you." She bit her lip. "It was after you found that picture in the supply room, the one with the thumbprint."

"The what?"

Before Indigo could explain, however, Dougal came stumbling into the Pigsty, half asleep. "What's going on? Why are you two sneaking about in the dark?"

Indigo stared nervously from Angus to Dougal and back again. Then she took a deep breath.

"I overheard my mum and dad talking at Christmas.

They were worried because of what had happened in the lightning vaults with Uncle Scabious, and then Principal Dark-Angel sent them a letter."

"Yeah, we all got one of those," Dougal said, rubbing his eyes, glancing sideways at Angus.

"Then Mum told Dad about a diary she'd written before she fled the castle, and I—I took it." She removed a small blue book from her bathrobe pocket and showed them the worn cover. "I know I shouldn't have, but I wanted to know more about the Dankharts, and Mum won't tell me anything."

"So that's what you've been hiding in your bag all this time," Angus said, putting two and two together.

Indigo nodded, looking thoroughly wretched.

But Angus understood, even in his sleep-deprived state. Indigo was both fascinated and appalled by her family connections. And she wanted to understand everything she could about the Dankharts, even if the truth was uncomfortable. After all, it was the Dankharts who shared her fascination with the weather. But she also hated the idea of anyone's finding out, so she'd hidden the evidence in her bag.

"But why didn't you tell us?" Dougal asked.

"I couldn't tell anyone, not even Germ. Besides, the diary was written years ago. There's nothing in it that could help Angus or his parents. I would have told you straightaway if there had been," she said earnestly.

Angus didn't doubt it for a second. Indigo was the most honest and trustworthy person he'd ever met.

"So why are you showing us now?" he asked.

"It was only when I saw that photo of Swarfe and Vellum that I realized . . . and I just knew I had to—"

Indigo opened her mum's diary and extracted a faded old photograph from the pages in the middle. "I found this hidden inside."

The photo showed a young boy and a girl sitting together on a trunk. Indigo's mum was laughing. And the boy . . . even with short hair and an innocent-looking face, he was obviously Scabious Dankhart. The resemblance to Indigo was striking, and Angus was glad she didn't have any pictures of her uncle after his ugly, malevolent transformation had taken place. But there was something else. Tucked into a corner, at the bottom of the picture, was another smudged thumbprint.

"I wasn't sure at first, but if you look closely, it's exactly the same as the thumbprint on that photo of Valentine Vellum and Swarfe. It matches the one on your dad's message, too."

Dougal frowned, looking skeptical.

"But how can you tell?" Angus took the photo and looked at it closely. "Don't all thumbprints look the same unless you study them under a magnifying glass?"

Indigo nodded. "That's why it took me so long to notice. But then you showed me that photo in the supply room, and I suddenly realized there's a lightning bolt inside each thumbprint. It's hard to see at first, but once you know it's there . . ."

Angus laid the photo of Swarfe and Vellum and the note from his dad on a table next to Indigo's photo, but the thumbprints were baffling, with barely visible zigzags, lines, and ridges. How had Indigo seen a lightning bolt? He picked up the picture of Indigo's mum and studied it from every angle. It was only when he squinted at it, through half-closed eyes, that he finally saw it. Running straight through the middle of the thumbprint was a very distinct lightning bolt.

"I can see it!"

Once he'd spotted it, it was impossible to ignore. He grabbed his dad's note and held it up against the photo. Indigo was right! All three thumbprints were identical.

"Indigo, this is brilliant!" He quickly passed the diary over to Dougal. "I never would have spotted it."

Indigo blushed.

"But I wonder who it belongs to?" Dougal said. "I mean, how come the same person's managed to smudge a thumbprint onto two separate photos and a secret message from your dad?"

Angus shrugged. "Maybe the thumbprints are a clue, and my dad's just trying to help us."

Indigo nodded enthusiastically. "All we've got to do now is figure out what it means."

They sat in the Pigsty, discussing the possibilities, until the first light of dawn began to brighten the sky outside the window.

At breakfast they were met by the appalling news that the silver lightning moths had escaped from the supplies department overnight and were now flapping about the Exploratorium, causing panic and chaos. Loud squeals could be heard coming up from stone tunnels and passageways as the moths swooped after terrified huddles of lightning cubs. The entire experimental division had to be sealed off while Catcher Sparks and her team tried to catch the silvery pests with some powerful magnets and giant strips of extra-sticky flypaper.

"If I ever get hold of the idiot who let those blasted moths out . . ." Gudgeon grumbled when Angus, Indigo, and Dougal bumped into him outside the research department.

Angus shot a guilty look at Dougal, who was staring down at the floor, his ears pink. Indigo looked thoroughly shamefaced and bit her bottom lip until it turned white. Luckily, nobody had the faintest suspicion that they had accidentally set the moths free. But if Gudgeon, Catcher Sparks, or Dark-Angel ever found out . . .

"We're already stretched to the limits as it is," Gudgeon told them, shaking his head wearily. "We've got icicle storms going off all over the globe, lightning catchers coming and going at all hours. If this carries on, we won't have enough experts left to run the Lightnarium."

Angus felt his face burn. The experimental division was

already working around the clock to repair battered storm vacuums. The kitchens were open twenty-four hours a day because of the high demand for tea and toast. And the supplies department was now in imminent danger of running out of rubber boots.

"Oh, but couldn't we help?" asked Indigo, trying to make amends. "I mean, the lightning cubs could work in the kitchens or clean out some storm vacuums."

Gudgeon shook his head. "The last thing Principal Dark-Angel needs right now is for you three to go wandering off, getting yourselves into trouble."

When most of the moths had finally been recaptured, however, Indigo got her wish, and all trainees were sent to help with the sizable backlog of cleaning and repairs that had now built up. Dougal was dispatched to the kitchens to peel carrots and potatoes. But Angus and Indigo were sent to the experimental division, where they were met by Catcher Sparks. She led them briskly into a familiar room filled with rusty coils of wire and large bolts. Angus, Dougal, and Indigo had spent many hours there during the previous term, removing pockets of earwax from hailstone helmets. To make matters worse, Percival and Pixie

Vellum were slouched against the wall, scowling.

"A party of lightning catchers has just returned from dealing with some icicle storms in Texas," Catcher Sparks said, pointing to a pile of weatherproof coats that had been dumped in the middle of the floor. They were covered in a thick, tarlike substance that smelled strongly of rotting fish. "Unfortunately, the lightning catchers were forced to run for cover across an extremely unpleasant swamp, and their coats now need cleaning thoroughly. You will find plenty of hot water, gloves, and buckets in the back."

"But that's not fair!" Percival Vellum folded his arms. "Why should we have to clean those horrible coats? It's not our fault some stupid lightning moths escaped."

Angus glanced furtively at Indigo, who was trying hard not to look anybody in the eye. Her face, however, was burning with guilt.

"Principal Dark-Angel expects everyone to help get Perilous back on its feet, and that includes you two." Catcher Sparks poked Percival in the chest with a bony finger. "I expect those coats to be spotless by the end of the day. And try not to get dirt all over the floor. It has just been steam cleaned after spillage from one of our oldest

storm jars." She strode out of the room and slammed the door behind her.

It was the most revolting thing Angus had ever done. The tarry substance proved highly resistant to cleaning. It oozed and dripped as he scraped the worst of it off. Then he quickly dunked each coat into a bucket of hot, soapy water and scrubbed away the dreadful stench, deciding he'd never eat sardines again.

The minutes dragged by at a snail's pace. Angus was convinced the disgusting heap of coats was actually getting bigger, not smaller. He was just wondering if Catcher Sparks would force them to stay all night to finish the job when—

"Watch where you're flicking that water, Munchfungus. It's going all over me!" Percival Vellum was glaring at him.

Angus shifted his bucket away from the twin, trying to keep the peace. But Percival hadn't finished with him yet.

"At least this is more interesting than those stupid survival lessons we've been doing with your uncle, Munchfungus," he said.

Angus clutched his scrubbing brush tightly. "Shut up, Vellum. I'm not interested in what you think."

"I'd rather clean a hundred rotten, stinking coats than go back into that Rotundra again," Percival continued.

Pixie giggled.

"But Angus's uncle is teaching us something really useful," Indigo said quickly. "You two wouldn't last five minutes in a real blizzard."

"Stop getting your rubber boots in a twist, Midnight. I couldn't care less if his uncle can knit an emergency shelter out of his own beard. He's still a McFangus, and who'd want to be one of those?"

"Yeah." Pixie snorted with giggles. "Our dad says that your uncle Jeremius ran away to the Canadian Exploratorium because Dark-Angel hates him, and nobody wants him here at Perilous."

"That's not true!" Indigo dropped her scrubbing brush into her bucket and stood up to face the twins defiantly. "Your dad's making things up! Just because everyone thinks he's a gormless gorilla."

"Does your uncle live on an iceberg back in Canada, Munchfungus?" Percival said, ignoring Indigo. "Does he share his lunch with penguins and spend his days digging for ice worms?"

"There aren't any penguins in Canada, you idiot," Angus said. He clenched his fists, resisting the urge to dump a bucket of dirty water over the sniggering twin's head.

"Is that why nobody ever sees your mum and dad around here anymore? Has Dark-Angel sent them on a *secret assignment* to your uncle's iceberg?"

Angus shot to his feet, accidentally kicking over his bucket of water. "Shut up about my mum and dad!" He flicked the coat he'd been cleaning at Percival Vellum, showering the twin in disgusting globs of filth and muck.

"Urgh!" Percival spluttered, staggering backward. "You're dead, Munchfungus! You and your feeble little friends will pay for that!"

Bang!

The door suddenly burst open behind them, making all four of them jump.

"What on earth is going on in here?" Catcher Sparks stormed into the room, her nostrils flared in anger. "I can hear your voices from the other side of the experimental division. And why is Percival Vellum dripping all over the floor?"

The twin glared at the lightning catcher but said nothing. The silence stretched on for several uncomfortable moments.

"Very well, if none of you are prepared to explain yourselves . . ." Catcher Sparks folded her arms. "Miss Vellum, there's dirty water all over this floor. Get a mop and clean it up at once, and then report to Catcher Trollworthy. She has some snow boots that need to be deodorized. Your brother will clean himself up and then proceed to the Octagon, where he will find a fresh pile of storm bellows waiting to be moved to the supplies department."

Percival groaned.

"And you two!" She pointed a finger at Angus and Indigo. "You will remain here until every single one of these coats has been cleaned. I will not tolerate this kind of behavior in my department!"

The stench grew steadily more disgusting as Angus and Indigo scrubbed coat after reeking coat. They were allowed to leave only after Catcher Sparks had checked all the pockets for any lingering specks of swamp.

"Ew!" Dougal wrinkled his nose as they finally entered

the Pigsty after dinner. "What have you two been doing? You stink of rotting fish."

Indigo explained quickly about the marathon coat-cleaning session. And Angus filled Dougal in on his argument with the Vellums.

"They definitely know something about my mum and dad." He pulled off his smelly sweater and flung it into the far corner of the room. The tarlike substance had somehow managed to work its way into his hair and now covered most of his clothes, face, and boots in long, sticky smears. "Vellum's been hinting at it for weeks now, making snide remarks. But how could he know anything personal about my family?"

"I've got two words for you," Dougal said darkly. "Valentine Vellum. He's always poking his nose into things that don't concern him, and I bet he's told those two gargoyles everything. Anyway, never mind about them now. I've been doing some digging."

"Into the lightning heart or the thumbprints?" Angus asked, hoping something could be salvaged from the day.

But Dougal shook his head. "Into Adrik Swarfe. I still can't believe he was ever a lightning catcher here at

Perilous. And then you found that photo in the supplies department. So I decided to find out more about him."

"And?" Indigo sat down on the floor beside him as Dougal spread out a pile of old *Weathervane* magazines. Angus kicked off his swampy boots and perched on an armchair.

"And you'll never believe what I've discovered. Adrik Swarfe comes from a long line of lightning catchers who go all the way back to the Great Fire of London," Dougal said. "And they've lived and worked at Perilous ever since. All of his ancestors were well respected; they believed in the Perilous philosophy about protecting mankind from the worst weather. Everyone says Adrik Swarfe is a brilliant inventor. He's got a real genius for it; he showed great promise in his early years at Perilous."

"How do you know all this?" Angus asked.

"Because Swarfe won the Lightning Catcher of the Year award two years in a row, before he scarpered off to join Dankhart. And the *Weathervane* covered the whole thing."

"There's a Lightning Catcher of the Year award?" Indigo asked as Dougal riffled through the magazines and plucked out a particularly moldy copy. A photograph of Swarfe covered the front page. His face, however, was hidden behind a gleaming trophy shaped like a lightning bolt.

"It's a really big deal! All the Exploratoriums across the globe can enter. There's an awards ceremony and a big celebration afterward. The winner gets a huge trophy and a lifetime supply of luxury all-weather lightning-proof leather jerkins. Then they do a lecture tour and demonstrations and stuff. Rogwood has won it loads of times. It was awarded to some guy called Kristof Wideflake two years ago, for his work with stretchable snow. And . . ." Dougal paused, suddenly looking uncomfortable.

"What?" Angus asked.

"Your mum and dad won it ten years ago for writing their *McFangus Fog Guide*. There's a picture of them collecting their prize."

Dougal pulled another *Weekly Weathervane* from the pile and pushed it toward Angus. Angus stared at the faded photograph dumbfounded. It was like discovering the world was no longer round. How could his parents have won such a major prize without ever telling him? He gazed at the picture, soaking in every detail. His mum and dad were both dressed in smart new leather jerkins, looking happy and relaxed. They were holding an impressive lightning-shaped trophy between them, standing among a larger group of lightning catchers, including Rogwood, Principal Dark-Angel, and Catchers Grimble and Sparks. It was the first time Angus had ever seen his parents with anyone else from Perilous. He studied the photo for several long moments before finally turning his attention back to his friends.

"S-so what did Swarfe win his award for?" he asked Dougal, who was patiently waiting beside him.

"According to the *Weathervane*, he did some really inventive work with extra-high-voltage lightning. It's far more formidable than the normal stuff; they've been using it to power the light fissures at Perilous. And that's not all."

Dougal picked up another magazine and flicked through a large section on Scottish rainfall patterns before he came to a column called "The Weekly Debate."

"Swarfe appeared in this editorial column a lot," Dougal said, "and it didn't make him many friends at Perilous, either. He was always going on about how the weather should be used for power, as a weapon. He thought that if you can control it, you have the right to use it."

Angus blinked. "But that's exactly what Dankhart believes."

"Yeah. He even tried to persuade Dark-Angel to let him hunt for the lightning vaults. He wanted to open them up again for experimentation."

"I'm amazed she didn't let him," Indigo said.

Dougal nodded. "Most of the lightning catchers hated the idea, though. And the only other person who really agreed with him at the time was Valentine Vellum."

"Vellum?" Angus said. "So they definitely knew each other?"

Dougal shrugged. "I know none of this helps us much with finding the lightning heart. . . ."

"Yeah, but at least we know a bit more about Dankhart's chief monsoon mongrel now. So why did Swarfe leave Perilous?"

"That's the really odd part." Dougal shuffled through the *Weathervane*s once again and retrieved a tatty, dog-eared copy. "From stuff I've read in other magazines, I managed to pin down the exact date he left, twenty-two years ago. But when I looked through the news for that week, most of it's been blacked out. All the photos have been removed, too, and three whole pages are missing." He showed Angus and Indigo what was left of the mutilated *Weathervane*. "It's as if no one wants to remember what happened, and they've literally ripped it from the pages of history."

Angus frowned. "So we still don't know why Swarfe left?"

"No, but judging by the state of this *Weathervane*, he must have done something really, really terrible."

It took five hot baths and four long days before the smell of rotting fish finally faded enough for Dougal to sit with Angus and Indigo at their usual table in the kitchens.

"Sorry! It's nothing personal," he said, still keeping his distance. "But you two were putting me off my breakfast."

Angus decided to stay out of everyone else's way until the last lingering whiff of fishiness had gone. He and Indigo therefore spent as much free time as possible in the library, searching for anything they could find about the strange lightning thumbprints.

Angus flicked through endless maps, old dictionaries, and an amazing lightning compendium, where he got totally sidetracked by some brilliant photos of volcanic lightning. There were whole sections on paleolightning, St. Elmo's fire, protons, and electrons. There were red sprites, green elves, and blue jets, all brightly colored flashes that appeared high above a thunderstorm and often took the shape of vegetables. He was deeply impressed by superbolts, cool-sounding upward lightning, which none of the lightning catchers had ever mentioned before.

But there was nothing that even hinted at the existence of the lightning thumbprints. The closest thing he found to it was a drawing of some rare finger-shaped lightning. He had no idea how that could help them solve the puzzle and find the lightning heart.

"But they've got to mean something important." Indigo sighed, browsing through a book on weather symbols. Since showing them her mother's diary, she'd been far more cheerful and bright and had stopped clinging so desperately to her bag. She had also been more willing than ever to discuss her uncle, which Angus took as a good sign.

He snapped his own book shut, yawning wearily. "Maybe we'd have more luck with the thumbprints in the mystery, riddle, and brain twister section. I'm going straight over there tomorrow evening and—"

He stopped talking suddenly. Familiar voices were drifting toward them.

"—and the good news is that Edwin Larkspur is now back at work in the museum and making a steady recovery."

Angus and Indigo peered through a gap in the shelves. Miss DeWinkle and Catcher Sparks had stopped close by. It was impossible not to listen to their hushed conversation. Especially as they'd heard hardly anything about the archaeologist and the museum theft for months now.

"Principal Dark-Angel has already sent Trevelyan Tempest from the London office to have a quiet chat with him at the museum, of course."

"And Mr. Larkspur still has no idea what happened?" Miss DeWinkle asked.

"Absolutely none, I'm afraid. He's suffering from severe memory loss. It's taken him weeks just to remember his own name. He had no idea he was an archaeologist until his colleagues showed him a collection of Viking hair-pins that he'd dug up. He seemed to think he was some sort of champion vegetable grower. Trevelyan says he's still asking all sorts of questions about slug repellent and worm farms."

"Oh, how terrible! Poor Mr. Larkspur," Miss DeWinkle said. "But is there any sign of the lightning tower artifacts?"

"They've completely vanished without a trace. And until Mr. Larkspur can give the police a description of the thieves . . ." Catcher Sparks said, shaking her head. "He's been moved to a quiet section in the museum archives until he's recovered his memory. Although there's no guarantee that he'll ever remember the exact details." There was a short pause in the conversation. Then—"What on earth is that dreadful smell?"

Angus almost fell off his chair in a panic. Indigo quickly sank behind a pile of books, trying not to stir the air around them.

"Heaven preserve us!" Catcher Sparks grabbed a hand-kerchief from a pocket in her leather jerkin and held it over her nose. "Has the new librarian been handing out fish-scented bookmarks? Or has Valentine Vellum been studying deep-sea charts again?"

"Perhaps we should find somewhere to sit in the snow-flake section instead," Miss DeWinkle suggested. "There's always such a crisp Alpine aroma."

And they made a hasty retreat.

Indigo gave Angus some special orange-scented shampoo to wash the last of the fishy smell out of his hair. And by the time they went up to the research department the next morning, he was feeling properly clean at last.

"It's a shame about Edwin Larkspur, though," Dougal said as they made their way under a low-flying sofa that was already occupied by several snoozing lightning catchers. "It would have been brilliant to see bits of an actual lightning tower. I mean, that's where it all started, wasn't it? It's part of our history."

Catcher Castleman was still supervising their daily duties. She led them straight up a long spiral staircase to a section of the department they had never visited before. Signs of frost damage still surrounded them on all sides, and the hall, which was finally beginning to dry out, was now full of the sweet, damp smell of decay.

"Luckily, the ice diamond spores did not creep into this particular room." The lightning catcher opened a door and led them into a modest library, lined on all four sides with a small number of large books. "Due to the dampness in the air, however, there has been a serious outbreak of bearded mold, which needs to be eradicated before it damages our most precious collection of holographic histories."

"These are all holographic histories?" Angus asked, surprised, gazing at the assortment of dusty books.

"Here at Perilous we have the oldest collection of holographic histories in the world," Catcher Castleman informed them proudly. "Sadly, many of them are rather frail and delicate and must be treated with great care."

Angus exchanged looks with Dougal and Indigo. In the previous term, they had encountered several holographic histories, none of which had been remotely delicate or frail.

"Each of the books will need to have its covers wiped down, inside and out," the lightning catcher explained, handing them cleaning cloths and bottles of misty mildew spray. "I will return for your midmorning break. In the meantime, this door should remain closed at all times. We cannot risk the mold's spreading."

And with that, Catcher Castleman left, closing the door behind her.

"This is brilliant!" Dougal grinned as soon as she'd gone. "Well, it's better than going back to the booby traps, anyway." He dragged a knobbly old book off a shelf and inspected it eagerly. "The early lightning catchers were really fond of holographic histories. I had no idea there were still so many of them left. They went out of fashion ages ago, so no new ones have been written for more than a hundred years now."

An hour later, Angus was beginning to understand why. The holographic histories were highly demanding and temperamental in nature and did not appreciate being riffled through for mold.

"Unhand my pages, young scoundrel! I must protest . . . Think of my ink!"

The second a book was opened, it began to recite its contents at full theatrical volume, getting louder and louder, until Angus's ears ached with the incredible noise. Some of the oldest tomes had lost their voices and

rapped the inside of their covers with walking sticks instead, to attract his attention. A small number of the histories were clearly beginning to disintegrate, pages crumbling with age, and they were now telling nothing but fibs and lies . . . along with some fairly disgusting stories about storm fleas, which Angus was certain he'd be having nightmares about for the next month.

"Don't these things ever shut up?" he yelled, wrestling a book on weather wisdom closed before it could tell him for the fourth time what a red sky at night meant. He had just managed to squeeze it back onto the shelf when—

"Oh no!"

Angus spun around. Indigo had tripped over a stack of books.

"I'm sorry!" she wailed as tomes scattered in all directions. And before they could stop it, the air was thick with the sound of frantic storytelling.

"Oh, save us from the noxious fumes that spilleth from the division of experimentation . . ."

"Doomed is the lightning catcher who does not heed the dangers of crumble fungus . . ."

"Quick! Grab them before they really get going!" Angus

scooped up the first book he could lay his hands on and thrust it back onto the shelf, where it wriggled furiously.

"Behold!" another tome boomed impressively.

He flipped it shut with his boot before it could say anything else, but there were still a dozen books scattered across the floor. He clamped his hands over his ears and dived on a large volume about historical Imbur ailments, which was now wailing, "The only cure for warts is to slice the root of a ginger plant, at the full moon . . ."

Squashed somewhere beneath it, yet another book was attempting to make itself heard: ". . . days of dark and old, when a fierce and terrible storm struck the city of London, that the lightning heart came into being . . ."

Angus froze. "What did that last book just say?"

"If you've got a problem with warts, I wouldn't take advice from someone who calls herself Carbuncula Blemish." Dougal grabbed the book on ailments and closed it with a loud snap.

"This has nothing to do with warts," Angus explained excitedly, fishing through the rest of the scattered holographic histories. "I could have sworn one of these books just said something about the lightning heart. Here!"

Buried at the bottom of the pile, and bound in battered leather, was a small tome entitled *Mysteries of the Great Fire, London, 1666,* by Crispin Pinny-Pencher. The storyteller was old and wizened, with sunken cheeks and a sinister glare. He was dressed in robes of plain brown, with none of the fancy pantaloons, feathered hats, or bejeweled shoes that most of the other storytellers were wearing.

"*Mysteries of the Great Fire*?" Dougal said, reading the front cover as Angus rescued the book. "But how could that have anything to do with the lightning heart?"

"No idea. But with any luck, we're about to find out."

Angus propped open the book on a small reading table where all three of them could see it. Crispin began his narrative without hesitation.

"Be warned! Those who are prone to great feebleness, fits of fainting, and sudden hysterics should flee before the terrible tale of the lightning heart can be told! Only those strong in mind and sturdy of shin should proceed beyond this point."

He pointed at each one of them with a long, crooked finger, his rasping voice cut short by a strangled hiccup.

"Hey, I know what this is!" Dougal said as Crispin

paused to consider his next line and to pick a scrap of puckered skin off his left nostril. "This must be one of the books in the famous holographic horror series. They were all narrated by the same creepy guy, but I don't think they were very popular in the end. They used to flip themselves open in the middle of the night and start telling horrible, spooky stories—gave people terrible nightmares."

Angus could totally understand why. What bothered him more, however, was the fact that the only mention of the lightning heart they'd ever discovered was in a series of books that had been designed to frighten people. It did not bode well. Crispin continued.

" 'Twas in the year of 1666, in the days of dark and old, as a fierce and terrible storm struck the city of London, that the lightning heart came into being. Mighty thunderbolts shook Londoners to their very bones. Lightning lashed out and lit up the skies. The tallest lightning tower was struck with a force that it could not withstand, and so the great fire started. The blaze spread quickly, destroying all in its path, with a heat so terrible, an inferno so fierce, a storm of such vicious sparks and such high danger that it curdled milk a hundred miles away."

A spectacular bolt of lightning suddenly illuminated the page behind Crispin Pinny-Pencher's head, making Angus and his friends jump in surprise.

"The people of London fled as flames scorched the sky. Thick black smoke filled every lung, extinguished every star—"

"I say, what rot!" A small scandalized voice squeaked from the pages of the book that Indigo was clutching.

"Shhh!" She snapped it shut quickly, before it could say any more, and shoved it onto the nearest shelf.

"'Twas only after the fires had burned themselves out, as the lightning catchers were searching through the blackened wreckage of London, that they discovered the terrible lightning heart. Formed when lightning struck, fusing the blood of a storm prophet with the lightning tower, it was a bloodred heart-shaped stone of great power."

"A heart-shaped stone, formed from the blood of a storm prophet!" Angus repeated, thunderstruck. "This is it! This is what we've been looking for!"

"You—you don't think Crispin Pinny-Pencher could have made the whole thing up, do you?" Indigo said hesitantly.

"Yeah, this lot has been telling the most outrageous lies all morning," Dougal added, looking doubtful.

But Angus shook his head. It was the first mention they'd found of the lightning heart anywhere. Crispin Pinny-Pencher had to be on to something.

"Well, there's nothing remotely useful in the rest of this holographic horror." Dougal flicked through the remaining chapter headings, ignoring the highly affronted look on Crispin Pinny-Pencher's face. "It's just a load of old waffle about buildings burning down and people fleeing. This storyteller's totally bogus, if you ask me."

Angus, however, was feeling far from downhearted. The lightning heart might have come from explosive beginnings; they might have heard about it from a creepy storyteller who enjoyed scaring the pants off people. But if it could help him stop Dankhart and the ice diamond storms . . .

14

THE UNEXPECTED MESSAGE

Thoughts of the powerful lightning heart filled Angus's head from the moment he woke in the morning until he finally drifted off to sleep at night. He spent every free minute with Dougal and Indigo, trying to work out how their brilliant discovery could help them prevent yet another storm from filling the Exploratorium with deadly, diamond-shaped spores.

"So we've got one secret message, two photos, and three lightning thumbprints," he said one evening as they sat in the Pigsty. A fire roared in the grate as an icicle storm pounded against the window outside. "We finally know what the lightning heart is. Now all we've got to do is find it."

"It might help if we knew what had happened to it after the Great Fire, when it was first brought to the island," Dougal said.

He turned to look at the holographic horror, which was open on the floor behind them. After revealing how the lightning heart had come into being, the storyteller had maintained a shrewd and stony silence.

"I bet he could tell us all sorts of useful stuff if he wanted to," Dougal added, giving Crispin Pinny-Pencher a prod with his finger to liven him up a bit. "I don't know why he's gone tight lipped all of a sudden. We couldn't shut him up a few days ago, and now he won't say a word."

"It might have something to do with the fact that you accused him of being bogus," Indigo suggested.

"Well, if he's going to be all moody about it, we might just as well shove him straight back into the research department and bury him under a pile of books on verrucae."

Crispin Pinny-Pencher scowled at Dougal. A lightning bolt flashed across the page behind his head, and he turned his back on the three of them.

Angus sighed and shuffled closer to the fire, warming his toes. The last few days had been frantic. Encouraged by their discovery, they had dodged Catcher Castleman and scoured random sections of the research department. They'd spent long hours in the library and even sneaked into the forecasting department, one of the easiest places to creep into unnoticed, in the hope that they might find something bloodred and heart shaped hiding in a secret cupboard. But so far, all they'd discovered was a stinking bag of rotting seaweed.

What if it was hidden inside the Inner Sanctum or the Lightnarium, where they had no hope of going? Angus felt his stomach twist into familiar knots. His mum and dad were relying on him; he couldn't let them down now, not when they were finally making progress. . . .

"Maybe we should have a look at the map again?" Indigo suggested.

Dougal unrolled an elaborate map of Perilous, which he'd drawn several days before, and spread it out across the floor.

"Well, it's definitely not in the forecasting department," he said, drawing a thick black cross through it. "All they've got in there is stinking seaweed and hedgehogs."

"And the only things they store up on the roof are bottling jars, buckets, and rain funnels," Indigo pointed out.

As Dougal reached over to cross it off the map, something shiny fell out of his pocket. "Oops!"

"What's that?" Angus asked.

"Oh, um, it's a lightning moth. Theodore Twill and his mates managed to catch some of the stragglers." Dougal picked up the moth carefully and cradled it in his hands. It had three bent wings and a slightly squashed look about it, as if it had been caught none too gently.

"Twill says they make really good pets," Dougal said. "They're only dangerous when they're flapping about in flocks. The rest of the time they follow you like a faithful dog. Clifford Fugg's already trained his to chase after Catcher Howler, and I thought it might be cool."

Angus stared at his friend in disbelief. After everything they'd been through with the dangerous silvery creatures, surely Dougal wouldn't dream of actually owning one?

"I've called him Deciduous, you know, after Deciduous Dewsnap. Or maybe even Cid, for short?"

And despite his misgivings, Angus couldn't help smiling.

Meanwhile, the dreadful weather continued. The icicle storms were showing no signs of fizzling out yet, with new reports coming in from the Caribbean island of Antigua. The gravity railway had frozen solid, meaning that all visitors, supplies, and messages had to be transported up and down the rock by a system of ancient baskets and ropes. Angus felt queasy just thinking about it.

Hot-water bottles were now being delivered to every lightning cub just before bedtime, along with extra mugs of piping hot chocolate and marshmallows. And Germ was giving them regular updates on the lightning catchers still in the sanatorium.

"They're all starting to show real signs of progress now. Doctor Fleagal's planning to release them in a few days," Germ said, happily tucking into his dessert one evening in the kitchens.

Despite the fact that Angus and Dougal were still sharing a bedroom with Germ, they'd hardly seen him for weeks now. He often came to bed long after they'd already gone to sleep, and he went straight back up to the sanatorium before they'd woken up in the morning.

"I only hope our dear old uncle Scabby isn't planning

any more ice diamond storms." Germ pushed his empty bowl away, yawning loudly. "I've got some serious sleeping to catch up on."

"Germ, don't!" Indigo whispered, turning pale. "Somebody will hear!"

"Germ's got a point, though," Dougal said, looking thoughtful. "I mean, there haven't been any new outbreaks for a while now, have there? Maybe your uncle Scabious has finally given up?" He whispered the last few words. Indigo looked grateful.

Tensions continued to simmer with the Vellum twins. Angus did his best to stay well clear of the hairy pair. But Pixie and Percival had gone strangely quiet all of a sudden, virtually ignoring Angus whenever they passed one another in the stone tunnels and passageways.

"What's come over those two?" Dougal stared as they encountered the twins for the third time in one day without drawing a single snide remark. "They've never been this quiet before."

Angus couldn't shake off the uncomfortable feeling that the Vellum twins were plotting something big. Percival had been building up to it for months now, dropping hints, making sarcastic comments, all with an unbearable air of smugness.

Angus returned to his bedroom early one evening, still brooding on the subject, only to find it bursting at the seams with lightning cubs. Brightly colored party balloons bobbed about on the ceiling; chips, hot dogs, and cupcakes had been thrown onto plates and scattered around the room.

"Spur-of-the-moment party!" Germ exclaimed, waving at him from the center of the happy throng. "The last of the frost shock victims has finally been released from the sanatorium. Thought it was a good excuse to celebrate!"

Angus elbowed his way into the room until he found Dougal perched on his bed.

"There was nothing I could do to stop him!" Dougal yelled.

At that precise moment there was a loud cheer as Germ grabbed one of the balloons, drew an ugly face with a thick black beard and eyebrows—clearly supposed to be Valentine Vellum—and popped it.

To his great surprise, Angus found the party mood was infectious. Nicholas Grubb and his friends challenged

Germ to a cupcake-eating competition, which showered the floor in a carpet of crumbs. Theodore Twill found an ancient record player and put on some music by a popular Imbur Island band called the Typhoon Trappers, which attracted several third- and fourth-year girls from the far end of the corridor. Indigo slipped quietly through the door from the Pigsty twenty minutes later, just in time to join in a noisy game of balloon basketball. It was only after Juliana Jessop told them some spooky Perilous ghost stories, with bloodcurdling sound effects provided by Germ, that an angry Catcher Mint finally appeared and ordered them back to their own rooms.

They returned to the Rotundra for their next cold-weather survival lesson a few nights later. For once, the early evening skies had cleared to a deep satin black, and a broad sweep of twinkling stars was clearly visible through the glass roof overhead. On the far side, the formidable-looking icebergs on the cold-weather training course stood glimmering in the moonlight. No one was attempting to cross it in the dark.

Angus felt his stomach lurch when he saw Jeremius striding toward them through the snow. He still had no

idea what to think about his uncle's dubious Dankhart connections.

"This evening we will be continuing our work with shelters," Jeremius announced as they stood shivering in the snow. "If you lose your emergency weather shelter or it gets ripped to pieces by an angry storm, you still need to find refuge. So tonight, you will be attempting to construct your very first igloos." An excited murmur swept around the cubs. Building igloos sounded like much more fun than boiling up survival stews.

"When built correctly, igloos are warmer, safer, and stronger than any tent. They are often used by lightning catchers when they're stationed in cold climates. And just to give you an idea of what yours should look like when you've finished . . ."

He led them past the snow dome and the fake snowman that concealed the entrance to it, over a small hill and down the other side, stopping before a range of raised bumps and domes. It took Angus several seconds to realize he was staring straight at an igloo village. It was an impressive sight. Some igloos were large enough to sleep ten lightning cubs. Others had sculpted reindeer guarding their entrances, complete with fearsome icy antlers. A few even had bloodred stained-ice windows, although Angus wasn't sure he liked those much.

"Wow!" Indigo said, standing beside him. "I never knew igloos could have turrets and towers." She pointed to one of the larger constructions in the distance, which looked like a mini medieval castle.

"These igloos were built by some fifth-year cubs a few days ago," Jeremius explained. "You will be starting off with a much more basic model." He stepped to one side so they all could see a plain igloo with no fancy flagpoles or crenulations. "And tonight you will be testing out just how warm and safe it can keep you."

"What does he mean?" asked Dougal anxiously.

"As I'm sure you've all noticed, another large party of lightning catchers has just arrived from Sweden," Jeremius continued.

It had been impossible not to notice. The lightning catchers had arrived with so much equipment that it had caused total gridlock for hours. And all trainees were now eating their meals at spare tables set up in the drafty entrance hall.

"They will be leaving tomorrow morning to help fight the icicle storms in Antigua, but in the meantime, they need some proper rest. And as there is already a shortage of beds up in the main Exploratorium, all you lightning cubs will be sleeping in the Rotundra tonight."

Shocked gasps and whispers broke out all around.

"Camping out will allow you to experience real survival conditions. It will test what you've learned from your lessons so far."

"That's assuming we make it through the night," said Dougal.

"Hope you've brought your teddy bear with you, Munchfungus," Percival Vellum hissed from behind them. "We wouldn't want you getting scared in the night."

Angus folded his arms across his chest, ignoring the sneering twin.

"You will find full instructions on how to build a basic igloo on page two hundred and thirteen of your survival guides. Felix Gudgeon and Catcher Castleman will be staying with us to help." Everyone turned to look at the two lightning catchers, who were stamping their cold feet in the snow. "Let me remind you, this is a serious survival exercise. It is not an excuse for pranks and snow-ball fights. Any lightning cubs caught messing about will find themselves in trouble. You have been warned!" He stared around at them all. "You will be working in teams of two. So find a partner, clear a patch of snow, and let's get started. Indigo, if you could join Angus and Dougal for the building part of the process? Millicent Nichols will not be joining us tonight."

"What's wrong with her?" Angus asked as they hurried over to a pristine patch of unused snow.

Indigo grinned. "Nothing, really. It's just that Doctor Fleagal thinks she might be allergic to snow."

"You're kidding!" Dougal said, his eyebrows raised in shock. "But isn't she already allergic to fog?"

Indigo nodded. "She breaks out in hives whenever we get near a rainstorm as well."

Dougal whistled. "She's not going to be much use as a lightning catcher if the only type of weather she can handle is dry." He flicked quickly through his survival guide as they walked. "Page two hundred and thirteen, two hundred and thirteen . . . Yeah, here it is. 'How to Build an Igloo in Ten Easy Steps.' It doesn't look too difficult."

Angus glanced at the page, which showed a series of diagrams with a smiling, happy lightning cub knee-deep in snow.

"According to this, the first thing we've got to do is mark out the base of our igloo. It looks like you've got to lie on the ground while Indigo draws a circle around you with a stick."

"How come *I've* got to lie on the ground?" Angus asked, stretching out reluctantly on the ice-cold surface while Indigo measured around him.

"Because I'm best at reading out the instructions, and Indigo's bound to be brilliant at actually building the thing." Indigo blushed, looking rather pleased all the same. "Right, steps two, three, and four say we've got to make igloo bricks out of heaps of snow and build them up in layers around the baseline. Each layer has to be angled inward slightly, so the whole thing meets in an igloo-shaped dome at the top. Otherwise, you just end up with a tower going straight up."

It was much harder than it sounded. After fifteen minutes, Angus could no longer feel his fingers or toes, and his gloves were caked in freezing ice. The igloo had already collapsed twice, burying Dougal under great lumps of snow. It was only on their third attempt, when Indigo took charge of the construction, that it finally started to take some sort of recognizable shape.

"Is it supposed to have this many holes in it, though?" Angus asked, threading his whole arm through a particularly large gap between two snow bricks.

Thirty minutes later, they were forced to take cover as the eight o'clock storm raced through the Rotundra, pelting anyone left unprotected with huge hailstones. Jeremius hurried the lightning cubs into one of the larger igloos, which had been decorated with icy snowflake murals.

"Sorry I haven't seen you three much in the last few days," he said, sitting with Angus, Indigo, and Dougal on a long seat carved into the side of the igloo.

"It's more like weeks, you mean!" Angus said, calculating quickly.

"Ah." Jeremius smiled. "I'm afraid things have been a bit hectic lately with the emergency training course. And then a flock of lightning moths sneaked in through the changing rooms a few days ago and ripped all our tents to shreds."

Indigo hid her face inside her hood. Dougal gulped loudly, turning pale. His hand shot protectively into his pocket, and Angus knew that he'd brought Cid, the lightning moth, with him.

"But if the moths destroyed the tents, where have you been sleeping?" Angus asked, hoping Jeremius wouldn't notice the guilt burning across his face.

"I've been camping out with the rest of the lightning catchers from the Canadian Exploratorium in some igloos on the far side of the Rotundra. Until all the moths have been caught, it's the safest place to catch forty winks."

As the storm continued to rage outside, Jeremius told them a long story about a famous igloo builder called Mungo Mortisehead, who had once created an impressive three-story snow dwelling—only to discover the following morning that he'd built it on top of a hibernating polar bear.

"You don't think they've got anything hibernating in here, do you?" Dougal asked as they finally left the shelter. The hailstorm had passed and was now pelting the deserted training course at the far end of the Rotundra.

The storm had damaged some of the unfinished igloos.

Angus led the way back to their own, hoping the walls didn't have more holes than when they'd left it.

"According to the survival guide, the next step is to fill in the holes between the bricks with snow," Dougal said, reading as they walked. "Then we've got to smooth off the inside, so water doesn't drip on our heads in the night, and . . ." He stopped suddenly and gasped. "Oh no! What's happened to it?"

Their igloo had been totally destroyed. There was nothing left but a lumpy heap of snow on the ground.

"It must have been the hailstones!" Indigo rushed over to inspect the devastation.

Angus, however, had just spotted some extra-large footprints, which definitely hadn't been there before the hailstorm. Someone had demolished their igloo on purpose.

"Hey, Munchfungus!"

Angus swung around.

Splat!

A snowball hit him square in the face, stinging painfully. He shook snow out of his hair. Pixie and Percival were doubled up in stitches, pointing and laughing.

"Shame about your igloo, Munchfungus!" Percival called. "It must have collapsed when Dewsnap looked at it."

"It was you two!" Angus raced over to the twins, plowing through the snow, with Dougal and Indigo hard on his heels. "You destroyed our igloo!"

"You'll have a hard time proving that, Munchfungus. It's your word against ours. And your mummy and daddy aren't here to take your side."

"Stop talking about my mum and dad!"

"Yeah," Dougal added, standing beside Angus. "Stop pretending you know secret stuff about them!"

"Who says we're pretending?" Percival checked over his shoulder. Jeremius was busy helping Georgina Fox with her snow bricks. There was no one else around. "We know exactly why nobody's seen them at Perilous for months now."

"And it's got nothing to do with them being on some stupid secret assignment for Dark-Angel," Pixie said, gloating.

"How . . . How do you know about—"

"About the fact that both your parents are losers and living in one of Dankhart's dungeons?" Percival sneered.

"I've already told you once, me and Pixie hear about everything that goes on around here. Our dad's one of the most senior lightning catchers. Dark-Angel tells him loads of important stuff!"

"You've got nothing to crow about, Vellum," Dougal said angrily. "Your dad's about as popular as stinkweed!"

"Shut up, Dewsnap. We'll see who's popular when the rumors start spreading."

"R-rumors?" Angus swallowed hard, feeling sick to his stomach. This was the moment the twins had been waiting for. "What are you talking about?"

"Well, there's no point telling everyone about your parents and their sad little dungeon. People might actually feel sorry for them," Percival said. "But just imagine if a rumor started going around that they'd been banished from Perilous for causing a deadly accident on a fog field trip? Or that Dark-Angel had stripped them of their lightning strikes for tampering with invisible fog?"

Dougal gasped in horror. "Drop dead, Vellum! You wouldn't dare!"

"Bad rumors stick like mud. You'd be finished at this Exploratorium, Munchfungus, you and your whole

ridiculous family. You'd never be able to show your face on this island again."

Angus clenched his fists, but Indigo quickly stepped in front of him, holding him back. "At least no one in Angus's family has ever been friends with Scabious Dankhart's chief monsoon mongrel," she said, her face red with determination.

A stunned silence fell. Angus and Dougal both stared at Indigo in surprise. Pixie turned to her brother, looking confused. "How—How do they know about—"

"Shut up, Pix!" Percival snapped at his sister. "They don't know anything. They're making it up."

"Oh, no, we're not!" Dougal said. "And we've got the evidence to prove it."

Angus rummaged through the pockets inside his huge coat, searching for the photo he'd stolen from the Lightnarium supplies room. He held it up, just out of reach, and watched the blood drain from Pixie's face. Percival's ears turned purple.

"I bet there're loads of people at Perilous who would be dead interested in this photo," he said, pocketing it again before the twins could make a grab for it. "Your dad was great friends with the creep who invented ice diamond storms, before he scarpered off to join Dankhart."

Percival clenched his fists. "You're a grubby little liar, Munchfungus!"

"Call me what you want." Angus shrugged. "But if you tell anyone that my parents have been banished from Perilous, I'll pin that photo up on the notice board in the kitchens, where everyone else can see it."

Percival was now puce with rage. He lunged suddenly toward Angus, growling like a grizzly bear.

Smash!

A large chunk of snow hurtled through the air and landed directly on top of Percival's head. He staggered backward, flabbergasted. Angus spun around to see where the missile had come from. Indigo was already picking up another heap of snow and aiming it at Pixie.

"You're dead, Midnight!" Percival threatened. "Nobody chucks snow at the Vellums and—"

Splat!

A large, slushy snowball caught Pixie on the back of the neck as she turned and ran for cover, and then a fierce battle broke out.

For several moments it was impossible to see anything but a blur of snowballs flying in every direction.

"Sorry!" Dougal yelled, after bombarding Angus by mistake. "Everyone looks the same in their cold-weather gear!" And he raced after Pixie instead.

Angus ran for cover as a stream of missiles came hurtling in his direction.

Smash! His hood fell down. His ear was full of freezing slush, throwing him off-balance. "Oof!"

Percival barreled into him sideways, knocking him over. "You're a stinking little toad, Munchfungus," he growled, pinning Angus's arms and legs to the ground. "I'm going to—"

Splat!

A large clod of well-aimed snow hit him full in the face before he could finish. Angus pushed him away and scrambled to his feet. Indigo had come to the rescue again.

"Thanks!" he said, staring at her with an awed expression. "Where did you learn to throw snowballs like that?"

"Germ." Indigo shrugged, beaming. "And Percival Vellum's got such a big head he makes an easy target."

Angus brushed himself off and was already arming

himself for the next battle when Jeremius strode briskly into view, his face like thunder.

"What is going on here?"

Angus dropped the new snowball he'd been planning to throw at Pixie's head and tried to look as innocent as possible. Percival scrambled to his feet, breathing heavily.

"And what has happened to this igloo?"

"Sir, the Vellums destroyed it on purpose, sir!" Dougal explained hastily. His glasses had been knocked askew. He'd been bombarded with so many snowballs he was now as white as an Imbur ghost. He pointed to the sad heap where their igloo had been standing.

Looking extremely angry, Jeremius nudged the remains with his boot. "I believe I warned everyone at the beginning of this lesson that pranks and snowball fights would not be tolerated. And yet you two have deliberately disrupted a valuable lesson on igloo building." He glared at the Vellum twins. "First thing tomorrow morning, I'm sending both of you up to Catcher Sparks to help flush out the storm drains."

"But, sir!" Percival Vellum protested.

"I will also be having a serious word with Valentine

about your disgraceful behavior. Now I suggest you finish your igloo before the next storm strikes."

Percival hesitated, still glowering with anger. Then he turned on his heel and stomped off, with Pixie stumbling after him.

"And as for you three . . ."

Angus held his breath, wondering if he, Dougal, and Indigo were also about to be sent up to Catcher Sparks. But Jeremius reached into his pocket and pulled out a familiar object the size of a matchbox.

"You and Dougal had better sleep in an emergency weather shelter tonight," he said, chucking it at Angus with a wink. "There's no time to start another igloo from scratch now. Indigo will be sharing an igloo with Violet Quinn and Georgina Fox."

"That was one of the best moments of my life!" Dougal said, a look of pure bliss on his face as Jeremius walked away. "I don't care if we can trust your uncle or not; that was absolutely brilliant!"

As soon as all igloos and tents were ready, Jeremius called everyone over to a large supplies igloo and handed out cooking pots and utensils. Dinner turned out to be another packet of special emergency stew concocted by the experimental division, which the lightning cubs heated over a small camp stove.

"What flavor is this one supposed to be?" Angus asked, prodding the bits that were floating on the surface with a spoon. After their mammoth igloo-building session and their snowball battle with the Vellum twins, he was famished. And he'd already decided to eat the stew, even if it contained storm fluff and thistles.

"According to the packet, it's beef stew and dumplings." Dougal wrinkled his nose, peering into the murky depths. "I'd rather eat frozen polar bear droppings than a bowl of that swill."

Despite Dougal's misgivings, they both ate the hot stew hungrily, reliving the glorious moment when Jeremius sent the Vellum twins packing. It was only as a chilly wind began to pick up that they decided to call it a night and entered the shelter itself. Angus hung his wet socks over one of the tent poles to dry. He changed swiftly into the striped pajamas he found wrapped inside his sleeping bag and then climbed inside it before his feet got cold. Dougal, however, had gone strangely still.

"What's wrong?" Angus asked, pulling the sleeping bag around his ears to keep them warm.

"I can't wear these!" Dougal swung around and held up his own pajamas in disgust. They were a sickly shade of pink and covered in fluffy white kittens. "These are *girl's* pajamas!"

"Nice!" Angus grinned, unable to help himself. "You should really think about getting yourself a pair next time you're in Little Frog's Bottom."

Dougal scowled. "What am I going to do? If anyone sees me covered in kittens . . ."

"Go and get some more from the supplies igloo," Angus suggested, still grinning.

At that moment, however, a ferocious gust of wind shook the entire tent and the first few flakes of snow began to settle on the roof with a thick *flump*ing sound. Dougal hesitated for a second, then—

"If you ever breathe a word of this to another living soul . . ."

Dougal pulled on the pajamas with as much dignity as he could muster and then jumped into his own sleeping bag. He grabbed his coat off the floor, where he'd dumped it, took Cid out of the pocket, and let him flap about the tent. "Well, he's got to stretch his wings for a bit every now and then, or they get all seized up," Dougal said, watching Cid fondly. "Theodore Twill's going to show me how to teach him some tricks next week."

Angus rolled onto his back and stared at the ceiling, listening to the sound of a storm that was suddenly raging outside. He was just wondering if the emergency shelter could withstand such a battering when he noticed something dangling from one of the tent poles, next to his damp socks. He reached up, still in his sleeping bag, and grabbed a small envelope. He instantly recognized the handwriting on the front.

"What's that?" Dougal asked.

"It's another note from Dark-Angel. Somebody must have delivered it while we were getting our cooking stuff."

"But why didn't she just wait until the morning? I mean, we're in the Rotundra, in the middle of a storm." The wind wailed outside, as if to confirm the fact. "What does it say, anyway?"

Angus tore open the envelope and read the message aloud.

"Angus,

I have arranged another storm prophet test for first thing tomorrow morning. Doctor Obsidian has assured me that the projectograms are now in a stable condition."

"Ha!" Dougal snorted, propping himself up on his elbow so he could listen and watch Cid at the same time. "That's what they said the last time, just before some fake ice diamond storm almost killed you."

Angus felt a flurry of nerves. He did not want to go through the same ordeal again. He continued reading.

"I have spoken at length with your uncle Jeremius, and he has given his permission for the tests to proceed, on the condition that he is in attendance at all times."

Angus looked up from the letter, frowning. "I wonder why Jeremius didn't mention something about it earlier, when we were talking to him."

"He's had a lot on his mind, what with ice diamond storms and lightning moths causing trouble all over the place," Dougal said as the storm shook the shelter from side to side. "Does Dark-Angel say anything else?"

"She just says, '*Gudgeon will escort you down to Doctor Obsidian. Please do not be late. I have included a map, showing the best route to the testing tunnels, in case you and Gudgeon should become separated. Please keep it with you at all times.'"*

Angus pulled a second sheet of paper out of the envelope. "Gudgeon already gave me one of these ages ago, when he first took me down into the tunnels."

He glanced briefly at the new map. It was almost identical to the one he still had tucked into the pocket of his pants. With one major difference. Angus stared at it and gulped. At the center of the map there was a very familiar thumbprint, with a lightning bolt running straight through the middle.

15

THE WRONG FOOTPRINTS

"What's up with you?" Dougal asked. "You look like you've just discovered you're Percival Vellum's long-lost cousin or something."

Angus grabbed his coat off the floor and rummaged through the pockets, searching for the secret message from his dad. He unfolded the note with shaking fingers. His heart skipped several beats. The two thumbprints were exactly the same.

Before he could show Dougal, the tent flap rustled and Indigo crawled inside, still wrapped up in her coat and boots.

"Hey!" Dougal grabbed an extra blanket and pulled it

around his shoulders before she could spot his kitten pajamas. "This is a boys' tent! You can't just barge in here without knocking!"

Indigo grinned, holding up a couple of small flashlights. "Catcher Castleman asked me to make sure everyone had one of these. Just in case. What's going on?" she added.

"Dark-Angel wants him to do more tests with the projectograms," Dougal explained. He reached out and grabbed Cid as the moth flapped past, before his wings got tangled up in Indigo's hair, and put him carefully back in his coat pocket.

Indigo frowned, resting back on her heels. "But I thought Jeremius had banned her from arranging anymore."

"Listen, none of that matters now!" Angus interrupted, excitement almost bubbling over. "I think I've found it! The lightning heart! I think I know where it is!"

It took several seconds for his words to sink in. Dougal's eyebrows slowly rose, disappearing under his bangs. Indigo's face was frozen in stunned surprise.

"But I—how— What are you talking about?" Dougal spluttered.

Angus waved the map and the note from his dad at them. "It's the thumbprint, the one on my dad's note. There's an identical one on the map that Dark-Angel's just sent me. And I suddenly thought, what if it's a signpost? You know, like X marks the spot. What if it shows us exactly where the lightning heart's actually hidden?"

Dougal grabbed the map. "You could be on to something! And if you're right . . . it looks like it's sitting right under the Rotundra, in the snow dome. We never even thought of looking for it down there!"

He handed the map to Indigo, who studied it, blinking. "But we still don't know who those thumbprints belong to. We've got no idea what they actually mean."

"Who cares what they mean?" Dougal grinned from ear to ear. "The only thing that matters now is that we've got another clue, and if it *does* leads us straight to the lightning heart . . ."

Angus studied the map again. After months of fruitless searching, after dangerous ice diamond storms, silver lightning moths, and stubborn holographic horrors, could they finally have found the lightning heart?

"So all I've got to do now is figure out how to use it," Angus said. "And then I can stop the ice diamond storms. Just like my dad—"

BOOM!

Angus sat bolt upright, his head hitting canvas. The ground suddenly shook beneath them, sending a shudder through every tent pole.

"What was that?"

"Oh, no!" Dougal gulped, turning white. "It's a hibernating polar bear!"

Angus struggled out of his sleeping bag. He grabbed his snow boots and tried to pull on his coat over his pajamas. By the time he'd finally thrust his arms through the correct sleeves, Indigo had already crawled back out into the freezing Rotundra.

Angus hurried after her and staggered through the thick snow until he found her standing next to a long, banana-shaped igloo. She was staring into the distance, a rigid look of horror on her face.

"What is it? What's happening?" asked Angus.

He stared around at the mass of small igloos before them until he finally saw it. At the far end of the Rotundra, sparkling in a thin sliver of moonlight, was a cloud of diamond-shaped spores. Flung high into the air, they had already formed a terrifying plume.

"It's an ice diamond storm!" Dougal gasped, plowing through the snow behind them. He'd accidentally dragged his coat on back to front, exposing the seat of his kitten pajamas. "We've got to tell someone before the spores spread!"

But the alarm had already been raised. A flustered Catcher Castleman was scrambling out of her own igloo, pulling on a heavy coat over her pea-green nightdress. She stared at the growing column of sparkling diamond-shaped spores in shock, then came marching over to them.

"Dewsnap! Quickly, boy, look at your storm timetable. What weather can we expect in the next ten minutes?"

Dougal unfolded the timetable from his pocket with fumbling fingers. "We're in the middle of a blizzard cycle, miss. Each blizzard lasts for precisely ten minutes, with ten-minute gaps in between. The next one is due to strike us in four minutes," he said, checking his weather watch.

"Midnight! Which direction is the wind coming from?"

Indigo checked her own watch. "I-it's an easterly wind, miss."

"Good. That will hold the spores back temporarily, long enough for us to reach the changing rooms safely. I am ordering the immediate evacuation of this Rotundra!" she announced. "We must alert the rest of the Exploratorium immediately! Get everyone clse up, now!"

"But, miss." Angus stood his ground, a growing weight pressing in on his chest. "What about Jeremius and Gudgeon?" Neither of them had emerged from any of the igloos nearby. "They're camping out with some lightning catchers from the Canadian Exploratorium. But I don't know where . . ."

Catcher Castleman glanced over her shoulder into the distance where a small cluster of igloos huddled together. Indigo gasped in horror. Angus felt his heart falter inside his chest. The igloos stood directly in the path of the ice diamond storm, dwarfed by the glittering cloud that was now rising behind them. It was obvious they would be engulfed by the deadly spores in a matter of minutes.

"We can't just leave them there!" Angus burst out. "They'll never get out in time!"

"Gudgeon and your uncle are expert lightning catchers and are perfectly capable of forming their own escape plan," Catcher Castleman said brusquely. "Helping them would place everyone else in unacceptable danger. I cannot risk it, McFangus."

"But we've got to help them!" said Dougal.

"We have to do something!" said Indigo.

"It is out of the question," Catcher Castleman said. "We are already wasting valuable time."

"But, miss," Angus pleaded, trying to swallow down a growing feeling of despair.

"I said no, McFangus!" She turned away abruptly and began to shout at the confused and sleepy lightning cubs who were now beginning to emerge from their own igloos. "Another ice diamond storm has just erupted inside the Rotundra! I want everyone to grab coats and boots and come straight back to me! Leave the rest of your possessions behind. And for goodness' sake, Quinn, there's no time to brush your hair, you silly girl!" Violet squeaked and dropped the hairbrush she'd been holding into the snow as Catcher Castleman marched toward her.

"I don't care what Castleman says, I've got to do something!" Angus said as soon as she was out of earshot. "I'm going to the snow dome right now. I've got to find out if we're right about the lightning heart and make this all stop! Jeremius and Gudgeon—" His voice broke. He could vividly recall his own brush with the fake ice diamond storm in the testing tunnel, how he'd been fooled into feeling the slow creep of the deadly frost over his fingers and into his bones, the blood freezing in his heart. Only this time it was for real. And if Jeremius had been trapped by the cloud, if Gudgeon had been overtaken by the spores before he could get out . . .

Indigo and Dougal were watching him intently. There was no need to ask if they were going with him. He could see the shock and horror in their faces, too.

"But how are we going to get past Catcher Castleman?" Indigo said. "She'll never let us go wandering off by ourselves."

Dougal gulped. "We'll have to make a run for it as soon as we get back to the changing rooms."

"Yeah." Angus nodded. "Castleman can't just abandon everyone else and come charging after us."

It was a flimsy plan, with a high possibility of failure. But there was no time to come up with anything better.

Catcher Castleman gathered everyone together, doing a hasty head count. Less than a minute later, she began leading them swiftly back toward the changing rooms. They trudged silently after her, Indigo trailing behind Angus, Angus following Dougal, who was hard on the heels of Violet Quinn at the back of the main group. Angus glanced over his shoulder every few feet. The plume of ice diamond spores was growing, spreading rapidly. In less than four minutes, it had already begun to advance across the Rotundra like a massive wave, coating everything in its path in crystal fronds. Angus gulped. He could no longer see the igloos. It wouldn't take long before the entire Rotundra, and everyone left in it, would be frozen solid. Including Jeremius and Gudgeon.

On through the endless snow they marched, heads bent against the wind, great sheets of ice battering them from all directions as the next ten-minute blizzard arrived and swiftly swallowed them up. Angus could barely see his own hand in front of his face, and for quite some time he wasn't entirely sure if he was following Dougal . . . or a stray emperor penguin that had wandered into the Rotundra by accident. He also had the strange sensation, all of a sudden, that the ground beneath him was moving. That it was gliding, almost.

"Ooff!"

He crashed into Dougal, who had come to an abrupt halt.

"What's wrong?" he yelled.

But as he spoke, the ten-minute blizzard suddenly subsided. The wind dropped away, the clouds cleared, and Angus realized, with a jolt of surprise, that they were no longer standing on solid ground. Instead, they were balancing on a tiny iceberg that was only just big enough for all three of them to cling to.

"I think we've come the wrong way!" Dougal whimpered as the iceberg wobbled dangerously in the water.

"But I don't understand!" Indigo gasped, holding tightly on to them both. "You've been following Violet Quinn!"

"Only until she got swallowed up by the blizzard, and then I had to follow her footprints in the snow instead."

Angus suddenly understood. In the confusion of the raging snowstorm, Dougal had accidentally followed the wrong set of footprints. They had somehow strayed onto the treacherous emergency training course and were now adrift on an iceberg. It was already floating away from the shore and across a large lake littered with dozens of similar icebergs. There was no sign of Violet Quinn, Catcher Castleman, or a rescue party. If they didn't act quickly, their hopes of escaping the Rotundra and finding the lightning heart would literally sink without a trace into the freezing depths.

"What do we do now?" asked Dougal.

Angus scanned the treacherous waters around them. They'd already floated too far away from the shore to return safely. "We've got to get across to the other side of this lake before the next blizzard hits."

Indigo nodded solemnly. "Iceberg hopping."

"Have you both gone completely mental?" Dougal gasped. "Iceberg hopping is only the most dangerous sport known to man."

"Well, we can't just hang around here waiting for the ice diamond storm to finish us off!"

Angus pointed over his shoulder, being careful not to lose his balance. The diamond-shaped spores, which had been slowed down temporarily by the ferocious winds of the blizzard, were now advancing across the Rotundra again, creeping closer by the second.

"This is like the worst nightmare I've ever had." Dougal gulped.

Indigo picked the quickest route, bravely leading the way, leaping from one terrible lump of floating ice to the next as they tripped, slipped, and scrambled their way across the lake. At the halfway point, they were hit by the next ten-minute blizzard. Snow and ice gusted around them, making it almost impossible to see.

BOOM!

Dougal yelped as something shot past them at high speed and crashed into the water, causing the iceberg to pitch and roll alarmingly.

"What was that?" Indigo yelled.

Angus checked his weather watch and felt his spirits plummet. "It's a snow bomb bombardment! The whole storm's riddled with them!"

His nerves were tingling; he could feel the fire dragon lurking, getting ready to erupt. If they got hit by a snow bomb, if any one of them fell into the lake and disappeared . . .

The deadly white missiles hurtled past, crashing and pounding, pummeling the surface of the lake into watery dips and hollows.

"Look out!" shouted Angus as the iceberg closest to them took a direct hit. It rolled and flipped, sending a wave up and over their snow boots.

SMASH!

They'd been hit! He was knocked off his feet. For several seconds, there was a confusion of white, and then suddenly he was sliding, headfirst.

"Argh!"

His whole body slithered over the edge of the iceberg and down toward the freezing lake.

"Angus! Hold on!" Indigo shouted from somewhere above him.

"I can't! There's nothing to hold on to!"

"Dougal, quickly, grab his ankles!"

"Hurry up!" Angus yelled.

His nose was almost touching the choppy waters; he tried to force his body back up the icy slope. But he was gathering momentum, like an escaped bicycle wheel rolling down a mountainside. He was seconds away from sinking to the bottom of the lake.

Above him, there was a desperate scuffling of feet.

"Gotcha!"

Hands grasped him by the ankles, yanking him away from the churning lake and back to safety.

"Next time you feel like taking a plunge, just give us some warning, okay?" Dougal stared down at him, ashen faced. Indigo looked equally pale and shaken. Angus lay on his back, breathing heavily, feeling extremely grateful that he had such amazing friends.

By the time they finally reached the far shore, the blizzard had blown itself out at last. Angus checked his weather watch. They had eight minutes before the next one struck. He glanced over his shoulder. The cloud of glittering spores was closing in from all directions, cutting them off from a clear route back to the changing rooms.

"There's another way out here, an emergency exit!" he said suddenly. "Jeremius told us about it during our first lesson in the Rotundra, remember? It's got to be on the far side of this obstacle course. It goes straight back to the changing rooms. We can get to the snow dome from there and find the lightning heart. It's the only way we can stop the ice diamond storm and save Jeremius and Gudgeon. Come on!"

Ahead of them, thickets of giant icicles poked up through the ground like a hall of frozen mirrors. Angus

led the way, weaving between the slender towers of ice as fast as his legs would carry him. On the far side, they were met by a sheer wall of frozen sea ice, thirty feet tall.

"It'll take far too long to run around it," Indigo said, standing back to get a good look at the problem. "I think we're supposed to climb it. Or— No, wait, up here!" She pointed. "There's a chute running right through the middle like a wormhole."

They climbed up to it, with the aid of some handy footholds cut into the ice. Indigo slid inside the hole, feetfirst, and disappeared. Angus followed, and suddenly . . . he was hurtling through the very center of the giant petrified wave, sliding over rippled sheets of sea-green ice. He gawped at the large schools of silvery fish accidentally frozen within its depths. There was a pair of knitted mittens, a solitary sock, and a packet of emergency survival stew with its contents spilled in a cometlike trail of icy gristle . . .

Thump.

He shot out the other end of the hole without warning, landing on his elbows. Indigo helped him onto his feet again, and Angus brushed himself off quickly. They were on the edge of a frozen marsh. Raised tussocks of snow-covered grass were scattered across it like random stepping-stones. The snow tuffets looked positively tame compared with the dangers they'd already faced.

"This is the last obstacle," Angus said as Dougal suddenly flew out from the hole beside him and landed with an "Ow!"

On the far side of the sprawling marsh, he could see solid ground. Beyond that was the back wall of the Rotundra. And set deep into the rock was a large, brightly lit door marked EMERGENCY EXIT.

"All we've got to do is get across this marsh," he said.

He placed a tentative foot on the tuffet closest to him. The frozen grass seemed solid enough, so he took a deep breath and jumped onto it with both feet.

"It's okay," he said, relieved. "Come on!"

Indigo stepped onto a tuffet beside him and dashed across the marsh at double speed, making it look like a simple game of hopscotch. Angus, however, found it far more difficult, and he moved cautiously. It wasn't until he'd reached the middle that he realized something was deeply wrong.

"What's going on?" he shouted as the tuffet beneath his feet stirred in a most unsettling manner.

"Oh no." Dougal gulped. "I don't think these are normal tuffets. I should have realized. They're clumps of polar sinking grass!"

"What?"

"They usually hibernate over the winter, but we must have woken them up. If anything lands on them, they pull up their roots and literally sink into the marsh. It's a defense mechanism, in case anything tries to eat their blades of grass. So if you're standing on one of them when it decides to sink . . ."

"RUN FOR IT!" Angus yelled as the grass beneath his feet suddenly gave a small shiver and promptly disappeared under the ice with a *plop*!

Angus leaped from one frozen tuffet to the next, barely hanging on by his heels as each one vanished at the mere touch of his boot. He launched himself off the last tuffet as it disappeared, landing on solid ground and temporarily knocking all the air out of his lungs.

"Dougal!" Indigo's voice was suddenly loaded with fear.

Angus looked up, still struggling to catch his breath. Dougal had taken a different route across the marsh. He was hurtling in from the left, but he was never going to make it. The last clumps of sinking grass were already shivering, getting ready to pull up their roots and submerge.

"Oh no!" Dougal shouted, valiantly trying to leap over two clumps of grass at once. "Oh no . . . ARGHHHHHH!"

The last tuffet disappeared, dragging Dougal down with it.

"DOUGAL!" Angus scrambled to his feet and ran to the edge of the marsh.

"I can't see him!" Indigo wailed, scanning the icy surface in a panic.

"I'm going in after him!" Angus had already removed his snow boots, desperately hoping that the sinking grass wasn't carnivorous, that Dougal would bob to the surface at any second like a popped cork and float over to them. But there were no air bubbles rising from the deep, nothing to prove that Dougal was still alive.

Angus ripped off his coat.

"Wait!" Indigo grabbed his arm. "Look!" She pointed to a disturbance on the icy surface, like a tiny whirlpool. The swirl grew rapidly, getting bigger and bigger, as if a plug had just been pulled from the bottom of the marsh.

Suddenly there was a great belch of boggy water . . . and a bedraggled Dougal was expelled from the depths with the force of a cannonball.

Thump!

He landed beside them in a soaking heap.

The polar sinking grass, clearly vegetarian after all, had decided to spit Dougal out again.

"What's wrong with him? Is he breathing?" Indigo bit her lip, looking tearful. He lay on the ground between them, twitching in his kitten pajamas, his coat soaked through. "Should we give him the kiss of life?"

"W-what? No! No way!" Dougal sat upright, spluttering and coughing, gulping down great gasps of air as the color rushed back into his cheeks. "Yuck!" He pulled a clump of sinking grass out of his pajamas. "This stuff smells like rotten eggs."

There was no time to be grateful that his friend was still alive. Angus glanced over his shoulder at the advancing cloud of diamond-shaped spores.

"We've got to get out of here and find that lightning heart, now! We've got to save Jeremius and Gudgeon!"

He dragged Dougal up by his soaking pajamas. All three of

them tumbled through the emergency exit and into the curved stone passageway beyond. Indigo slammed the door shut behind them. They had escaped the ice diamond storm at last.

They ran until they reached the empty changing rooms. It was clear that Catcher Castleman had been forced to take the rest of the lightning cubs back up to the Exploratorium without them, to raise the alarm. Dougal peeled off his soaking wet coat and grabbed a dry one, rescuing Cid, his soggy lightning moth, from his pocket first. And they set off again, darting straight down into the dark passageway that led to the snow dome.

It felt creepily quiet after the howling wind in the Rotundra. Dougal squelched beside him, leaving a wet trail of foot-prints. Angus checked his weather watch, panic rising in his chest once again. It had now been at least thirty min-utes since the ice diamond storm had erupted. They'd wasted loads of time getting across the emergency training course. But there was still a slim chance. If they found the lightning heart in the snow dome, if it could somehow stop the spores and unfreeze everything in the Rotundra, including Jeremius and Gudgeon, before the unthinkable happened . . .

"I don't believe it!"

Indigo had skidded to a halt behind him.

"What?"

She pointed to a figure slumped on the ground. He'd clearly been knocked unconscious. Angus had run straight past him without even noticing.

"Hey, that's Catcher Greasley," he said, taking a closer look. "I recognize him from the dirigible weather station."

Dougal frowned. "What's he doing here?"

"He must have been trying to escape from the ice diamond storm," Indigo said. "It looks like he's fallen and hit his head."

"You stay and make sure he's okay," Angus decided quickly. "Dougal and I will grab the lightning heart. Wait here!"

He hurried on, around a bend in the passageway. Three more strides, and they'd be outside the heavy snow dome door. It would take both of them just to tug it open. He skidded to a halt again.

"What now?" Dougal blurted out from behind him.

Angus swallowed and pointed.

The door was already open.

16

THE LIGHTNING HEART

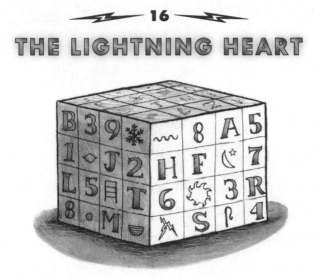

Ten feet inside the door, something small and heart shaped rested on a neat, round table.

"Wow! The lightning heart! We've found it!" Angus rushed to the table and paused. He took a deep breath and picked it up.

Smooth and warm to the touch, it fitted easily into the palm of his hand, like any tumbled stone or rock he could have picked up from the beach. But Angus knew, the second his fingers touched the marbled surface, the second he traced the bloodred veins and fissures that ran deep within the lightning heart, that he'd never seen anything like it before. He swayed dizzily. Was it the stone that was

suddenly making him feel light-headed or their frenzied escape from the Rotundra?

"This is weird. I thought we'd have to tear this place apart to find it!" Dougal said.

"Yeah, me too." Angus glanced around the snow dome for the first time. Aside from the light fissures along the walls, several lamps had been lit, filling the cave with deep, eerie shadows.

Angus frowned. He'd been expecting some sort of trouble, or an elaborate system of booby traps. This was too easy.

"The lamps!" he gasped, suddenly understanding. "Somebody lit the lamps before we arrived."

Dougal frowned. "But nobody knew we were coming down here. We've only just figured out where the lightning heart is."

"Look, we've got to get back up into the Rotundra before—"

Thud, clunk, clink!

Angus spun around on his heels.

"NO!" Dougal yelled as the steel safety door swung shut.

Angus ran, grabbed the largest bolt, and tried to slide it back again, but it refused to budge.

"I can't move it," he said as the horrible truth dawned on him. "We're locked in! *Indigo!*" He hammered on the door, pounding it with his fists. "It's no use. She can't hear us!"

"INDIGO!" Dougal joined in, pummeling the steel loudly. "Why isn't she answering?"

"It doesn't matter. We don't need help!" Angus pointed to the set of stone steps in the corner. "They lead straight up to the fake snowman and out into the Rotundra."

He raced across the cave. He was already wondering how to activate the lightning heart when a flicker of movement caught his eye, and he stopped dead in his tracks. A tall figure was coming down the steps toward them. The man was wrapped in a sweeping emerald coat. A hood was pulled down low over his face, leaving just the tip of his dark goatee visible.

"Listen," Angus began urgently, "I don't know who you are, but—"

"My name is Adrik Swarfe."

"S-Swarfe?" Angus stared at him, astounded. None of

this made any sense. They had come tearing into the snow dome to save Jeremius and Gudgeon and had somehow run straight into Dankhart's right-hand man instead.

The man lowered his hood. Both his shoulder-length black hair and goatee were flecked with gray. His eyes were inquiring and intelligent. He looked nothing like the villain Angus had been imagining. He could easily picture Swarfe walking the halls of Perilous and arguing with the other lightning catchers about the best way to tackle icicle storms.

"What are you doing here?" Angus demanded. The glass dome above their heads was already covered in diamond-shaped spores; fierce winds howled around the Rotundra. They were wasting precious time.

"We are both here for the same reason, Angus—for the lightning heart."

"The lightning heart belongs to Perilous and the storm prophets," Angus heard himself saying, without really understanding what the words meant. "You betrayed the lightning catchers. You fled to join the monsoon mongrels, to work for Dankhart!"

"I am flattered that you know so much about me," said

Swarfe, keeping his distance from them both. "But you are quite wrong, Angus. The lightning heart does not belong to the storm prophets. It belongs to my family."

Angus glanced at Dougal, who was quivering from head to toe.

"When the lightning tower was struck, on the night of the Great Fire, it fused with the blood of my own ancestor, Benedict Swarfe, to create a heart-shaped stone of untold power—an illustrious family heirloom."

"Your ancestor?" said Dougal.

"The lightning heart has been passed down through my family for hundreds of years since that terrible day. It allowed my ancestors to perform powerful deeds beyond the ability of any normal storm prophet. It enhanced their natural talents and made them formidable. But when the last of the storm prophets in my family died, so too did the power of the stone. Nothing could be done to revive it, and it has lain dormant ever since, a relic of our past."

"So it's broken?" Angus gasped. "It won't stop the ice diamond storm?"

"It has not been easy to lure you down here this evening, Angus," Swarfe continued shrewdly. "It has taken months of meticulous planning. I had help, of course, from within these very walls."

Angus stared at Dougal, and he knew they were both thinking the same thing—if Swarfe had an accomplice, it had to be Valentine Vellum.

"But I knew exactly how to start. I deliberately staged a conversation in the dungeons at Castle Dankhart. I spoke of a plot to cause mayhem and chaos with a series of icicle storms around the globe. I made sure your parents overheard. I allowed your father to smuggle a secret message out of the castle to his trusted brother, Jeremius. Jeremius would have recognized a forgery instantly. So I let Alabone send a real and urgent message inside a Farew's qube. Jeremius set off for Budleigh Otterstone the instant he received the message, in order to remove you to the safety of Perilous—the only place he could be sure to protect you, and the very place that I wanted you to return to."

"Oh no." Dougal gulped, as flushed as his pink pajamas. "A Farew's qube! I should have worked it out sooner."

"What?"

"If you change the letters around, Swarfe spells Farew's.

It comes from his name. He invented it!" Dougal pointed a shaky finger at the monsoon mongrel.

"I then had another Farew's qube placed carefully in your bedroom, Angus, on Christmas morning—a mysterious, anonymous, tantalizing gift sure to gnaw away at the edges of your imagination. An object that refused to reveal its secrets, but that surely contained something wondrous and important. I knew that once you'd discovered Jeremius had been sent an almost identical qube containing a secret message from your father, you would instantly assume your own Farew's had a similar note inside."

Something explosive was happening deep inside Angus's brain, the truth suddenly crashing down upon him like another snow bomb bombardment.

"*You* wrote the message inside my qube!" He glared at Swarfe, hope sinking fast.

Swarfe had tricked him. The message had been a clever forgery, designed to make him believe that he was acting on his dad's urgent wishes when all the time . . . He'd been guided and used without ever realizing what was happening, and now he'd put them all in terrible danger.

"I waited until the lightning catchers were preoccupied

with icicle storms and ice diamond spores. I forged a note from Dark-Angel. I knew you had received similar notes, that you would not question the appearance of another. It showed a very distinctive thumbprint that you'd seen for the first time on the message from your father . . . which could have no possible meaning until you saw it again, on a map. It was the key to solving the mystery of the lightning heart at last!"

Angus swallowed, feeling sick.

"A well-placed ice diamond storm was all that was needed to send you scurrying down here, so courageously, to find the lightning heart and rescue your uncle Jeremius and Gudgeon. I brought the precious stone back to Perilous and broke into the Rotundra, meeting very little resistance on the way."

Angus thought of Catcher Greasley, slumped in the passageway outside. He bet Swarfe had knocked him unconscious.

"I placed the lightning heart on the table, where you could not fail to find it. For there is only one thing capable of reviving it from its dormant state, Angus . . . and that is the touch of a living storm prophet."

Angus squeezed the stone tightly in his hands. He felt nothing but a vague tingling in his fingers. Was Swarfe wrong about the stone? Or was it, too, a fake, just like the note from his dad. Would it fail to stop the ice diamond storm? Or were his own storm prophet skills simply not strong enough to bring the lightning heart back to life? Fake or not, he had to try!

The ice diamond storm was still raging inside the Rotundra above them. Swarfe was edging slowly away from the steps that led up to the fake snowman, drawn toward the lightning heart like a magnet. If Angus could just entice the monsoon mongrel farther. . . .

He shot a furtive glance at Dougal, then back at the stone steps, hoping his best friend could somehow read his desperate thoughts. Dougal hesitated, slipping his hand into his coat pocket, and nodded once.

"But I don't understand," Angus said, turning back to Swarfe. "The lightning heart doesn't work. I can't feel anything."

"You must give it time, Angus. The lightning heart is frail and old. It requires a gentle drip feed of storm prophet contact before it can accomplish great deeds once again. But I first had to lure you down to the very edge of mortal danger, where it would sense your fear and desperation and be shaken from its long sleep at last. Once the lightning heart has been fully restored, Angus, it will revive my own dormant storm prophet skills, the powers I inherited from my ancestors that lie sleeping in my blood, and you will no longer be the only storm prophet in existence." Swarfe smiled, inching closer to Angus and farther away from the steps. "The lightning heart will be mine to command. The skills that Dark-Angel has been trying to coax out of you with fake ice diamond storms will exist in me. But it will not end there. Why stop at one lightning heart when two, ten, or twenty can be brought into existence."

"But that's impossible!" Dougal said, looking horrified.

"On the contrary. When Edwin Larkspur and his team of archaeologists discovered some interesting artifacts under an old paint factory in London, the possibilities suddenly became endless. The objects were still warm, still infused with the violent power that had helped create the lightning heart so long ago. It was a remarkable stroke of good fortune, one that I could not ignore."

Angus's brain had gone into overdrive. Swarfe had deliberately broken into the museum and stolen the artifacts months ago.

"With my own special skills, I will create an electrical storm to rival the one that started the Great Fire in 1666. I will use it to strike the lightning tower artifacts and fuse them together with the one crucial component that was present at the making of the first lightning heart. Do you know what that is, Angus?"

Angus didn't have to guess. The holographic horror had given them all the terrifying details. The third element was the blood of a living storm prophet. Swarfe was going to steal every drop of blood from his veins. He shot a desperate look at Dougal.

"The time has come for us to leave the Exploratorium, Angus." Swarfe was pulling on his gloves, moving farther away from the steps. "You will travel with me to Castle Dankhart. In a few hours you will be reunited with your beloved parents, and then we will begin our work, restoring the lightning heart to its full potential before creating a new generation of lightning hearts that will unleash more power than you can imagine."

"NOW!" Angus yelled.

There was a sudden flash of silver. Dougal shot forward, throwing Cid high into the cave. The lightning moth flexed his wings, circled the snow dome once, and dove straight at the shocked monsoon mongrel.

"Get this thing off me!"

"RUN!" Dougal shouted.

Angus sprinted up the steps and pushed the fake snowman out of his way as he tumbled into the Rotundra at last. He was hit by a fierce gust of glacial air. Large drifts of ice diamond spores were being driven in every direction by violent winds. The Rotundra was unrecognizable. The horizon had been obliterated, along with every familiar landmark. Giant crystal fronds had spread across almost every inch of snowy ground, wall, and ceiling like a malicious, choking fungus.

"Hurry up!" Dougal hurtled up the steps behind him. "Cid won't stop Swarfe for long!"

Angus cupped the lightning heart in both hands and closed his eyes, willing it to come back to life again and give them a small glimmer of hope, but . . .

"Nothing's happening!"

"Can't you make it do something?"

"How? It doesn't exactly come with an instruction manual!"

"But you're a storm prophet!" Dougal shouted above the howling winds. "This is the worst weather Perilous has ever had. Shouldn't you be feeling *something* by now?"

Angus scrunched his eyes up tight. Dougal was right. He had to let his storm prophet senses punch through the fear in his brain and take control at last. It was now or never; there would be no second chances.

"Oh!"

The stone convulsed. Angus gasped as the bloodred veins and fissures began to pulse. The lightning heart was beating once again! He felt its power blazing through every inch of his body. And he suddenly knew what had to be done.

"Look out!" Dougal yelled, pointing toward the snow dome, where an angry-looking Swarfe had just emerged at the top of the stairs.

Angus turned and stumbled, trying to make a run for it, but Swarfe was already closing in. He lunged and grabbed Angus by the wrist.

"Let me go!"

"Not until you give the lightning heart to me, you foolish boy!" Swarfe hissed in his ear. "It cannot withstand such powerful forces. I will not allow you to destroy it."

He twisted Angus's arm behind his back, forcing him to drop the stone. Then he dove greedily into the snow after it. But Dougal had beaten him to it. He grabbed the lightning heart and lobbed it.

"Angus, catch!"

Angus grasped it with the tips of his fingers and felt an instant surge of power.

BANG!

The fire dragon appeared at last, a blaze of roaring color in the bleak whiteness. The dazzling creature hovered above him for a fraction of a second before it reached out with the tip of its wing and touched the lightning heart.

CRACK!

Sparks flew; deep veins and fissures fractured inside the stone with the force of a mighty frost quake, and the power of the ancient lightning bolt was released at last.

Angus dropped it and flung himself behind a rocky outcrop as lightning burst from the fractured heart in a thousand fiery splinters, each striking the glass ceiling above.

CRASH!

Hundreds of crystal fronds shattered and fell, smashing into the ground. Ripples of lightning swept through the Rotundra in a blistering wave, liquefying ice diamond spores into drops of harmless rain. Angus cringed as the inferno surged across him like countless fire dragons. Gigantic rolls of thunder followed, shaking every inch of frozen ground. And then, suddenly, an eerie silence fell.

Angus waited, half expecting more explosions or a second swell of deadly ancient lightning, but all that was left was a steady *drip, drip, drip* as a deep thaw set in.

He rose slowly from behind the rocky outcrop. The lightning heart had exploded into a million tiny pieces, its remains now smeared across the snow like a bleeding wound. There was no sign of Adrik Swarfe. Angus wondered if he, too, had been vaporized. And Dougal . . .

Dougal lay in a crumpled heap on the ground. For the second time that night, he was showing no signs of life. Angus scrambled across the snow toward him, gripped by a feeling of dread. He had to get help now! He ran . . . and collided with something solid.

17

THE LAST PROJECTOGRAM

"**A**ngus!" Jeremius grabbed him by the elbows, holding him upright. "What happened? Are you all right?"

"Swarfe!" Angus managed to gasp, feeling desperately relieved that Jeremius was still alive. "Swarfe was here, and Dougal's hurt!"

Jeremius nodded. "Stay here! I will deal with Swarfe."

"But Dougal?"

Jeremius was running through the melting snow before Angus could say any more, closely followed by Gudgeon.

Then strong hands were grasping him by the shoulders, turning him away from the snow dome and his friend, back toward the changing rooms.

"I think it might be best if we leave the others to it, Angus."

Rogwood steered him carefully back across the Rotundra, where Dark-Angel, Catcher Castleman, and at least thirty other lightning catchers were all staring at the devastation. They walked silently up through the stone tunnels into the Exploratorium. There was a buzzing in Angus's ears as he slowly played back every scene inside the Rotundra like a slow-motion movie, and each time it ended with Dougal lying lifeless on the ground.

"Please go straight down to your room, Angus, and do not talk to anyone on the way." Rogwood was speaking again. They had reached the spiral stairs that led to the lightning cubs' living quarters. "I will join you in a few moments."

Angus walked wearily down the deserted stairway and along the corridor to his room. He pulled off his snow boots, dumped his damp coat on his bed, and sat in a chair by the fire, suddenly feeling too exhausted to take off his socks.

Rogwood appeared a few minutes later with a tall mug of warm milk from the kitchens, which Angus sipped numbly.

"I am sorry, Angus, but I must ask you to explain exactly what happened tonight," Rogwood said, watching him closely. "Miss Midnight has been most informative, but—"

"Is Indigo all right?"

"She is perfectly fine. When she realized that you were locked inside the snow dome, she assisted Catcher Greasley back to the changing rooms and then ran up to the Exploratorium, without a map, to fetch help. Were it not for her quick thinking and bravery, we might not have discovered you and Mr. Dewsnap for some time."

Angus swallowed hard. He couldn't believe that Indigo had braved the tunnels without a map. If she had taken a wrong turn or run into trouble on her own . . . He hardly dared ask the next question, for fear of what the answer might be.

"And D-Dougal?"

"I will speak to Doctor Fleagal as soon as he has examined Mr. Dewsnap properly. But I have just been informed in the kitchens that Dougal is now conscious and asking a large number of questions. Unfortunately, there is no sign of Adrik Swarfe. It seems he made his escape through the snow dome before Jeremius and Gudgeon could catch him."

Angus slumped back into his chair, finally feeling an enormous weight lift. Nobody had been killed by the ice diamond storm. Somehow, both Jeremius and Gudgeon were safe. The lightning heart had been destroyed. Adrik Swarfe's plans had failed.

"Now that we have covered everyone, I would be grateful if you could explain what happened with Adrik Swarfe. Principal Dark-Angel will want to speak to you, Angus, and soon. Doctor Fleagal will also be on his way shortly, to examine you thoroughly, and I believe it would be better to keep some of the details of your adventures between me, Gudgeon, Jeremius, and your closest friends," he said, raising his eyebrows at Angus. "Swarfe undoubtedly had an accomplice, and until we can prove beyond any doubt who that might be . . ."

Angus wondered if he should mention his suspicions about Valentine Vellum. But Rogwood was already waiting for him to begin his account of events. Angus took a deep breath and explained everything as swiftly as he could, from the appearance of the mysterious Farew's

qube in his bedroom on Christmas morning to the moment their efforts to open it had finally paid off, revealing what he thought was a note from his dad inside.

Rogwood nodded, looking thoughtful. "Swarfe knew that once you'd discovered the message, nothing, including ice diamond storms, would stop you from finding the mysterious lightning heart. The storms, however, kept the rest of us conveniently busy."

"But, sir, I don't understand . . . he tried to set off two ice diamond storms in my bedroom," Angus blurted out, suddenly realizing that only he, Dougal, and Indigo were aware of this fact.

"Hmm. Perhaps Swarfe felt it would provide some extra urgency to your quest, once the real storms had begun. I do not believe he meant to harm you at that time. Although it appears you had a lucky escape in the research department." Rogwood considered him carefully. "It seems Swarfe is unaware of your habit of turning up in places that you are not supposed to be."

Angus smiled sheepishly, deciding not to tell Rogwood about the incident in the Lightnarium supplies room and the accidental release of the lightning moths. He quickly described the events that had led them across the emergency training course and down into the snow dome, where Swarfe had revealed the truth about the forged notes and his intention to take Angus back to Castle Dankhart.

"He was planning to make more lightning hearts!" Angus explained. "He was going to use my blood and the museum artifacts."

Rogwood shook his head sadly. "I'm afraid there is very little hope that the lightning tower remains will ever be recovered from Castle Dankhart. An important part of our heritage has vanished forever. But Swarfe can do very little with them now that you have slipped through his fingers."

And then Angus came to the moment the lightning heart had finally awakened in his hands. He paused, trying to recall the exact feeling of the powerful stone, hardly daring to believe that he and Dougal had come through the ordeal without getting themselves frozen.

"But, sir, why did the lightning heart shatter? I mean, Swarfe was wrong, it wasn't fragile at all. I could feel how strong it was."

"It is quite simple, Angus. I believe Adrik Swarfe failed

to understand what would happen when a young and talented storm prophet got his hands on a very thirsty stone. He had no idea that you could revive it in a single moment of great need. Or that the lightning heart would respond so readily. And although I believe you did feel its full power for a brief moment, in the end it was indeed too fragile, and it shattered. Such an object of wonder is less important, perhaps, than the person who is holding it," Rogwood said wistfully.

"You should be very happy with your efforts, Angus. I realize you must have a great many questions about your storm prophet skills after everything that has happened tonight, but I'm afraid now is not the time to discuss it. I assure you, however, that we will return to the subject, and soon. Sadly, I fear we must," he said, shaking his head. "All I will tell you for now is that storm prophets do not use their most potent skills until they are faced with the worst possible danger. You have only experienced brief glimpses of that power, and for my part, I would be very happy if it were to stay that way for many years to come."

Angus sat quietly, trying to make sense of Rogwood's words.

"Your mother and father would be very proud of you, Angus. No one could have tried harder. It is a credit to your loyalty that you did not ask for help. I believe Swarfe understood that much when he formed his plan. He could see your potential."

"Is there still no word from my mum and dad?" Angus asked, already knowing what the answer would be. But he had been desperately clinging to the hope.

"Nothing has been heard from them since Jeremius received the note from your father, Angus. I am truly sorry."

"But they've been there for months now. Dankhart could be starving them."

"I think even Scabious Dankhart is intelligent enough to understand how important your parents are to him. And if he is not, then Adrik Swarfe almost certainly is. They will not perish in those dungeons, Angus, I can promise you that. We will get our chance to rescue them, and in the meantime"—he smiled kindly through his toffee-colored beard—"they are armed with the happy knowledge that Scabious Dankhart makes mistakes."

Angus stared down at his hands, trying to hide his tears.

He had thought that he and his dad were in it together somehow, that they were fighting against Dankhart and the monsoon mongrels. He sank farther into his chair, wishing that the message from Castle Dankhart had been real.

It wasn't until the following morning, after Doctor Fleagal had forced him to drink a disgusting tonic that tasted exactly like an emergency survival stew, that he was allowed out of bed and up to the kitchens for a proper breakfast.

Indigo was already waiting at their usual table, a deeply anxious expression on her face.

"Oh, thank goodness!" She leaped up from her chair to give him an awkward hug, accidentally squashing the toast he was carrying in the process. "Catcher Sparks knocked on my door last night. She told me both you and Dougal were fine. I wanted to go straight down into the Pigsty to see for myself. But if Rogwood had caught me . . ."

Angus wolfed down a plate of poached eggs as Indigo described the chaos and panic that had taken hold of the Exploratorium in the hours following the dramatic events in the Rotundra.

"Everyone got woken up and brought into the kitchens, just in case there were any more ice diamond storms," Indigo told him, helping herself to a slice of his squashed toast. "Violet Quinn had to be taken up to the sanatorium with hysterics. Theodore Twill was running around telling everyone that the ice diamond storms had woken up a top secret herd of woolly mammoths, causing a stampede through the Rotundra."

Angus grinned. He stared around the kitchens, which were still buzzing with excitement and rumors. Nicholas Grubb and his friends had joined forces with some fourth-year girls, and they were all huddled around one large table. Catcher Sparks was talking quietly with Miss DeWinkle and Catcher Castleman, demonstrating something complicated with a pile of sugar cubes and a spoon.

Ten minutes later, Jeremius appeared, with Gudgeon trailing behind him. Angus jumped out of his chair, abandoning the rest of his breakfast, and he and Indigo raced over to meet them. Jeremius pulled Angus into a tight, rib-cracking hug before explaining exactly how they'd both managed to escape the ice diamond spores.

"The storm went off right behind us. We knew Catcher Castleman would get all the lightning cubs back to safety, but we also realized that if we tried to make a run for it, we'd perish."

Angus remembered the dreadful plume of diamond-shaped spores about to engulf the igloos and shivered.

"So we blocked the entrance to the igloo with extra snow, to stop the spores from drifting inside, and kept our fingers crossed. It was an extremely close call. The weight of the crystal was starting to crack the roof of the igloo. If we'd been trapped in there for much longer . . ."

"Then there was a great commotion," Gudgeon said. "The igloo started collapsing around our ears, and the spores were melting, thanks to you and that lightning heart." He shook his head in disbelief. "I told Jeremius you'd be off doing something risky, wrestling with polar bears or getting yourselves into trouble. And I was right. Only you three could get trapped under a snow dome by a lunatic monsoon mongrel. Adrik Swarfe always was a sly one, mind," he added.

"You—you remember Adrik Swarfe when he was a lightning catcher, here at Perilous?" Indigo asked, surprised.

Gudgeon nodded, his face grim. "I reckon he's been keeping that old lightning heart up his sleeve, just waiting . . . I'll never forget the day he deserted this Exploratorium, or the trouble he left behind him like a stinking trail of dead fish."

Angus stared at Gudgeon, desperate to ask more. But—

"I'm so sorry, Angus. This is all my fault." Jeremius gripped him tightly by the shoulder.

"What? No! Of course it isn't!"

Jeremius quickly steered him away from the others so they could talk in private. "I have not been completely honest with you, Angus. I do work at the Canadian Exploratorium, but I spend the rest of my time trailing monsoon mongrels around the globe, trying to prevent them from causing trouble with the weather."

Stunned, Angus held his breath, waiting for more.

"It is top secret, dangerous work. I turn up in odd places at odd times, and occasionally the danger follows me. It was easier for your mum and dad to pretend I didn't exist. Evangeline sent cards and letters every Christmas, but I have watched you grow from a distance."

"So all that stuff about not getting in contact, about

being on a solo expedition before you turned up at the Windmill . . . ?"

"It was partly true. I was trying to disrupt the activities of some monsoon mongrels who were experimenting with volatile icicle storms," Jeremius explained.

"But you told Doctor Fleagal that you got the scar on your chin when you were staying at Castle Dankhart," Angus blurted out, determined to uncover the whole truth this time.

Jeremius looked surprised. "Perhaps this is not the best time to discuss that particular adventure. But it was one of the most dangerous of my life. If I had learned anything that would help get Alabone and Evangeline out of those dungeons, I would have used it without hesitation. I am sorry, Angus. I have not been a very good uncle. I should have told you about the message from your dad as soon as I arrived at the Windmill, but I didn't want to get your hopes up. I thought you might believe the message could somehow lead to plans for a rescue. But it was a serious error of judgment on my part, and I apologize for underestimating both you and your friends." He shook his head and stared down at his battered snow boots. "If you had come to me, or Gudgeon or Rogwood, with the note inside your own qube, none of this would have happened. I'm supposed to be keeping you out of danger, and instead . . . Your mum is going to kill me when she finds out what happened here last night."

Gudgeon joined them again, chuckling. "She'll do more than that, if I know Evangeline. She'll be chasing you across that Rotundra with a flock of angry lightning moths."

Angus couldn't help smiling. The thought that his mum, dad, and Jeremius might all be together in the same room someday, even if it did involve lightning moths, made him feel slightly more cheerful. The thought that Jeremius had been on his side the whole time, that he could trust his uncle as much as Dougal and Indigo, made him want to burst with relief.

He and Indigo were allowed to visit Dougal up in the sanatorium later that day, under strict instruction from Doctor Fleagal not to tire him out. Dougal looked extremely pale, but he was enormously pleased to see them both. They chatted quietly about Rogwood's and

Gudgeon's escape until Doctor Fleagal disappeared into his office and Germ had gone to clean out some vomit buckets. Then—

"So, what happened?" Dougal asked, suddenly agitated. "How come we both haven't been frozen solid by the ice diamond spores? The last thing I remember is lobbing the lightning heart over to you, and then my fingers started to freeze. . . ."

Angus told them everything he could remember about the lightning heart, how it had come back to life in his hands and how he'd accidentally destroyed it.

"Wow! I bet Swarfe wasn't happy about that," said Dougal.

"Using Cid was a brilliant idea," Angus said, thinking back to Dougal's moment of inspiration when he'd set the lightning moth loose in the snow dome. "Where is he, by the way?"

Dougal frowned. "Swarfe trampled him to the ground. There was nothing left but a few coiled springs and a wing tip."

They spent the rest of the afternoon discussing the fact that Swarfe could not have carried out his despicable plans alone, that someone inside the walls of Perilous had helped him.

"It's got to be Valentine Vellum!" Dougal hissed. "I mean, they worked together in the Lightnarium."

"And Angus found the photograph to prove it," said Indigo.

"Yeah, and Vellum was the only one who agreed with him about trying to find the lightning vaults and opening them up again."

"It might also explain why Gudgeon hates him so much," Angus said, thinking it through, "if he believes Vellum's in it up to his rubber boots, too."

"But what can we do about it?" Indigo said. "We can't accuse him of planting ice diamond storms all over Perilous without some proof."

"I'm not sure Dark-Angel would believe us even if we caught him in the act," Angus said. "She's the only person in this whole Exploratorium who actually seems to like him."

"She's also the only person who can get rid of him," Dougal pointed out with a sigh.

▲　▲　▲

Two days later, Dougal left the sanatorium with strict instructions not to get overexcited about anything. Catcher Grimble also returned to the research department and resumed the supervision of their duties as lightning cubs. "I don't even mind if he calls me Agnes anymore." Angus grinned as the doddery old lightning catcher struck up a heated argument with his favorite hatstand.

The weather, too, was showing welcome signs of improvement. All ice diamond storms had now ceased. The icicle storms were finally fizzling out around the globe. Warm spring sunshine began to melt the deep drifts of snow and ice, allowing lightning catchers from Greenland, Canada, and Scotland to return to their own Exploratoriums at long last, which also meant that Dougal and Germ could reclaim their bedrooms.

"Ew! I don't know who's been sleeping in here, but it reeks of cheesy feet," Dougal complained, opening the window and letting some fresh air in.

Angus was also glad to have some privacy back. He put the Farew's qube away in his bedside table, along with the forged note, which he couldn't quite bring himself to throw away, even though he knew it was a fake.

And then the moment he'd been dreading arrived.

"Hey, Angus!" Edmund Croxley stopped him as he was about to leave the kitchens two days later. "I've got a message from Principal Dark-Angel. She wants you to meet your uncle in the entrance hall immediately."

"Hang on a minute." Angus grabbed Edmund's arm before he could disappear. "Did Dark-Angel look like she was in a bad mood?" He had a horrible feeling that he was in for it. The last time he, Dougal, and Indigo had tried to tackle a notorious villain on their own, she'd sent him straight back to the Windmill as a punishment.

He met Jeremius a few minutes later, but instead of heading up to Dark-Angel's office, his uncle took him down toward the Rotundra.

"There's no need to worry," said Jeremius, smiling."This has nothing to do with iceberg hopping or polar sinking grass."

"Then what . . ."

"I think it's better if I let Principal Dark-Angel explain it to you herself, Angus."

The principal was already waiting for them in the

changing rooms, with a serious-looking Rogwood and Gudgeon.

"Ah, Angus. I trust you are feeling rested after your ordeal?" She began with a slightly less frosty smile than usual.

"Er . . ."

"I have brought you down to the Rotundra, because Adrik Swarfe left something behind before he fled," she continued. "It was intended for you. It might be best if you study it by yourself first. We will wait out here for a few moments, to give you some privacy."

Angus glanced at Rogwood, who nodded. Jeremius simply smiled.

"Go on, boy," Gudgeon urged. "There's nothing waiting to freeze your brains or suck your blood this time."

Angus entered the snow dome warily, just in case. Now that Swarfe was gone and the ice diamond spores had melted, it had a much brighter, cheery feel. But Angus shivered anyway.

He'd only taken a few more steps when he saw it. Flickering slightly at the far end of the cave was a projectogram. Angus approached it suspiciously, wondering if Dark-Angel was planning to put him through one last training session. It was only when he stood directly in front of it that he finally understood. Angus swallowed hard. His mum and dad gazed back at him. Their leather jerkins were tattered and torn; their hair was disheveled; their faces were thin, pale, and gaunt. They were standing in a dungeon; it was bleak and grim, with no natural light.

Swarfe had left the projectogram behind on purpose—a cruel parting shot, designed to fill Angus with fresh despair and torment. But Angus spotted something, a detail so insignificant that he was certain nobody else, including Swarfe, could have noticed it. And he felt his heart leap.

His dad was holding the small white pebble that he'd kept as a souvenir from a great family trip to the beach. The message was crystal clear. His mum and dad had not given up yet. They intended to return, to complete the stone-skimming game with Angus. It was better than any note scribbled inside a Farew's qube. It was a secret, personal sign, sent straight from the dungeons of Castle Dankhart.

"I must thank you, Angus."

Angus turned. Dark-Angel had followed him into the snow dome. She was now watching him with great interest.

"Adrik Swarfe would have caused us a great deal of trouble with a newly revived lightning heart. It is a shame that it was destroyed during the events in this snow dome. It might have proved useful to us here at Perilous. And it was extremely unwise for you, Mr. Dewsnap, and Miss Midnight to try and tackle such a dangerous person without the help of the lightning catchers." She frowned for a fraction of a second. "But I am willing to overlook any foolishness on your part on this occasion."

Angus gawped at her in surprise. He'd been expecting another telling-off; this was almost more puzzling.

"Once we have examined the projectogram for any clues it may provide about your parents, and their exact whereabouts in Castle Dankhart, you are welcome to take it if you wish."

"What, seriously?" Angus said, amazed. "I mean, thanks very much, Principal Dark-Angel."

"I have also asked Jeremius to escort you back to the Windmill and stay with you there until you have fully recovered from this distressing episode. It is not a punishment, Angus," she added hastily, seeing his face fall. "Perilous is your home now. You will continue your training as a lightning cub. But I think it is also time you learned more about the other storm prophets that once lived and worked at this Exploratorium. And that requires a small detour."

"A detour?"

"I will say nothing more about it for the moment, Angus," she said, almost kindly. "Your uncle will explain when you are thoroughly rested. And I will see you upon your return to Perilous." And she smiled briefly and left him alone with the projectogram once more.

"Well, you're not the only one who's being sent home this time," Dougal informed him when Angus returned to the Pigsty later.

"Catcher Sparks just put up a notice in the kitchens," Indigo explained. "Principal Dark-Angel's giving everyone two weeks off."

"She's what?"

"Yeah, the decontamination team wants to give the whole Exploratorium a thorough cleaning, and the supplies department needs to restock; they've completely run out of weatherproof gear," Dougal said with a shrug. "And the kitchen staff is exhausted."

For the next twenty-four hours, the lightning cubs' living quarters were buzzing with the excitement of the unexpected holiday and the sounds of disorganized packing. Angus persuaded Theodore Twill to give Dougal another lightning moth.

"Wow! Thanks, this one's even better than Cid." He grinned. "No wonky wings."

Several spur-of-the-moment parties broke out, but the biggest and loudest took place in Germ's room. Angus and Indigo thoroughly enjoyed a mad pillow fight with Nicholas Grubb and Juliana Jessop before Catcher Mint finally broke up the celebrations.

And then the moment came to leave. Angus dragged his bulging bag out to the gravity railway in the pleasant morning sunlight, wishing he and Jeremius could return to Feaver Street for another visit instead.

"Cheer up, we'll be back before you know it," Jeremius said, joining them in the long queue that had already formed. "And I've just had word from Maximilian. He's finally got the pods back under control. Although he seems quite excited about his latest invention . . . something called an instant inflatable ice storm stopper."

"Well, that doesn't sound hazardous at all," Dougal said with only a slight hint of sarcasm.

Indigo looked mildly concerned. "But not everything your uncle invents is dangerous, is it?"

Angus considered the question carefully. Dangerous was tackling Adrik Swarfe with the powerful lightning heart in a Rotundra full of lethal ice diamond spores, or leaping across drifting icebergs in the middle of a heavy snow bomb bombardment. Nothing Uncle Max invented could ever come close to that. And Angus couldn't wait to return to Perilous, after his mysterious detour, to start their next adventure.